PUBLISHING

THE QUANTUM STATE

ABRAM SMITH

First published by City Limits Publishing 2021

First edition

ISBN: 978-1-955631-14-3

Editing by Kimberly Macasevich
Cover Art by Daniel Cantos

For my sister, Clara

CHAPTER 1

I had no idea what dangers the following months would hold. I had no idea what I was about to start. Nevertheless, all I knew right now was that my black lab puppy, Bubbles, was licking me on the face to wake me up.

Today was the day I was set to leave for college—more precisely the Massachusetts Institute of Technology. Being accepted at sixteen years old was one of my greatest accomplishments yet. I was two grades ahead of where I should be and was entering the university after my sophomore year in high school.

For the majority of my life, my goal had been to go to MIT. Engineering had inspired me before I left elementary school.

More recently, I had decided to major in Quantum Engineering, a new and exciting career field. I had always had a particular interest in physics, specifically quantum physics.

I opened my eyes and realized my door had been opened. I guess it was time to wake up.

I hopped out of bed and walked downstairs to the kitchen. Bubbles trotted behind me all the while.

"Good morning, Alan," my father said as I entered the kitchen. He was sitting in one of the chairs with a cup of coffee, watching the news.

"How did you sleep?"

"Pretty good."

"Good. I made some pancakes this morning. I just put them on your plate, so they should still be hot."

"Great, thanks." I sat down at the table and looked at the TV. "So, have they figured out how to resolve themselves yet?"

"Nope."

"Any agreements on denuclearizing China?"

"No."

"Are there—"

"Just listen to the news. That's all they talk about."

I nodded and read the headline on the news segment.

SECOND COLD WAR IN FULL SWING AS UNITED STATES AND CHINA STOCKPILE NUCLEAR WEAPONS

The Fox News anchors barely held my attention, but I listened closely enough as they spoke.

After the COVID-19 pandemic was contained, the United States announced they believed China leaked the coronavirus intentionally. China denies all of these claims, but the United States says they have proof of this. This has caused a cold war situation between the two countries, and both continue to stockpile nuclear weapons.

The U.S. and China each believe the other may be plotting an attack on their country and they prepare their nation's response.

Citizens will be notified by their local officials if any immediate actions must be taken.

"It's been this same stuff for years now," I told my dad. "Can't they just stop talking about it?"

"I wish they would. Maybe there's something else on a different channel." He clicked a button on the remote and the channel switched to CNN.

"Ugh. Same junk." The new headline was the same thing.

THEORIES ABOUT ORIGIN OF COVID-19 SURFACE BRINGING PRODUCTION OF NUCLEAR WEAPONS WITH THEM

He flipped off the TV as my brother and mom came down the stairs. Bubbles ran over to greet them. "Good morning," my mom said. "I can't believe the big day's already here. Promise you'll call every week?"

"I'll call every day if you want me to."

She wiped her eyes and came to hug me.

"It's not even time for him to leave," my dad said. "He's still got an hour or so." Mom shot him a look then came back to me.

"Why don't you go finish eating?" she told me. "You're going to need that food for your drive." I would need energy for my drive to school. MIT was around five hours from where we lived in Philadelphia, and I had only been driving for a few months.

I picked up my fork and began to eat my pancakes. Bubbles was lying right by my feet, hoping for a tiny bit of my meal.

"So," Dylan said. "Today's it. Thirteen years went by pretty quickly. Then subtract five because I can't remember them. Eight years we've been together."

"Goes by so fast."

"Yeah. Remember when we were really little, and we built that . . . what was it . . . a boat?"

"Of course. Didn't it stay afloat for a while?"

"I think so. That was the beginning of your engineering career. That boat . . . we had a great time with that." He sighed. "I wish we could still do stuff like that together. I mean, today, once you're gone, you're gone."

"We'll still see each other. All the time."

"I hope so. I'm really gonna miss you, Alan."

"Me too."

I finished my breakfast, secretly sneaking a couple of bites to the puppy. The hour before I had to leave seemed to go by in mere seconds. It was finally time. Time to start my own life. Time to get out into the world. A couple of years before expected, but still, my adult life started today.

As we walked onto the front porch so I could get into my car, everyone seemed to be sad in their own way. For my mom, she was quietly crying. My dad was staring at the ground, trying his best not to think about what was about to happen—which was odd. He would always think about the future and how we could do something better. "Efficiency is the key," he would always tell me.

Then my brother just stared right into my eyes. He and I had always been so close. It seemed like leaving him would end our relationship. I would miss him so much.

We all just stood there for a moment, thinking about what was about to happen. I didn't even know if *I* was ready for this.

"Alan." My mom came up to hug me. "I want you to always remember I love you so much. You'll do great out there." She gave me a big squeeze and I went to my dad.

"You will be great out there. You can and will do this." We shared a hug and I went on to my brother.

"I'll miss you, brother," he said. "I know you can do this. You're the bravest and smartest person I know."

We hugged and said our final goodbyes as I walked towards my car. Bubbles attempted to follow me.

"I'm sorry girl, but you've got to stay here." I knelt down to the ground and gave her a hug while she gave me kisses on my face.

I stood up and opened my car door. "Bye, everyone," I said solemnly. "I'll come home all the time. I love you all." I entered my car and turned the key. My brother went over to grab Bubbles and she went with him.

I pulled out of the driveway, turned on to the street, then honked my horn as I pulled away. My life had begun.

***

After arriving at the university, I did all of the check-in and registration work, then was assigned to my dorm in Fenton Hall. I found room 606 and began to move all of my stuff into it.

It was a pretty standard room that included a bed and a desk. I didn't even have a roommate. The best thing about it was having my own bathroom. My parents had saved enough money to be able to allow me to have that. Even though they were the ones to buy it for me, they were both jealous that they never had that option.

For the week or so, I spent time getting to know the campus and reviewing my schedule. Classes would begin on September 4th. My first class was Quantum Physics. I tested out of all other core physics classes.

I still had a few days until the fourth. I hated all the waiting. In the meantime, I decided to go to lunch. It was that time anyway.

As I walked to the cafeteria, I examined some of the displays on the walls. There were so many different achievements, discoveries, and projects by the MIT student body. I just hoped I could live up to that.

I remembered back to high school when I was taking all of those advanced classes. It would be the same here, taking classes with people two grades ahead of me once again. Even so, there were so many other questions running through my mind. Would the other kids like me? Would the professors just overlook me because I was young? Would I be made fun of because of, well, me?

It shouldn't matter, but my height bugged me. Being shorter than everyone in my grade level was rough, but being in classes with people two grades ahead of me? It felt so out of place. I knew I could easily do the academic work, most of the time even better than they could, but the social work was the real challenge. The biggest problem was that I never fought back against all of the school bullies. I just let them continue to pick on me and pick on me and I never said anything. I was kind of afraid to. If I did, it wouldn't take much for them to knock me out.

Instead, the people I stood up to were teachers. For some reason, I felt I could talk to them, maybe even better than other kids. I was never afraid to get my point across. If there was something wrong with one of my grades on a quiz, I went to them to have it fixed. I was able to respectfully tell them they had made a mistake, communicate the issue, and then figure out how to fix it. I could definitely thank my parents for that.

Growing up, my dad always had extremely high intensity levels. Efficiency was a main topic throughout the day, along with hard work. If you weren't holding something the right way to move it, we're going to fix it. When you got something out of the refrigerator the wrong way, we're going to fix it. His methods of problem-solving were not always the most diplomatic, but they had helped me to succeed in life so far.

Then my mom, like my dad, had always been a hard worker with a lot of smarts. Her work with me was the reason I was at MIT right now. I mean, my dad is very smart, but if I got a B in a class, he wouldn't really care that much. Now, my mom on the other hand would help me to improve. Any time I missed something on a test, she would ask, "Do you understand why you got the question wrong?" If I did, then we were set. If not, then we needed to fix it.

One thing that was not tolerated in our household was laziness. If I got that B in a class because I didn't *try*, that would be a whole different story. Both my mom and my dad would be on me for that.

That was the reason I was so successful . . . my parents. They each taught me. Some ways were different, but some were the same. At the time, I may have not known everything I was learning, but it sure paid off now.

I finally received my lunch and sat down at an empty table. I hadn't met any friends yet—making friends was not my strong suit.

As I ate my chicken salad, I looked around the room. I saw groups of friends having great conversations. There were times I wished I could know what that felt like. This was one of them.

I continued to look around. Standing in front of the wall nearest me was a man in a suit. I wondered who he was and why he was just standing in the cafeteria. I dropped it from my mind, as it didn't matter that much—or so I thought.

I finished my lunch and threw away the trash. As I walked out of the cafeteria, back towards my dorm, I thought I saw something—or someone—following me as I turned a corner. I turned around but didn't see anything.

I kept walking back to my dorm, but at a slightly faster pace. I turned another corner and felt I was being watched again, just like I had before. I looked back again and just saw a shadow behind the wall. Could it have been that man in the suit?

I greatly quickened my stride and finally made it back to my dorm in less than a minute. Maybe I was overreacting. Maybe it wasn't anyone at all.

Or maybe it was.

CHAPTER 2

Once I was back in my dorm, I felt a bit uneasy about what I had just seen. I decided it was nothing; I was just being paranoid. I opened my laptop and began some homework. The year hadn't even started, but I already had things to do for my English class.

I finished the assignment in a couple of hours and decided to head down to the common room. When I got there, I sat down in a chair and looked at the TV. The nightly news on NBC was playing, still droning on about the same thing they had been covering for years.

I then decided it was time to try making some friends. There were a few students scattered throughout the common room. No one seemed to notice me. I walked by one of the kids and said hello, but he didn't respond and just went back to talking to one of his other friends.

I could feel it already starting. That all-too-familiar way no one would pay attention to me since I was younger than them.

I decided to go back upstairs to my dorm room. I could just do something by myself there, maybe read about the stuff going on on Mars. But, as I was leaving the common room, the same man who I had seen in a suit was standing in the room with his eyes on me.

I immediately went up to my dorm room. For some reason, I didn't feel this was a coincidence. Either this guy worked for MIT or he was following me.

But of course, he had to work here! Why had I not thought of that? The university wouldn't let some stranger on campus, much less in the cafeteria or in the dorm if they weren't employed here. I had immediately only seen what could have been wrong. Nevertheless, there was some part of my gut telling me that he did *not* work here and might be looking for me.

I needed to calm down. This was not an issue. There's not some random guy in a suit trailing me. That didn't make any sense.

That whole idea changed when I heard a knock at the door. I looked through the peephole. It was him.

I backed away from the door as quietly as I could and made sure it was locked.

I heard another knock, this time a little harder. I didn't make a move.

Then after a minute of no knocks, I went and looked back through the peephole. No one was there. So, all this might have not been a coincidence at all.

***

My thoughts of being followed began to vanish over the next couple of days. I had not seen the man anywhere around campus since he had come knocking on my door.

Today was my first class at the university. Quantum Physics. It was at eleven o'clock this morning.

I woke up around eight o'clock. I made myself breakfast and went to my bag to make sure I had everything I needed. Well, more like the *one* thing I needed. Just a laptop.

The morning passed by pretty quickly. Around 10:45, I left my room with my computer bag and began my walk to class.

I used the map I had been given at registration to find my way around. About five minutes before eleven, I reached the building with my class and stepped through the door. I walked down a short hallway and found the correct room, comparing its number with the other paper I'd been given for my first semester's schedule.

I walked in and found a seat at an open desk. It was a nice flat workstation with charging outputs for phones and laptops. At the front of the room was my professor's desk with a nameplate reading, "Dr. Phylus Boctrum." Soon after I sat down, the class began.

"Okay, students, class is in session," Dr. Boctrum said. He was a middle-aged teacher wearing a lab coat over a formal dress shirt with black slacks. "Welcome to your first class of Quantum Physics. My name is Dr. Phylus Boctrum, and I will be your instructor for the duration of the semester. On your desks, you will find a syllabus with lists of test and quiz dates, point values of assignments, and the topics we will cover this semester. You will also find a key code and instructions for access to your online textbook. Please open your laptops and follow the instructions to access the book. You have three minutes. If you need any assistance, do not hesitate to ask. Go ahead and get started."

Dr. Boctrum seemed to be a fairly good teacher so far. He sounded particular, yet someone you could talk to when you had a question without the fear of being shot down. It was funny how I could immediately tell detailed traits about someone after hearing just a few words.

I got out my new laptop and went to the website. I entered the keycode and accessed the textbook. I navigated to the table of contents and found a list of topics that would be covered. I noticed some remarkably interesting ones, but I did not get a chance to check them out before Dr. Boctrum started talking again.

"I assume all of you are on the textbook. Please navigate to the first chapter: An Introduction to Quantum Mechanics. I assume all of you have a basic understanding of Quantum Mechanics. Quantum Mechanics and Physics are physics related to very small pieces of our universe. I don't mean something the size of a bug, cells, or even something like the organelles of a cell. I'm talking about the size of electrons and photons, quarks and gluons, some of the smallest things known to exist. We will be studying the physics of these tiny things. But before I start teaching, we have a pre-test."

Audible groans arose.

"I understand many of you may not want to take this and want to get straight into the class, but I need to see what you know first. The test has been assigned to you in your textbook platform. Don't worry if you don't know much of the material. This test is designed with an extremely high ceiling which allows me to see your true level. Begin."

I started the test. The first few questions were easy—as easy as high school material. *What is Wave-Particle Duality?* Simple.

After these, they became a little harder, but still not too difficult. I continued to answer questions and eventually finished after around an hour. A few minutes after I had completed my test, Dr. Boctrum started talking again.

"Thank you all. Your scores will be reviewed and reported to you as soon as possible. Class is dismissed. Homework is chapter one. You can find the assignment, again, on the textbook platform."

I turned off my laptop, grabbed the syllabus, and put these into my bag. As I was walking out of my first ever college class, a kid, at least three years older than me, stopped me outside of the classroom. He was at least eight inches taller than me and probably outweighed me by sixty pounds.

"Hey, *kid*. What are you doing here? You look a little young to be here," he sneered, "Are you *lost?*"

I had expected to be taunted by the other students just like I had in high school. Learning from my past experiences, I knew I had to stand up for myself, but for some reason, that day, I didn't.

I didn't respond and he taunted, "Oooh, he's too young *and* afraid to talk. Little pathetic twerp."

He walked away and joined a clique of friends, his cruel laughter echoing all the while. As I started walking back to my dorm from class, another kid came up to me, but he seemed closer to my age, or at least a freshman.

"Don't worry about Jake. He's the 'cool' kid here. Personally, I would love to take a whack at his nose. I've seen him a few times around campus, and he's not nice to *anyone*. My name's Daniel, but you can call me Dan."

"Hi, I'm Alan. Alan Barnes," I responded

"Nice to meet you! How did you like Dr. Boctrum?"

"He was pretty good."

"I thought so too. Well, anyway, would you like to work on that homework tonight together? I looked at it, and chapter one is quite long."

"Sure, I'd love to!" This was a perfect opportunity to make a friend. I didn't get too many of these.

"Well, you don't know my address. Here, I'll just text it to you. What's your phone number?"

I gave it to him as he entered it into his phone. "There we go," he said as he finished.

Out of the corner of my eye, I saw him again. The man in the suit. He was walking towards us. Urgently, I asked Dan something. "Do you know who that man is?" I said. I subtly gestured behind us.

"No," he responded with a frown on his face. "Why?"

"We need to go. Come on."

I walked very quickly alongside Dan who looked very confused about why we were leaving the place so promptly.

"What's wrong?" he asked.

"That guy's been following me the last few days. I have no idea who he is and a couple of days ago he even tried coming up to my dorm room."

"Have you told anyone?"

"I didn't think it was anything. He was first watching me in the cafeteria, then in the common room, came up to my dorm room, and now he's following us." I paused for a second. "Is he still there?"

Dan looked behind his shoulder as did I. Dan shook his head. He wasn't there anymore. "Where'd he go?" I asked him.

"No idea. You need to tell someone about this. If someone really is following you, it needs to be reported. Especially if it's some random, conspicuous adult in a suit."

"But what if it's nothing?"

"But what if it's something?"

CHAPTER 3

Dan had texted me his address and what time I could come over. I had about thirty minutes until I needed to leave, so I decided I would take a look at the homework. Unfortunately, I remembered I had more homework from my other classes, so I was hoping to get a good start before I left. As I was working, though, I got a very mysterious message from Dr. Boctrum. I read it not knowing what to think:

> Mr. Barnes, come to my office in ten minutes. Do not bring your cell phone or anyone else with you. This is a mandatory meeting. If you do not attend, you and I will have an unpleasant conversation about your university attendance. See you soon.

The two parts that stuck out were that I should not bring my cell phone and that this was mandatory. He even made it seem like I would be expelled if I did not come—so I guess my only option was to go.

What about Dan's invite, though? He was the only person who even seemed to notice me. I needed to make a friend. It would be a lonely four years if I didn't. But then again, I would not be here for the next four years if I skipped this meeting with Dr. Boctrum.

Was this legitimate? Why would a professor call me to his office after classes had ended? Maybe they did this at colleges all the time. I decided to go, but I took my cell phone with me. I left the dorm and walked through campus.

On my way, I had a million questions on why he would want to see me. I was, as Jake had cruelly reminded me, a little young for college. What if he thinks I need to be in a more beginner class? Maybe my pre-test was such a failure that MIT was sending me home. I had no idea. I got to his office right on time and knocked on the slightly open, recently polished wooden door. He seemed to be talking with someone. Through the crack, I could see Dr. Boctrum and another man who happened to be in a suit in deep conversation. It was him. It was that man. The guy who had been following me. I panicked—I needed to get as far away from that office as I could.

"Come in," he said. But I was already on my way out of there. Not even realizing it, I was already running. After a couple of seconds, the door behind me opened and Dr. Boctrum emerged.

"Mr. Barnes!" I heard him call. "Where are you going?"

I continued to run and got out of the building. I kept moving towards my dorm room. Once I got there, I could report it. Or, there was always the option of clicking one of the emergency buttons scattered around campus.

But what if it wasn't really an emergency? What if that man in the suit just wanted to talk to me? I looked behind my back as I slowed down. Boctrum was still walking towards me. He wasn't running, so he was a good distance away.

I decided to turn around and confront Dr. Boctrum. I walked towards him. The man in the suit was nowhere to be seen. Once we were right next to each other, he asked me, "Where are you going?"

I needed to tell him what was going on. "That man . . ." I gestured towards the building Boctrum had just come from. I was a little out of breath. "He's been following me. I don't feel safe with him there."

Boctrum seemed to know what I was talking about. "Did you ever think that maybe him following you was for a good reason? One that had no danger involved?"

"What do you mean?"

"I mean, did it ever occur to you that he was trailing you because he needed to talk to you?"

"No, I just—"

"He is a fine man. No one is here to hurt you. Rather, we are here to talk about something with you."

"What?"

"Top secret." He dropped his voice to a whisper. "We can't discuss it out here."

I looked at Dr. Boctrum. Why did he want to discuss something with me? I was about to say no but then decided something. I had no evidence that something bad was happening here. *You have no evidence that something good is going to happen either,* a voice inside of me said. I ignored it and responded to Boctrum. "Okay, I'll do it."

"All right. Then let's head back to my office and we can talk things over."

We walked back towards the building. Neither I nor Boctrum said anything on the way back. We entered the building and found his office. Still, there was the man in the suit, standing near the desk, a computer in front of him.

The unknown man clicked something on the laptop in front of him then addressed me, "Why did you bring your cell phone?" How did he know? I had it in my pocket, but it was not visible at all.

"How did you know?" I asked him.

Responding, he said, "The government has access to anything and everything on your phone, including audio and location."

"Do you mean to tell me that the government can watch and listen to anything they want on my phone? Wait . . . are you from the government?"

"Yes, the government can access anything they want on your phone. I am a government employee and was able to track your phone. I am also able to turn off its tracking, which is what I did when you entered the room. It would have been much easier if you would have just left it in your dorm so we wouldn't have had to go through all this trouble."

"So, you're from the U.S. government? Why are you here and why do you need to see me? And why did you need to turn off the government's access to my phone?"

Dr. Boctrum had been quiet but began to talk, although it was completely off subject. "Did you find that the pre-test you took today seemed quite easy? It tested on post-doctorate Quantum Engineering topics."

"I mean, it wasn't incredibly hard," I replied, attempting to be humble.

"Then would you be surprised when I told you that you received a perfect score?" My heart almost leaped out of my chest. What? A perfect score? That is impossible. No way could that have happened.

"Sir, are you telling me I received a perfect score on a diagnostic for post-graduate studies?"

"Yes, Mr. Barnes, I am." He paused. "Though some of my colleagues believe you cheated, I think otherwise. I think you legitimately got a perfect score on the test."

This was a complete shock. I never thought I would even get *half* of the questions correct, much less get *all* of them correct.

I had no idea what to say. "There is no way . . . I . . . Why am I here?"

"I'll tell you why you are here." The man in the suit was talking again. "Your teacher has never seen a student like you. No one has ever even come close to a perfect score. The reason I have been spectating you and trying to talk to you the last few days is because we thought you could be a candidate for the USQDA. Now that we've seen your test scores, we know for sure you are."

"What did you say? The USQDA? What is this? Why are you here? Who are you?"

"I'm getting to that," he responded with a tinge of annoyance in his voice "I am Agent Bruce. I work for a secret government program called USQDA. That stands for the United States Quantum Defense Agency. This is a secret government program only the president and our employees know about. Our primary focus is on creating quantum weapons for the United States military."

'What in the world? What is this? Why were they telling me? Was this all a joke?' I didn't say anything, but I'm quite sure my mouth hung open a bit. Agent Bruce seemed to notice my shock.

"We are here to recruit you. This is a very selective job position. We are here to see if you want the job."

"But why do you care about me? Why don't you tell someone more important? Someone who can make a difference."

"You are the one who is most important right now. The one who could make the difference. Anyway, the fewer people who know about our agency, the better. That's why we are so selective about who we tell and who we don't." He paused. "Do you know about Area 51?"

"Absolutely." Why did Area 51 matter anyway? I continued. "It's a highly secretive Air Force base that no one knows anything about. Many people think it has aliens or some other type of extraterrestrial life. But what does that matter?"

"It does not have aliens, nor any other extraterrestrial life. Aliens were used as a cover-up; the fake information intentionally was leaked from our agency itself." He didn't answer my question, but I was intrigued to learn about these secrets.

"If it is a cover-up, what is actually at Area 51?"

"It is our headquarters, where we collect intel on other countries' progress with quantum weapons and engineer our own."

There is a quantum defense agency that engineers quantum weapons? Why do they need me? Are they going to experiment on me, see the effects of quantum radiation? Maybe test the effects of a new principle when in a different environment like a live subject? I had no earthly idea, so I asked, "What does this have to do with me? Do you want to experiment on me? If so, I'm sorry, but I want no part of this agency."

"You are obviously one of the most intelligent people in the United States in the field of Quantum Mechanics and Engineering. Of course, we

ABRAM SMITH

are not going to *experiment* on you. We are offering you a position in our agency. We have done background and security checks to verify you are a valid candidate for the USQDA, and you are. You would work in the Quantum Research and Development Unit."

If finding out I made a perfect score on the diagnostic was a shock, I have no idea how I would describe this—Area 51 is really the headquarters for a *quantum defense agency* that oversees everything involving the quantum realm and its possible weapons to be used against man. This was *petrifying*?

It was Dr. Boctrum who spoke this time. "I also work with the USQDA. I do undercover scouting on new developments here at MIT with projects and recruits. You will be the first person I successfully recruited, assuming you accept the offer. Speaking of the offer, here it is." He gave me a paper and I examined it.

United States Quantum Defense Agency Offer

Name: Alan Barnes
Location: Massachusetts Institute of Technology
Candidate: Quantum Research and Development Unit
Age: 16 Years
Main Reason for Consideration: 100% on Quantum Engineering
Postdoctoral Diagnostic
Offered Salary: 300,000 United States Dollars annually
Details: Housing, food, and utilities included in addition to salary

This was the offer? 300,000 dollars, and housing, food, and utilities were included? This was impossible. There was no way this could be a legitimate job offer. It was too good to be true.

Dr. Boctrum began speaking before I could open my mouth to say anything. "I would personally recommend you take it up. If you do decide to decline it, as it is ultimately your choice, your memory will be altered so you don't remember this conversation. It is your choice."

Agent Bruce looked at me, "Unfortunately, we are unable to allow you to leave this office without your final answer. What do you choose?"

I thought about it. Accepting this job would mean ending my college career and heading straight into the workforce as a sixteen-year-old. Then again, according to my diagnostic score, I didn't really need the four years of education. Also, the paycheck would be better than anything I could possibly ever receive from any job, especially at sixteen years old. I think I had made up my mind.

"I'll take it. I want the job."

"Wonderful," Agent Bruce replied with a look of satisfaction on his face. "Welcome to the United States Quantum Defense Agency.

***

After Agent Bruce left the office for a call, it was just Dr. Boctrum and me in the room. He congratulated me and told me how selective the USQDA really was. He explained ways to keep my identity hidden from others. If for some reason, though, someone did find out about it, I would need to immediately call the USQDA Quantum-Brain Interaction Unit (QBIU) for memory alteration. Dr. Boctrum explained to me how these changes are conducted.

"Using this new kind of technology," he began, "machines can pinpoint the brain cell that holds the part of the memory. A quantum device then can go and destroy the cell, or sections of the cell. These advanced machines can perform very precise memory 'blasts,' as we like to call them. After the procedure, we can explain a new story, leaving the subject with no recollection of an event. If you were to say you didn't want the job, we would have memory blasted you."

"Wow. That's amazing." Up until now, I had always thought memory alteration was only something that happened in sci-fi movies. I also thought this quantum agency, the Area 51 truth, and quantum weapons were all fictional before today. It makes me wonder what I will know tomorrow if I've learned this much today. This thought made me even more eager to start my

work, so I asked Dr. Boctrum about it.

"You will begin work as soon as possible. A transport vehicle will be here for you tomorrow morning, so pack up tonight. One thing you might want to do first is to tell your parents about a government job opportunity you have taken. You may tell them the reason you will end your college education is because of your perfect diagnostic score. One thing you may *not* do is tell them what type of work you are doing. If they ask, tell them, by law, you cannot tell them."

"All right. Is there anything else I should know? Things that might impact what I do over the next few hours before I go to bed?"

"Just be careful what you talk about. It is easy to let something slip when it's so fresh on your mind. You can go back to your dorm for the night. We will call you when the transport vehicle is here so you can get your bags."

"Thank you. I look forward to tomorrow." He smiled as I walked out.

So, the man in the suit wasn't bad after all. There was such a thing as the United States Quantum Defense Agency. I was just offered the best job I could ever imagine. Life was full of surprises.

CHAPTER 4

As I walked back to my dorm, I couldn't stop thinking about what I had just learned. *'There's a secret quantum defense agency based at Area 51. The alien stories were a cover-up.'* Wow.

As I entered my door, I laid down on my bed and pulled out my phone to call my parents. I needed to let them know about my decision. When I saw my screen, though, I was reminded I was going to go do homework with Dan. I had a couple of texts from him that said, "Where are you man?" and "U here yet?"

I texted him back: "Sorry I couldn't make it. Dr. Boctrum emailed and needed to urgently talk to me so I had to go."

It took a few minutes for him to respond by saying, "Why?"

I dreaded the response I would be forced to say. "I'm sorry, I can't tell you. It's complicated." After saying it, it sounded a lot like a lie, even though it wasn't.

"You can't tell me? What did he say anyway? Was it about the homework? You should have at least let me know you weren't going to make it."

"I know. I'm sorry. It wasn't about the homework."

"Then what was it about? Why did he need to see you so urgently?" Dan was very inquisitive.

"I can't tell you. I want to, but I can't."

Dan never responded.

So, within minutes of finding out about the most secret agency in the United States, I'd already lost a friend because of it.

I've never been able to make friends easily and I thought I had one.

I wasn't so sure about the United States Quantum Defense Agency anymore. I mean, what's going to happen when I can't tell my parents about my job? Are they going to reject me too? What about my brother? There's no way he would stop talking to me, but you never know. Now that I know all this new, secret information, will I ever be able to live without it?

I fell to sleep with these thoughts on my head, all the "what ifs" pestering my brain until the sunrise. I decided to not tell my parents. Not yet, at least. I didn't want to lose all contact with them, too.

***

As he had said, Dr. Boctrum had the transport vehicle ready for me in the morning. He called me to let me know it was here and that there would be someone coming up to help me with my bags. After just moving into the dorm, it was a pain to pack everything up again. I was incredibly grateful to have someone help me move out, though. Once they got there, we had all of my things moved out in around five minutes and the van was waiting for me. As soon as we entered it, we left for the airport.

It was a quick ride to the Boston International Airport, and as soon as we got there, we boarded a private jet, a luxury I had never experienced, despite the wealth of my parents. Things were extremely fast-paced at this USQDA. Within twenty minutes of leaving from MIT, we were already on a private jet, flying to Nevada.

The agent that helped me with my bags was very nice. He gave me some more information on the agency while we flew. One question I still had, though, was exactly why this agency was such a secret.

"Sir, may I ask you a question?"

"Absolutely," the agent said.

"Why is this agency such a secret? Wouldn't it be good for the entire world to know how powerful the United States is, kind of a 'Don't mess with me' message?"

He paused, thinking. "By letting the information about our agency into the world, every country would know that it is possible to make quantum weapons. They would start trying to engineer the weapons themselves to match our power. Imagine other countries with as powerful weapons as we are creating."

I imagined another country with that type of weapon and immediately realized why the USQDA was so secret. I also realized why no civilian knows or ever will know about Area 51.

***

We landed at Area 51 and exited the plane. According to the agent who flew with me, I would be meeting with the director of the USQDA, Timothy Beck, once I got there. As I walked off the plane, I saw Agent Bruce walking towards me. He told the other agent that he would take it from here. We walked inside one of the buildings on the base, past many Airmen who apparently also worked with the USQDA.

In this building, it seemed like any other workplace: meeting rooms, offices, cubicles, etc. To our right, there was another door labeled, "Special Operations." We walked through it and found a hallway. We walked a few yards and turned left, finding two elevator doors. We clicked the button to enter, then Agent Bruce inserted his ID in what seemed like a hidden opening, then the elevator on the right opened.

We stepped into it, and instead of going up, the elevator went down, even though we were on the ground floor. We rode into the earth and eventually stopped. We walked out, then saw a huge work floor with what seemed like technology from decades ahead. Quantum nanotechnology was everywhere. I mean, this tech was advanced. So advanced. I had never seen anything like it.

Before I could examine it anymore, Agent Bruce led me away and towards the offices. I had also noticed everyone on the floor seemed to be positioned around some center object, although I could not see what it was.

We passed some offices and stopped outside what looked like the largest one. On the nameplate, it said, "Director Timothy Beck." We knocked and heard a voice from inside say to come in. Agent Bruce stayed outside of the door and gestured for me to walk inside.

When I entered, I found a man sitting at the desk, presumably the director. "Welcome, Mr. Barnes, to the United States Quantum Defense Agency. Take a seat." I pulled out a chair opposite him and he began to talk again.

"I see you have already met Agent Bruce, one of the lead agents here," he said. "My name is Timothy Beck." He had brown hair with some grey and was probably in his early 50s. He had a small beard and wore glasses. "I am the director of this agency. I am glad my friend Phylus—the instructor of your Quantum Physics class at MIT—noticed you. For years I have worked here, and I have never recruited someone as young as you. Nevertheless, Phylus was legitimately surprised to have someone as advanced as you in his class. He's never seen someone with as much knowledge and potential as you."

As I have always been ahead in academics compared to other kids my age, I was used to being called "young" by instructors, students, and other adults. Sometimes, though, it made me frustrated when adults referred to me that way. I should be treated like any other one of their students, and in this case, treated like any other employee.

"You will be assigned to the Quantum Research and Development Unit (Unit 1), which happens to be the largest unit. Just so you know, other units consist of the Quantum Intelligence Unit (Unit 2), the Quantum-Brain Interaction Unit (Unit 3), and the Quantum Disaster Unit (Unit 4). Each of these units is managed by a manager. Under each manager, there is a group of scientists for internal operations, and there is one head scientist. This does not apply to Unit 2. They have a group of agents with one head agent for external operations and intel collection.

"Based on your performance, you can be promoted by your unit manager. Agent Bruce will show you to your workspace. I look forward to working with you. We have not had a breakthrough in finding a new type of quantum weapon for a while now. I hope you will allow this agency to advance with our discoveries."

"Thank you, sir," I responded.

"You are welcome. Here is your Identification Badge. You will use this to enter the elevator to this building. You will also have on-base housing which you will use this ID to enter. If you check the reverse side, you will find the address."

"Thank you very much, sir."

I left the room and Agent Bruce began leading me to my workspace. As we approached, I could not believe my eyes. The technology I was witnessing was like nothing I had ever seen before. The computers seemed to be pulled straight out of a sci-fi movie. That wasn't much different from everything I had learned over the past few days, though. To my left and right were my primary coworkers, Agent Bruce explained. One was Marisa and the other was John. They would apparently be the ones I would work with most. He also told me that they would help me get set up.

I guess it made sense they were the ones I would work with most. As I looked around, I saw that there was no one under the age of thirty here other than John and Marisa. That must have been who Director Beck was talking about.

As I walked up to them, I introduced myself. "My name is Alan Barnes," I said. "I was just recruited by this agency while at MIT."

"Hello," John said. He was a bit taller than me with large glasses and short brown hair. "My name is John Ross. This is Marisa Palmer. I have been working here for a month or so. I was recruited right before my first year of college would have started."

"Hi, I'm Marisa. I've been working here for the same amount of time as John. I have really enjoyed working here so far."

It took me a second to find words. Marisa was one of the most beautiful people I had ever met. Her blonde, silky hair and wonderful hazy brown eyes made me lose track of my thoughts.

"Nice to meet you," I said, still admiring her.

"We need to get you set up," John told me. "It shouldn't be too difficult. We just need to get you your computer login and get your 3D modelers synced with your computer." That was one of the first things I noticed when I looked at my workstation. That modeler was years ahead of anything I'd ever seen in my life.

"Let's get you going," Marisa said. She was still the prettiest girl I had ever met, and I'd had a slight difficulty focusing for the rest of the day.

CHAPTER 5

After John and Marisa helped me get set up, the Quantum Research and Development Unit and the Quantum Intelligence Unit were set to have an urgent meeting over the current crisis between the United States and China.

John, Marisa, and I walked towards the meeting room. It was large enough to easily fit thirty people around the table. We took a seat, and moments later, Director Beck stepped in and took a seat. At the chairs to the left and right of him were the managers of either Unit. Next to the managers were the lead scientist of Unit 1 and the head agent of Unit 2. All these people had laptops sitting in front of them. A television mounted on the wall behind Director Beck had the logo of the USQDA: an atomic model with the acronym written out across it.

The director was the first to speak. "Thank you all for coming. I would like to introduce you to our newest member, Alan Barnes." I heard mumbles of welcome around me.

"As you all know, the U.S. is in deep tension with China. On the news, it has shown we have been speeding up the production of nuclear weapons. This is true, but there is more, as many of you know."

I had known both countries had been stockpiling nuclear weapons, but I had not known there was more to the story, but after everything I'd learned over the past few days, I don't think anything could have surprised me anymore.

"Our agency has also sped up the production of an extremely dangerous and destructive quantum weapon. Of course, the media only knows about the nuclear part because of the nature of our agency. I would also like to add that we will all be working at a faster and more efficient pace over the next few weeks, months, or years. It all depends on how our politicians handle the situation.

"Now, more than ever, it is imperative that the USQDA remains a secret. We may *not* give China the idea that we are running an undercover agency that is researching and developing quantum weapons. I would like my Quantum Intelligence Unit manager to explain where we believe China is with its quantum developments."

"Thank you, Dr. Beck," the Intelligence Unit manager said. "As of right now, we do not think China has any knowledge of our operations. We also do not have any evidence that they have any type of quantum agency. We believe they are only producing nuclear weapons.

"Unfortunately, we think they, like us, may have a secret government group researching the possibilities and uses of quantum weapons. We believe that, if this is the case, we are much more advanced than China. Again, as Dr. Beck said, it is vital that we keep our agency a secret, now more than ever."

"This is very true," Director Beck said. "As a result, I need the Quantum Research and Development Unit to step up with their production. I will need all employees to work their hardest so we can produce an ideal quantum weapon as fast as possible. For tonight, though, everyone may leave the building and return to your home. Get a good night's rest before we begin our work tomorrow. Be thinking about how we could create a quantum weapon that makes Hiroshima look like a pop-bottle explosion. Our goal is to make a weapon that can do unmatched damage, not so we can necessarily use it, but to deter other countries from harming us. You are all dismissed."

I began walking out of the office with John and Marisa. When we returned to our station, Marisa showed me how to take my laptop with me from my workstation. I would have figured it out, but I allowed her to help me so we could talk a bit.

I grabbed it and walked with them out of the work floor and to the elevators. We again had to scan our IDs. We rode the elevator up and I remembered the address was on the back of my ID badge. I looked at it. "Do you know where F3 is?" I asked them.

John showed a smile. "I live in F4! That means we're neighbors!"

"Great!" This could be a second chance to make a friend.

We stepped off the elevator and began to walk out of the building. We said our goodbyes and Marisa turned to walk the opposite way towards her housing, but John and I continued to walk in the same direction. We walked together up to the same building and he showed me where our doors were.

"This is great!" I exclaimed.

"Yes!" he said. "If you want, you can come over tonight."

"I would love to! But as Director Beck said, we need to get a good night's sleep, so I shouldn't stay up too late."

"Okay, that's good. I'll have dinner too."

"Perfect! I'm looking forward to it!"

I walked towards my own apartment and scanned my ID badge to enter. I noticed there was also an electronic combination lock on the door. I assumed I could set it up if I wanted to use that to unlock my room. I figured I could just use my badge, so it didn't matter that much.

As I stepped in, I realized this was a pretty nice place to live. On my right, there was a kitchen with a refrigerator, dishwasher, sink, oven, stove, and microwave. In front of me, there was a living room with a couch and a television mounted on the wall. It also had a desk. To my left was a door. I entered it and found a decent-sized bedroom. Attached to the bedroom was a bathroom and a closet. I walked inside the room and started to look around. I looked in the bathroom to find a nice shower, sink, and toiletry area. Off the bathroom was a closet. I poked my head inside, just to see the size. Instead of seeing an empty closet, I found it filled with clothing. It had a suit, work clothes for my regular job, and casual clothing for the weekends and other off days. I went back to the living room and kitchen area and decided to check out the refrigerator. I mean, if the closet were filled, why wouldn't it be filled too? I opened it up to find it filled with food. I opened the cabinets and found them also stocked. This apartment was definitely an upgrade from my dorm at MIT.

I went over to John's room later that night. I had gotten familiar enough with my home by that point. I opened my door, stepped outside, and then shut it behind me. I then went over and knocked on his door. He opened the door and welcomed me inside.

"Hey, John! Thanks so much for inviting me!"

"No problem! Sit down at the table." My room also had a table, which was on the outer edge of my living room. Our rooms were identical, other than the fact that his was more personalized because he had lived here longer.

As I sat down, I saw he had made spaghetti, one of my favorites.

He sat down across from me and we began to talk. We started first talking about college. He had planned to go to Purdue, but he was recruited by the USQDA before he was able to start. He told me that the same thing happened to Marisa. He told me about his family. He said he had two sisters, who were both younger than him. One was 13 and one was 15.

I told him about my family, about how I had a younger brother. He was also 13. I also found out he had skipped a grade somewhere in school, so we were less than a year apart in age. John was also apparently a whiz with computers and an incredible hacker.

We continued to get to know each other until I looked at my watch and realized it was almost nine o'clock. I was tired and needed to get to bed. Also, talking about our parents and families made me remember I needed to call them and tell them I had gotten a job.

Hopefully, whenever I would call home, my dad would be in town. As he was a pilot, he was gone a lot. My mom had gotten a job as a doctor once Dylan and I were old enough to stay at home by ourselves. I spent a lot of time with just my brother at home. He and I had always been really close. I knew I would miss him so much now that I was out of the house.

My thoughts about Dylan abruptly ended when I remembered the time. "John, I'm sorry, but I need to get going," I told him. "As the director said, I want to get a good night's sleep."

"All right. Thank you for coming."

"Thank you for inviting me!"

"No problem. Come anytime."

As I was standing up to leave, I remembered I had a question for him. "Is it just me, or does everyone we work with seem way older than us, and it's kind of awkward?"

He thought about it. "That's how I felt on my first day. Then, after working with them a bit, it was fine. They seemed to respect my opinion and didn't care about my age."

That made me feel better. "Good! Well, I'll see you again tomorrow. Goodbye."

"See ya," he said as I left the room. I hadn't blown this friendship yet. It might work.

***

Back in my own apartment, the thing on my mind was the USQDA, of course. I had been thinking a bit about a new type of weapon that could work. It wasn't much but could be something to go off of.

I also decided to call my parents. It seemed that that needed to be what I should do. I dialed them on my cell phone, and they answered after a couple of rings.

"Hello," my mom said as she answered.

"Hey, Mom. I just wanted to call and tell you something big!"

"What is it?" She seemed to be suddenly excited.

"I did so well on an assessment, I have been recruited."

"Wonderful! Recruited by whom? I'm sure you told them you needed to finish college first."

"Well that's the thing, Mom, it was a now-or-never kind of thing."

"Are you saying, that after all your hard work in high school, less than a week after you start college you dropped out? Surely not." She said that with a laughable tone.

I had no idea how I could respond to this. "This job was . . . perfect for me. It even includes housing, water, meals, and clothing. Everything!"

She seemed to be partial to the idea. I mean, they had already paid for most of my college. They wouldn't want me just running off to some random place. "Where and what is it? Are you going to be okay there? Honey, tell me more about this." She asked inquisitively.

This was the dreaded question. "I . . . I can't exactly do that."

"Why not?"

"Well, it's with the government."

"C'mon, what do you do?"

"I really can't tell you."

"What . . . you . . . you don't even trust your own mother?" She called for my father. "Maybe you should talk to him. I think he's just fooling around with us. He's saying that he got a job and dropped out of college." She handed the phone to my father.

My dad said, with a bit of anger in his voice, "Are you kidding us? Did you really drop out? I mean, what could be a good enough job to do that?"

"I can't tell you," I responded. "I want to, but I can't. They told me I can't."

"Who told you this?"

"Well, it's with the government."

"Ah, so that's why it's so secret. And what job would they have available to a sixteen-year old that had to do with quantum engineering?"

"I can't tell you."

"Then why don't you ask them. We need to know what this is. And I need to figure out how to get all of my money back from MIT." He began to mumble to my mother, "Can't even tell his own parents . . . what kind of job is this?"

Then before he hung up, I heard my mom say, "Wait. Don't hang—" The phone went dead.

This is what I feared might happen. I thought that the same thing that happened with Dan might happen again here.

It surprised me so much, though, that it actually happened. I never thought they would actually stop talking to me. I mean, it sounded like my mom wanted to keep talking, but I doubted my father would want me to talk to her. Even from Nevada, which was over halfway across the country from where I was, I could still almost hear them fighting.

I fell onto my bed in despair and put my head on my pillow. It was over. I had lost connection with them. My parents had stopped talking to me. That quick. One phone call. That was it.

CHAPTER 6

After I had finally fallen to sleep, I had a dream.

I walked up to the doorstep of my parents' house and rang the doorbell. I had home to visit them for Christmas. I rang it again and heard shuffling inside. My father opened the door enough to see who it was, then slammed it before I could say a word. I woke up with tears on my face.

I looked at the clock. Six o'clock. I needed to take a shower after falling asleep without changing my clothing or cleaning myself. Today was my first full day of work at the USQDA and I needed to make a good impression.

I walked out of the bed and towards the bathroom. I half expected my puppy, Bubbles, to come with me, then remembered I wasn't at home anymore. After my shower and getting dressed (I picked a nice pair of khakis and a blue button-up shirt then threw on a lab coat that came past my knees), I made myself a quick breakfast of eggs, bacon, and toast as I tried to forget that awful dream.

I finished my meal and put my ID around my neck, grabbed my cell phone and computer, then walked out of my apartment. As I stepped out of the door, I saw John walking down the hallway, not too far in front of me. I hurried to catch up with him and called for him.

"Hey, John! Wait up!" He turned around and saw me.

"Hi! How was your first day in your new apartment?" he asked.

"It was fine," I said, lying. Everything *wasn't* good. I had just lost the connection with my parents. I continued, pretending that it had never happened. "So, I wanted to ask you, what exactly do we do when we get to work? What's our project?"

"Well, since I've worked here, this is the first big project announced by the director. Before, we were just studying the properties of quantum everything. I assume before I got here, they had been working to make sure quantum weapons would work, and I guess they did. I bet the agency was probably set up in the first place just for studying the possibility of a more powerful weapon than a nuclear bomb. It might have just been named something like 'Specialty Defense' and have been part of the CISA. I'm not exactly sure."

"Okay, then. What else happens when we get to work?"

"Our unit section usually has a meeting about any new discoveries in the mornings before we go to the work floor."

"All right." And before we knew it, we were in the building with the elevators and swiping our cards for access. We stepped inside and began going down. We continued to chat all the way until we were back to the work floor.

We walked out of the elevator and over to our workstation. Marisa was already there and said hello, and I hoped I didn't blush.

"The meeting this morning is in Room 6," she told us. We walked over there and eventually reached the door. As we entered, we noticed we were some of the first people in the room and sat down in a small triangle. Soon after, though, it began to fill up. The manager walked in with the lead scientist and the room fell quiet.

"Good morning," he began. "I hope everyone is well and rested. We need to get straight to business. Like the director said yesterday, we need to develop a weapon the world has never seen. One they have never even dreamed about possessing. One that makes Hiroshima look like a pop-bottle explosion. Does anyone have any ideas on what we could do to start? If so, speak now."

I had an idea that I had begun to imagine last night. It wasn't much, and it might not be significant, but I thought I should tell the unit.

"Anyone, anyone?" he said.

Another person spoke up before I could. "Well, I have an idea. What if we were to use . . ." I began to lose track of this person's idea. It didn't make any sense and didn't seem realistic, much less feasible.

I knew mine was better, but it was only my second day here. I didn't want to sound like a know-it-all in front of all these adults. I was, indeed, still a child.

Despite my anxieties, I knew I needed to say something. After the first person was finished, another person began to speak. I started to lose hope—and confidence—of ever getting my idea out there.

People continued to talk, but none of these ideas seemed any good. I did not want to say anything like "Oh, that idea stinks," or "You know, that's going to work," even if I wanted to. I just knew that what I was thinking would work.

Finally, when it seemed like it might be a perfect time to release my thoughts on my idea, I was interrupted yet again. The only difference this time was that this person *did* indeed have an attainable and practical idea. She seemed to have put some work into thinking about it. She explained it like this:

"Okay, so my idea, essentially, is a more powerful version of a nuclear bomb." She began quietly. "I call it a 'quantum nuclear bomb.'

"The way it works is not too difficult and it would be possible to pull off. The device would be dropped from an aircraft. Then, inside of the shell, a series of events would happen. First, a small object would go quantum, small enough so it is on the scale of protons and neutrons. We would have something like uranium in the middle of the shell as a core. The object that has gone quantum would speed towards the uranium or whatever we use. It would dismantle and destroy the nucleus of the atom, releasing loads of energy, like an atomic bomb." She seemed to be gaining a lot of confidence now in her explanation. "Some of these atoms that have been broken apart will try to recombine. From here, we can, again, shrink an object and speed it towards the nuclei with more protons. When this breaks apart, it will release even more energy than the first time. This would all have to be done lightning fast as the initial blast from going quantum—that's right, going quantum releases energy—would break the shell. Then, we would have the second blast from nuclear fission. Finally, we will end with a blast coming from the energy released when the nuclear fusion occurs and the atoms recombine. The size of the blasts would be determined by the size of the bomb itself."

"That is a brilliant idea," the manager said. "This is possible. How big would the explosion be?"

"Based on my calculations, it would be around three times larger than the standard nuclear bomb. The first time the object goes quantum, it releases some energy, then the nuclear fission, then the fusion, then going quantum the second time, then the fission, then the fusion. I know that sounds complicated, but all these blasts would be very close to each other, but they would be far enough apart that they are separate shock waves, which does more destruction.

"We could do the cycle (going quantum, nuclear fission, then the nuclear fusion) more times than that, but it would be too hard to make the bomb's internal parts go that fast. It could mess up the entire explosion if it went too rapidly."

"This is a very good idea. Does anyone have anything to add or anything that could be a problem," the manager said.

I knew my idea could be even better than that, but the last performance was intimidating. If no one liked my idea, no one would respect me from here on out.

I decided if my idea was needed, I would tell them, but if not, I would keep it to myself.

***

Immediately following the meeting, we got to work on the quantum nuclear bomb. Everyone was assigned to a primary component, which included a group researching how fast the nuclear fission and fusion would occur, what material was needed to be used for the core (which was the part that would be blasted), and how exactly we would make the objects go quantum and hurl towards the core.

I was part of the group that would find out how we would control something that has gone quantum and speed it towards the core.

The first thing we did was look at the previous studies at the USQDA. One of their breakthroughs a while ago was taking an object and shrinking it so it is in the quantum realm.

This so-called "realm," the scientists believe, is not a magical reality. It's just an isolated system of very, very small objects. According to their theories, this allows an object to come back to our realm—also known as our regular life. This has not been studied as much, but they believe it is possible.

When an object shrinks to where it is on the scale of atoms, it has a mind-staggering density (the ratio between mass and volume).

The diameter of a proton is one-millionth of a nanometer—that's 10^{-12} millimeters. Imagine shrinking something, just the size of a *millimeter*, to that size. You would have to shrink it so, so much. The problem is that it stays its same mass. It works like a trash compactor. If you pick up a bag of garbage, put it in a compactor, then pick up the compacted version, they will feel the same weight. It's the same thing with going quantum, but it is compacted much, much more.

The reason there's a problem with having such a dense object is that everything has gravity. For everyone on earth, every time someone jumps, it pulls the earth *slightly* up. Of course, we would never notice a change because the earth is so much more massive than us, but everything is pulling on everything else.

When you have something as dense as an object shrunk to the quantum level, we must remember to not shrink it too much, so it becomes a black hole.

A black hole is something with so much density, it has overwhelming gravity that not even light can escape. For our earth, it would have to become the size of a golf ball but retain the mass of the earth. If a black hole was accidentally created, it would become more powerful until it was either the only thing left in the entire universe, or it was consumed by another black hole. That was the risk in this project, even though it was very minimal.

Nevertheless, the Quantum Disaster Unit has a plan. After we had finished the meeting and settled on the idea, Unit 4 had a meeting. I assume they were assigned to figure out how to immediately enlarge the object if it were to approach becoming a black hole. If it makes it to the estimated density of 2×10^{19} kg per cubic meter, atoms collapse on themselves. From there, it is impossible to stop it. No way to escape. No way to live.

A thought that had occurred in my head, though, was if the space-time fabric *did* exist, it could exist on a smaller scale also, assuming Einstein was correct. It means we don't have to have something the density of a black hole to still draw in matter. We could have something, still with incredible density, but less than a black hole, work on a smaller scale. This had my mind racing until John snapped me back into reality when he needed my help creating a model.

"Hey, Alan. We need to create a model on how we will shrink, propel, and control the objects." Of all the times to be interrupted, now was not one of them.

I started to help him, but these thoughts were still on my mind. For some reason, I felt like it could work. I knew that it would work.

CHAPTER 7

Our group finished our assignment in about a week. We knew how we could shrink and compact the object because of previous studies, but the rest we figured out ourselves.

We found that if we shrunk our material while it is moving in the direction of the core at a certain speed, it splits apart perfectly, releasing maximum energy. This allows us to not have as many internal functions running at the same time—others would have been some type of propeller and controller for making sure the object collides correctly with the core.

Today, we had a test of our new weapon in the desert terrain surrounding Area 51. We were testing a much smaller scale version of the weapon. We would take these results, then scale them up to the size they would be on the full-scale version.

The only problem with doing tests outside of the underground headquarters was security. That was a topic the Intelligence Unit had worked on recently. They were to make sure we had a secure testing environment. We had to make sure no one found out about what we were doing.

As a precaution, we blocked all satellite data for the Area 51 location. We replaced the current live feed with a previously recorded video feed. We had also set up a tent for the people running the test and for blocking any video feed from anyone that may be spying on us. Lastly, we completed the testing at night. This allowed us to remain undercover. Around 12:30 AM, the staff headed out to the test site.

I had seen the inside of the tent. It had a 1-inch-thick tempered glass box set up in the middle, around one cubic foot. Then, around the box, was another plastic box, which was supposed to block any glass pieces from flying. The device (which looked like a small steel box) was placed inside the two boxes. The explosion should not be too large, so there were not too many safety concerns. There were also multiple slow-motion, high-definition cameras to capture the event.

On standby, of course, was the Quantum Disaster Unit. They always seemed to be anywhere and everywhere. I never was working when one of them was not spectating me.

Finally, the test administrators and Director Beck settled in to watch. For a few seconds, we stood there, then the director told the operator to go ahead. We were all standing on the open side of the tent, probably a good hundred feet away, looking inside.

Beforehand, our unit had predicted there would be six consecutive bangs. These would be from the energy released from going quantum, from nuclear fission, then from nuclear fusion. This would then happen again, totaling six waves of energy.

The operator started to countdown. "5, 4, 3, 2, 1, now."

I heard three loud noises—pop! boom! bang!—within a matter of less than a second. That was it. There should have been six waves, not just three. That means the second cycle didn't work, and it was supposed to be even more powerful than the first because heavier elements would have been destroyed.

First, the Research and Development Manager, Director Beck, the operator, and the administrator walked inside to take a look at the results. They came back outside with stern faces and told the rest of us to come in. I walked in with some of my coworkers to check out the scene.

The glass was broken, but not the plastic. The glass was evenly spread out on the outskirts of the plastic box, meaning it had an even blow, which was good.

In my head, I concluded the 'pop' was the object going quantum, the 'boom' was the atoms breaking apart, and the 'bang' was them recombining. It looked like the energy from going quantum just rattled the glass, the energy from the fission broke the box and sent the pieces flying, and the fusion pushed the pieces of glass to the edge of the plastic box.

Before I was able to think about it more, new people came into the tent and I had to leave. After the group came out of the tent, Director Beck announced we would have a meeting to discuss the results.

We all walked back towards headquarters while everyone had quiet conversations about what happened. When we entered the building, we all rode the elevators down and entered a large meeting room. We each sat down in a chair and looked at Director Beck.

"Well, that did not go exactly as we had planned, but was nonetheless successful," he said. "The part about going quantum, splitting the atoms, and then recombining went perfectly. Our problem was that, before the second cycle could occur, the components had already been blown up by the energy released from the first cycle. There was just too much time between the fission of the first cycle and the going quantum in the second cycle.

"I would like us to review the video of the test." The television behind him began playing the recorded version of the quantum weapon. Like I thought, the cycle had only occurred once, and the waves corresponded with what I had thought.

"This idea worked, but either we will need to accelerate the time between the fission and going quantum or leave it the way it is. By leaving it the way it is, it will release about as much energy as a nuclear bomb, so there would not be much of an improvement in that regard.

"The best thing about this test is that we can build off this. We can take what we have and figure out a way to make it better. It is very early and— how may I help you?" An agent had just walked into the room. He whispered something in the director's ear. The entire room fell silent.

When the agent was finished, Director Beck cursed then said to us all, "Well, well, well. It seems we have some new information. Apparently, the test we just ran emitted some quantum radiation, which was expected. That is a recognizable type of radiation that can only be produced when something goes quantum. The USQDA developed a shield that can block almost all of the release of this energy over a year ago. It prevents the detection of the identifiable radiation.

"I was just informed, though, that this shield was not in place. This means the entire world is now potentially aware of our operations. For example, if China happened to pick up a trace of this quantum radiation, they will know we have the technology to create quantum weapons. Then, they will start their own agency, most likely creating a relentless and uncontrollable weapon that could destroy cities, states, our country, and maybe the world." He cursed again. The room was now quiet enough that all I could hear was the heavy breathing of Director Beck.

"That means our entire country is now in jeopardy because we have failed to block this radiation from escaping. So, we may have just a *slight* problem." The director slammed his fists on the table and stormed out of the room with the agent.

The entire time, John had not made eye contact with Director Beck. He continued to look at the ground and fidget with his fingers. As we were leaving the room, he told me four words before he walked away into the darkness of the night:

"This is my fault."

CHAPTER 8

I went back to my apartment thinking about what John had said. He was the person who had caused all of this—the one who had put the millions of people in the United States at risk with one mistake?

How could he do such a thing? I'm sure someone had instructed him to put the shield in place.

I assumed the USQDA was probably going to fire him, in which case he'd have his memory cleared from the time he has worked here. I couldn't let that happen to him. I had to do something.

I fell to sleep with these thoughts on my head—about John, about the agency, about the country, about China, and about the rest of the world.

***

I woke up at my regular time, despite the events of last night. I made myself breakfast, got dressed, and headed back to work.

I entered the building, navigated to the elevators, and rode one down. Not too many people were there when I arrived. Definitely a lot less than usual. When I went to my workstation, I noticed John's bags there. He must already be here.

While I was getting ready before our usual morning meeting, I saw John walking out of Director Beck's office. He looked depressed. When he saw me, he just gave me a sorrowful "Hi." We went to pick up his bags and I asked him what was going on. He responded, "I just got fired. Apparently, 'I'm not reliable enough to work with during these times.' They're going to wipe my memory." He said that with unbearable despair.

'No! Not John!' He and I had become such good friends over the last few weeks. I couldn't have him leave the agency. If they wiped his memory, he wouldn't remember me at all.

Then, before even attempting to respond to him, I started towards the director's office.

"Where are you going?" he asked sadly. I continued to walk and found the director's door was ajar and I knocked on it. He told me to come in.

Director Beck looked like he had stayed up all night, probably because he had. He looked so exhausted; I didn't even know how he was awake.

"Sir, I was wondering if there is another option with what to do with John," I asked him.

"No, I'm sorry," he responded without looking up from his desk. "He seems unable to fulfill the needs of his current position."

"Please, Director, just give him another chance."

"I'm sorry, but I can't do that. We can't risk it."

"Here, I have an idea."

"I'm telling you; he's fired."

"Just give me a second. You said China most likely has a clue that the U.S. has an agency for quantum weapons because of John's error. Right?"

"Yes."

"Well, what if I go undercover and work for their new agency if they create one? I can convince them I am on their side and feed them fake information. Then I can give you exactly what they are doing, making John's mistake worthwhile." I had been formulating this idea on my way here. It seemed like it could work.

"No. It's too dangerous. If you were discovered before you could tell us, that would put the United States in grave danger. Plus, how does that make John any more reliable?"

"They won't discover me. I promise," I said, attempting to avoid the last question.

"We don't even know if they have an agency yet. Also, how would we get you in there as an employee?"

"If they do create an agency, they will be eager to know what the U.S. knows. If I get on their side, they will *need* my information and will do a lot to retrieve it from me."

Director Beck sat there, thinking, then looked up at me. "If they do decide to make an agency, we will talk more about this later. But your friend, John, is still fired."

"Maybe we can turn this around and end the war. Maybe his mistake can be the reason we defeat China."

Again, the director sat there, looking annoyed. "Okay, okay! He's on probation. We won't wipe his memory but he's going to be heavily monitored. Now, go back to the work floor; I have business to attend to."

"Thank you, sir."

I left his office and went to tell John the good news. I also told him about my plan.

"Wait, you volunteered to work for China as a spy to let me keep my job? No way! You can't risk your life for my job."

"It's done. You're not fired and now we have a way to defeat China."

"I can't let you do that."

"Sorry, but it's finished."

Throughout the rest of the day, he continued to thank me for saving his job.

***

That day, we began working to attempt to fix the new weapon we had tested last night. Our goal was to figure out a way to have the multiple cycles fire faster, causing more of an energy release in the explosion.

My work was interrupted later that afternoon, though, when an agent came up to me. He told me I needed to go see Director Beck. When we reached his office, Director Beck told me to come in and sit down. The agent remained standing like people from his unit always did.

"My agent has informed me that China has indeed started a quantum research facility. I have agreed to allow someone to go undercover to their new agency, but I'm not sure if you are the one. I feel like one of our agents is more qualified for the position."

My spirits fell when he said this. "But, all due respect, sir, wouldn't it be better if someone who has worked with our projects went. Someone more specialized in the science part of quantum engineering?"

"Yes, but it is less likely that an agent will make a mistake."

"But they know less about the science part," I said, then quickly added, "No offense," when the agent standing in the room looked at me. I continued. "China will want information, and they will take it if it comes from a more reliable source like an engineer."

He thought about it for what seemed like an eternity. "Okay, let me think about it. I will brief the agency on the final plan today. Tomorrow, the selected person will depart. We will talk to you about the fine details of the operation later if we decide you are the best person for the job."

"Thank you." I left the room and went back to work, determined to work as hard as I could to make myself look the best candidate. Even John, later that day, said, "Dude, why are you working so hard today? Director Beck must have convinced you to work hard so you don't get put on *probation* too." He subtly gestured to the two agents a little over ten feet behind us. "You don't want to end up like this, being watched all the time."

He was right. I didn't.

CHAPTER 9

Later that day, a quick meeting was called for the entire agency. Instead of us all trying to fit into a single meeting room, Director Beck came onto the work floor and briefed everyone on the plan.

"Hello everyone," he began. "I want to explain exactly what will happen tomorrow. We have deliberated, and we believe Alan Barnes is the best candidate for this mission. As many of you know, he will be heading on an undercover operation to China. He will act as a spy for us." He continued explaining to the agency the general idea of what would happen. He also addressed me individually during the briefing and instructed me to come to his office early the next morning so they could tell me about exactly what would happen.

So far, there didn't seem to be many objections to what would happen or that I would be the one to do it. I was still so surprised they had chosen me for the job. I wondered why they didn't choose someone else. Anyway, it didn't matter. I would be the one to do it, and I needed to be ready.

After I left work, I went back to my apartment and began to pack up all of my things—again. I went to bed early with the thoughts of what I would be doing for my country over the next few weeks. We still weren't sure exactly how long I would be in position, but it would have to be long enough to see what they are doing and feed them the incorrect information.

When I woke up the next morning, it was just like any other day. I was to go to work and we would go from there. I needed to meet with the director first thing.

I left my home and entered the building above the USQDA then rode the elevator down to the headquarters, stepped out, and walked over to Director Beck's office. I walked in and saw him waiting for me. We were going to discuss the fine details of the operation.

"Hello Mr. Barnes," he said. "I'm glad to see you. I need to tell you all the details of your operation. First, you, today, will board an airplane to the Beijing Airport. Intel has confirmed their new agency is located in its capital. You will not be riding in a private jet, but just in a standard passenger jet. Once you arrive, things become a little tricky. We will need to get you in touch with one of their authorities. We are going to have to play this part by ear. After this, assuming you are into the agency, you will be telling us exactly what happens.

"Of course, they will be eager to know everything about what the United States is doing. When they ask, you will need to tell them this agency has been going for about a year and we just figured out how to go quantum. That should make them feel like they can easily catch up to us. When you help them, you will need to be incredibly careful about the way you tell them your information. You can explain to them the United States is planning a quantum attack with an enormously powerful weapon on Beijing. Tell them you have no idea what it is, but you wanted to keep them protected.

"They will probably, at some point, try to confirm you are not a spy. For your answer, you could say something like, 'There is no way for you to see if I am a spy other than my word. But I can assure you I am not. I want to help you. I cannot let the U.S. destroy your capital and your country.' Of course, this is all just speculation on what may happen. Our goal of this entire operation is to help the U.S. end this cold war in our favor.

"Finally, you will permanently have a two-way waterproof radio device in your ear for the operation. This will allow you to talk to us and for us to talk to you. We will also be able to hear every conversation you have. On the bright side, most of the people there should speak English. Many of the scholars that will probably be recruited will know English. Do you have any questions? We will be in constant contact with you on your mission to answer any questions if or when you have them."

I did have a question. A really important one. "What happens if everything goes wrong? What happens if they discover who I am? What do I do?"

He paused. Instead of frowning, the director smiled. "Optimism, Mr. Barnes. Have optimism. Of course, in the event they do discover you, we will know and will be able to work from there. Another good thing about us being able to hear everything you hear. Do not worry. You are part of the strongest, most advanced country in history. I assure you that you are backed with the entire United States military." That made me feel slightly better. "Do you have any more questions?" he asked me.

I shook my head. "I'm ready. Let's get this party started."

He nodded with a look of satisfaction on his face and pointed for me to leave his office.

***

At around ten o'clock, the USQDA gave me an unmarked government car to drive to the airport. I was wearing casual clothes and was taking a suitcase with some of my possessions, including a passport the USQDA had given me.

I got to the airport, went through security where we had a health screening to check for COVID-19, even though it had been gone for years now, and found my gate. In my ear, I had my communicator. I checked to make sure it still worked.

"Check, 1, 2. Check. Do you read me?"

"Yes, we hear you," the person on the other side responded.

"My flight leaves soon. When I get there, we will need to find a way to find an authority."

"Yes. Also, as soon as you get there, we will be monitoring the area to see with whom you can get in contact."

"All right." Less than an hour later, I boarded the airplane. Luckily, it only had one stop, so it wouldn't be too long before I got there. The thing I wasn't sure about was the time change. I had never traveled out of the country, so such a drastic change was going to be a new concept for me.

I found an aisle seat on the plane and was sitting next to another single passenger. Soon after I found a seat and all luggage was packed away, the airplane began to move. We reached the runway and took off.

I fell asleep after reading part of an engineering textbook and stayed asleep for a few hours. I then watched a couple of movies and read some more of my book. It was hard to believe I would be a spy in less than twelve hours as I was relaxing, sleeping, and reading on an airplane.

Eventually, we reached our stop in Tokyo. I had a one-and-a-half-hour layover, then would board another plane to go to Beijing.

I navigated to my gate and sat down in another chair, waiting for my flight to be called. Eventually, it was. I boarded, took off, and finally reached Beijing. When our plane landed, we all disembarked. We then had to go through customs, which went smoothly.

Now was the hard part. I was out of the airport and needed to find an authority. I looked around. I didn't see anyone. Then, suddenly, a police officer came into sight after coming around a corner. I went up to him, and he spoke in Mandarin. Luckily, I had learned how to say I spoke English. "Duìbùqǐ, wǒ zhǐ huì shuō yīngyǔ," I said.

After I said this, he responded, "What's the issue? Why do you need me?" He had a thick accent and did not have the correct grammar but could be helpful nevertheless.

"I need to talk to an authority about a national security issue. It is urgent."

"I'll get you to talk to authority. Come with me." For some reason, he did not seem to question me at all. He was just taking me to a leader. That worked for me.

In my ear, I heard, "Nicely done, but you must be careful about how you present the information to the Chinese official. He will most likely take you to the police station or somewhere similar." He was right. We walked a short distance to a police station. When we walked in, the officer told a person in the lobby something in Mandarin. He was probably explaining the situation.

The person in the lobby asked, "Where are you from?"

I answered, "The United States. I have an urgent security matter and must warn your country."

He then spoke to the officer who brought me in. They seemed to have made some type of decision about me. The officer again said, "Come with me."

I followed and realized I was heading towards the tip section. He stopped there and pointed to the sign. I told him thank you in English and he walked away.

The person at the tip counter started speaking to me in Mandarin. Again, I said, "Duìbùqǐ, wǒ zhǐ huì shuō yīngyǔ." She stopped talking, then handed me a form, which was in English luckily. The form was labeled "Crime Information Document" and was for filling out a tip. It asked for a name and phone number, which I put down. Then it asked for urgency on a scale of 1-10. I circled 10 then filled out the details of the fictional crime. I put down just "National Security."

I handed it to the woman at the counter when I had finished filling out the form, and her eyes lit up a bit. She used her office phone to call someone, and in about a minute, another, more official-looking police officer came to where we were. She handed him the form and this man began to speak to me in better English than I had experienced so far.

"And you say this is an urgent matter? National Security? Come with me."

I walked with him. While on my way, I concluded he was the police chief. We walked into his office and he told me to sit down.

"So, what type of issue is this?"

In my ear, I heard something. "Just say quantum. Nothing else," they told me.

"Quantum," I responded to the chief.

He paused for a second. He stared at me and looked flustered. He knew. He knew there was an agency. Instead, he responded with, "What?" His attempt at having no idea what I was talking about was not working.

"It's a quantum issue. I know China has just formed a secret agency. I know you know too." The police chief seemed at a loss for words, then checked to make sure the door was completely closed.

"Keep it steady. Don't say anything crazy," my earpiece sounded.

"What do you know," he asked me. "That is classified. How could an American like you know anything about it?"

"I previously worked for the quantum agency in America."

I paused as I heard the USQDA say, "Now tell them we are plotting against them."

"They are plotting against you. They plan on attacking soon. I don't think it will be for at least a month because they just found out about going quantum. I know China saw the quantum radiation."

This police officer seemed astounded. "Why are you telling me this?" he asked. "Shouldn't America keep this to themselves?"

"I am telling you this because they want to destroy you. They want to destroy your country. They want to take over." He seemed even more shocked.

"You said you previously worked for the U.S. agency. You must have just left it if you know about our agency. It was just started after we recognized an interesting type of radiation coming from Nevada. How can we trust you?"

"If I were still part of their agency, I wouldn't be here. There's no way that stupid director would allow me to be here. He'd say, 'It's too dangerous' and 'No way.'" I made a mental note to apologize to Director Beck later. "I also would not be here to warn you of their plans if I were still part of the agency. I can't let them destroy you. You must be warned."

"Brilliant. You played that perfectly," I heard in my ear.

The police chief seemed to believe me. "Let me get you in touch with our director. And, know this: any funny business and we'll arrest you on the spot." He seemed to be very on edge, as would I if I just found out the opposing country found out about our most secret agency.

"Yes, sir."

"Let's go." He paused. "What's your name again?"

"Alan Barnes." Everything seemed to be going according to plan. Hopefully, it would stay that way.

CHAPTER 10

The police chief and I left the station. We boarded a taxi and they took us to what looked like a regular office building. When we stepped in, it just looked like an ordinary work facility. It reminded me of the normal offices above the USQDA, but I knew there had to be more somewhere, just like in the U.S.

We found an elevator and rode it up, rather than down in the USQDA. In my ear, I heard, "Okay. You are in a perfect position. Talk with the director and convince him you are on his side."

After we reached our floor, the police chief told me to step out of the elevator. When we did, we found an area that looked like any other floor. There were offices and meeting rooms. These seemed to be in good condition. As we continued walking, we found some walls that had recently been taken out to create a work floor. It was much smaller than ours back in the U.S. This was obviously just created for the new Chinese agency.

We kept walking and found a good-sized office. Sitting at a desk inside was a man in a suit who seemed to be around the same age as Director Beck. They even seemed to look similar: same face shape, both wore glasses, they had the same color eyes, and both had grey hair.

The police chief walked in with me. He told me to wait where I was and went up to talk to the director. He whispered to him.

The director nodded and then told him something which I couldn't understand, most likely asking him to leave. He strolled out of the room, leaving just the director and me.

He addressed me with near-perfect English. "So, I hear you have some information for me regarding our national security."

"Yes, sir. The United—"

"I know, I know. My coworker has informed me. The United States is planning an attack on our country using some type of quantum weapon. You also said they have just recently discovered you can go quantum, so they are not extremely far in the design stage of a weapon. You predict that it will be at least a month before they attack."

"Yes, sir."

"Well, if your information is accurate and you are on our side, we have nothing to lose here." I let out a breath I didn't realize I had been holding. "Still, we are not sure if you are really on our side. If you happened to be a spy, we would lose our secretive advantage." My thoughts intensified again.

"Be careful. We are on thin ice," my earpiece said.

"How did you know about our agency in the first place? How do you know so much about us?" the Chinese Director asked.

"As I told your head of police, I previously worked for the United States' agency. Recently, we performed a test proving we could, indeed, go quantum. Soon after this, I discovered my agency did not just want to *know* how to do this. They want to *use* it. They want to produce an all-powerful weapon to destroy you and your country."

"We also detected a spike of regular radiation during that test. What was this?"

I responded, being careful. Really, it was the atoms splitting apart, but I said, "I am not sure. I never had high enough clearance to know everything about every test they ran." I hoped he believed my lie.

"Okay. Still, how do we know we can believe you? What if you are a spy?"

I had no idea how to respond to this. "Sir, you will have to trust my word. There is no way for me to prove to you I am not on the United States' side except my word. I assure you I am here on your behalf. I do not agree with the actions of the United States. They should not plan deadly attacks on any other country. Why would I be here and tell you what I was doing if I *didn't* want to help you?"

He sat there and thought for a second. "You seem pretty believable, but there is actually a way for us to confirm that you are really on our side. Something our Chinese government has perfected is the polygraph, a classic device commonly referred to as the lie-detection test. We will be able to tell exactly if you are on our side or the U.S.'s side." *'Oh no.'* They brought up the lie detector test. I had read about them before. They used to be much less advanced than they are now, but today, they were almost always accurate. There was essentially no way to trick it, especially if they had improved upon it.

I nodded hesitantly, but I still don't think the director noticed the hesitancy. "I must prove to you I am on your side." I was secretly terrified. Really, inside, I was screaming. I had no idea what I would do. This is not something I had considered. I'm sure the USQDA had thought of this, but I guess they either chose not to mention it to me or forgot to.

"Wonderful. We will be setting up the test as soon as possible so we will be able to verify your authenticity. If we find you are on our side, great! You will be able to assist us from here on out. If not, you will be imprisoned."

Oh man. It was over. I could go ahead and give up right now if I wanted to. But I had to try. The United States needed me. I needed to do my service for my country. "All right," I said. That sounds good to me." I had no idea how I was going to avoid the inevitable fate to come.

"Until then, you may sit in a spare office. I believe there is a television in there you may use. I will show you to it." He walked me down the hallway and we entered an empty office just like he said.

"I'm sorry, but we will need to lock the door from the outside just in case you are not on our side," he told me, then added, "Which we doubt. We will come and get you as soon as we are ready for you."

"Perfect. Thank you."

"Thank *you*," he responded.

I now had most likely a couple of hours, or less, to learn how to avoid being caught by a highly advanced machine that is meant to detect any form of deception.

The odds were not in my favor.

***

An hour and a half later, the director came into my room, saying the examiners were ready for me. During the time I had sat in the empty room, I pretended to watch television. Really, the USQDA had been telling me exactly how to pass the test.

A polygraph was a machine that tracks different components in my body, including heart rate, blood pressure, respiration, and skin conductivity (a way to check my sweat levels).

They had told me there would be some things called control questions. These would just be initial questions. These would be based on anything from my past and were broad questions. Something like "Have you ever lied to someone close to you?" They use these to track your initial response to a threatening question that does not relate to what they are attempting to find out.

Eventually, they get into relevant questions which they compare to the control questions. For example, a relevant question might be "Are you on our side?" If you are innocent, you usually have a greater response to control questions. If you are guilty, you have a greater response to relevant questions.

To pass the test, you must throw off the control questions and make sure you have a big reaction to them. You must make your breathing unsteady and offbeat. You can also hold your breath which can affect your heartbeat. If you make yourself nervous before the test, it is better. Your hands will begin to sweat, and your pulse and breathing may change. Another strategy is to try and stimulate your brain with something like a difficult math problem to throw off the control questions.

Once you notice they ask a relevant question, allow yourself to stop stressing and try to relax, taking deep and steady breaths.

The goal is to make yourself have a much larger reaction to the control questions. If this does occur, you can trick the test. In my case, I *must* trick the test. If I attempt to think about being imprisoned, that should simulate enough anxiety.

I continued to walk with the director. He led me into a dimly lit room with a black chair that had many instruments on it.

I sat down and test administers connected some devices to me. Some were on my fingertips, for sweat monitoring, a blood pressure cuff on my arm, and tubes placed over my chest to record my breathing rates.

In my ear, I heard, "You can do this. Just remember what we taught you. We will not talk to you during the test because you need to be focused on tricking it. The instruments connected to you may pick up a stimulus that could be detrimental to the results if we were to talk to you. Good luck."

The examiner began speaking with me, first starting with some easy questions.

"What is your name?"

"Alan Barnes." I tried thinking about going to prison and felt my heartbeat rise.

"Now—only answer with yes or no. Have you ever committed a crime other than a minor traffic offense?"

"No." This time I tried increasing my breathing.

"Have you ever told your parents a lie?" I'm sure I had.

"Yes." This question may have legitimately caused a noticeable response.

"Have you ever lied to a teacher?" I remembered back into second grade when my teacher asked me if I had broken a pencil in half. I said no, but really, I had done it.

"Yes." I attempted to change my breathing patterns, which seemed to make my heart rate change.

"Why are you in China?" This seemed to be a more relevant question. I tried to relax a bit to make my answer seem valid. "Are you here to warn us about a potential attack by the United States."

"Yes."

"Did you have a high enough clearance to know the details of the weapon they are developing?"

Again, I tried to relax. I thought about my brother. I can see him saying, "Breathe, Alan, breathe. You are doing great."

I answered the examiner, "No. I—"

"Yes or no answers only," he interrupted. "Did you know any specific details of what was going on inside the agency?"

"No."

"When was the last time you had contact with the United States' quantum agency? Was it when you figured out their true intentions?"

Using the same strategy that I had used so far, I answered, "Yes."

The examiner continued to ask me questions like this. I continued to stay calm and relaxed. I felt like I was doing a rather respectable job.

Finally, he asked the last question. "Are you on our side? Are you really here to help us?"

I tried the hardest I had ever tried at something in my life to stay calm. I answered, "I am on your side. I am here to help."

The examiner looked at his computer screen and did a few things. He told me to stay where I was, then he left the room to talk to the director.

The director came into my room a couple of minutes later and began to speak. "The polygraph has given us our results. It seems that you are being totally honest, and you are really here to help us."

I let my breath out, literally. Yes! I had passed! "Great job," my earpiece sounded. "You tricked it."

"We are going to incorporate you into our system," the director said. "I want you to come with me into my office and we can talk some more about how you will assist us in our operations of defending ourselves from the United States."

"Great," I responded. We walked down a hallway and entered his office. He sat down behind his desk and I sat opposite him.

"I am incredibly grateful for what you have told us. I mean, you have saved our country by—"

A man had just walked into the room. He told the director that he needed to come with him.

"Mr. Barnes, just stay where you are. I will return shortly."

"All right," I responded. He left the room and I was the only one left.

In my earpiece, I heard, surprisingly nervously, "We would usually tell you to look around and get us some information, but you are too new. If someone saw you, you would be imprisoned on the spot." They seemed to be worried about something. I guess it was me being imprisoned.

After they said this, I thought about it. '*Why would they not want me to discover some new information?*' I decided to do the exact opposite of what I was supposed to do. I mean, the director was gone, and I was sitting in his office unaccompanied.

I began quietly, stealthily standing up so I could check out the office. I walked to the other side of his desk. It seemed to be just like any other desk, nothing out of the ordinary. I tried opening the top right drawer, and it did.

Inside, there were just pens, pencils, and a notebook. I tried some of the other drawers and they contained other small, insignificant things, such as a stapler, an empty filing drawer, and so on. Finally, I tried opening the bottom right drawer, which was the only one I hadn't tried yet. As I attempted to pull on its handle, I found it was locked.

Why was there a locked drawer on this desk? Why only one? I didn't even see a keyhole. Of course, I didn't have a key so there was no way I could get inside anyway. If I tried forcing it open, I'm sure the director would notice the drawer didn't lock anymore when he got back.

I decided to give up and go back to my chair where I was supposed to stay, still wondering what was in that drawer. As I stood up, though, I noticed there was a small, very intricately designed silver key sitting on the director's chair. No way this was it. It must have fallen out of his pocket. I picked it up, but there was nowhere for me to try it. I looked around and still couldn't find it. The key seemed to perfectly match the desk, though. I could just tell this was it.

I searched for a little longer and was about to give up. But then I saw it. On the underside of the desk, there was a tiny little latch. I reached for it and slowly opened it. Underneath was the keyhole. I found it!

I inserted the key to see if it would work and it fit perfectly. I turned the key to unlock the drawer then pulled its handle. It opened.

As I slowly pulled it, I realized it needed some real effort to get it out. I gave it a good tug, then found that the drawer was not made of wood like the rest of the desk. It was steel, disguised as wood from the outside.

Inside, there was a single file folder. It said, "U.S." on the label. I had no idea what it was. I opened it and found one piece of paper.

Labeled at the top, it said, "Alan Barnes–Polygraph." I continued to look at the document and found my results. In the first section, it was the control questions. For each question asked, it listed my answer, my heart rate, my breathing patterns, my sweat levels, and more. I looked at the results of the controls.

Then I continued to look at the paper and found the stats for the relevant questions. I looked at them and was dumbfounded. No way.

My reactions to the relevant questions were considerably larger than the ones to the control questions. Why did they think I was on their side? Right on the paper, it even said, "Greater response to relevant questions. Result: FAIL."

What was going on here? It was obvious I was on the United States' side. Something was going on here. I committed the page to memory and put the paper back into the folder, put the folder back in the drawer, and closed it. I tried pulling on the handle and found it had automatically locked after I had closed it.

I put the key back onto the director's chair exactly where I had found it and headed back to my own seat.

Soon after I had sat back down, the director came back into the room. It was so soon after that I was lucky he hadn't caught me snooping around. "Sorry, I had to take care of that," he said. I tried to look like I had been sitting there the whole time. "I need to let you know some more information about our progress. Although this agency is less than a week old, we have already begun figuring out how to make something go quantum. We believe we are almost there.

"In the meantime, I want your help with creating a weapon. You are an engineer, correct?"

"Yes, sir," I said.

"Good. While our scientists work on going quantum, which we are sure is possible, you will work on the weapon. Any ideas at all are accepted. Let me show you to your office where you will be able to work. By the time you have fully developed your idea, we should be finished." He walked me to where I would work, talking more about his agency on the way, but I wasn't completely paying attention. All I could think about was that paper.

If they knew I was lying, why was I still here? Why were they allowing me to work? They were setting me up; I knew it, but I didn't know what they were setting me up for.

I needed to figure it out. My life depended on it.

CHAPTER 11

The Chinese director had told me where my office and apartment were located and gave me my ID. To get to my apartment, you had to leave the office building and walk a short distance.

I had done this yesterday after work. Like the USQDA, there was food available; the cabinets and refrigerator were stocked.

Last night, the USQDA communicator (who had spoken with me the entire time during the operation, probably under the supervision of Director Beck) talked to me. "So, the Chinese director wants you to engineer a weapon. Most likely, he currently thinks it will take a while. When he eventually asks for your idea, give him part of the idea we came up with. The one where we launch a quantum object at uranium. If and when you help build it, we will give you instructions on how you can sabotage it and come up with a good cover story.

"During the time they expect you to work on your idea for them, though, work on a new one for us. If you think of anything worthwhile, you will need to tell us. This time is perfect for engineering a weapon for the U.S. They need to think you are actually working on something and not just sitting there. You might as well help the USQDA"

"Got it," I responded.

"We are in a good spot. Starting tomorrow, you will be able to tell us their progress and we will know what to do from there."

"Thank you," I responded.

"Thank *you*." But I never said anything about the paper I found. It just wasn't time yet. I still wasn't sure who I should trust and what was going on within this Chinese agency. Maybe the results were printed wrong.

I doubted it. I really did.

THE QUANTUM STATE

I only slept a couple of hours that night. I was too distracted by everything going on in my life. Less than a month ago, I was an MIT student, set on a course of success. Now, I was part of the most secret agency in the United States acting as a spy in a foreign country that was in a cold war with America.

I didn't know if I could handle this. It was just too much for a sixteen-year-old boy.

It had to be done, though. My actions in this country could help the U.S. finally end this war. My actions could save countless lives if China decided to attack the United States.

Then again, what was that paper I found? Why was I still here? I knew something was going on, but it didn't seem to be in my favor.

I woke up that morning in my new apartment. I got dressed and made myself breakfast. Luckily, the apartment had American-style food. I wondered how they already had it stocked when I got here. I guess once they confirmed the polygraph test, they sent someone to do that.

But, again, why was I still here? They didn't really confirm my test. I mean, what if they were double-crossing me while I was double-crossing them? Like a double-double crossing. I was being a spy, pretending to be on their side while on the United States' side, but they knew I was on the U.S. side but was pretending to tell me they thought I was on their side. Thinking about all of that hurt my brain. That was the conclusion I had come to. Except, there was one other much more likely conclusion. What if the printout was simply just wrong? That made sense. That's what I decided to believe.

I left the apartment with my ID and walked out of the building. Stepping into the morning air, I began to walk the short distance to the building containing China's agency. I opened the door and found the elevator. I entered then rode the elevator up to the floor where I was yesterday. Once I stepped out, the Chinese director greeted me.

"Good morning, Mr. Barnes," he said. "We are so, *so* close to going quantum. Yesterday, after you were back in your apartment, we made a breakthrough. Tripentoctium. That's it."

Oh no. No. They *did* figure it out. The new element. It came out a few years ago, and someone thought it could be used to go quantum. That might have been the inspiration that started the USQDA. But now that China had it, quantum supremacy was not something the United States had anymore. They got it. How did they figure it out? My mind was racing. That was the key to getting something compressed enough to go quantum. I had no idea how they could have gotten their hands on the idea. Before I could keep thinking, the director continued.

"We discovered it works to help with the compression. We might be finished with making something go quantum by the end of today. If possible, I need the weapon design by the end of today. You may go to your office. I just wanted to tell you the good news!"

"Yes, sir," I responded. "I'm so glad you figured it out!"

"Did you know?"

"Know what?"

"That Tripentoctium is the key?"

Of course, I did. That was what allowed us to go quantum, though it was still hard to keep something there for longer than a couple of milliseconds. Without it, going quantum would still only be a scenario from sci-fi movies. I had to lie. "No idea. Now that I think of it, I might have heard it mentioned a few times, but they never gave me enough clearance to do anything with it or even know what it really was."

"All right then. Go ahead and get to work."

When I entered my office, it had a rather large stack of blank paper for the designs I would soon be creating. It also had a touchscreen computer if I wanted to do designing that way. The technology was advanced but not nearly as advanced as the United States'. I assumed the USQDA had reached quantum nanotechnology supremacy, contributing to their futuristic tech.

China would no longer be that far behind after their breakthrough.

As I sat down, the USQDA talked to me. "They figured it out. We expected that. Don't sweat it. But right now, go ahead and create a model with our old design for them. We need to give them something that actually makes sense. Do not include every detail, though. After you finish that, start working on something for us. You should have almost all the tools that we had to create something new."

I began working on the sketches for China. I finished it in around half an hour and began working on a new idea.

For a bit, I just sat there, thinking. I had, indeed, thought of some ideas recently for a weapon. I had tried to share one at that first USQDA meeting. Then, while working on the new weapon at the USQDA, some more thoughts had occurred to me, about the space-time fabric existing on a smaller scale, about the black hole density, and so on.

I began to formulate an idea. I wasn't sure if it would work, though. If it did, it would end this war for the country that got their hands on it first. If the U.S. got it, they could do so much with it and still not necessarily use it against another country. If China got it, they would probably use it in a much more powerful version than intended. That means I would need to be very secretive about where I kept my design.

I began to draw my new idea, which was based on Einstein's theory of space-time fabric. If we could take something large and make it go quantum, it would, of course, retain its pre-quantum mass. It would be incredibly dense, and our goal would be to make it have a density slightly less than a black hole. That means, even if it weren't necessarily a true and complete black hole, it would still suck in matter surrounding matter, assuming the space-time fabric works on a smaller scale.

The super dense quantum object would work as a ball on a blanket held above the ground. At first, the blanket is flat. Once a mass is applied, the fabric dips. Anything around the ball and its indention would move towards the ball. That is how this would work. A black hole makes a dip in the fabric so much that it is impossible to stop anything from entering it. It is also impossible to stop it from pulling in general.

If the object we shrink doesn't become the density of a black hole, it *would* be possible to stop. We could use it as a weapon on a certain area then stop it once it completes its purpose. That would make it a much more controllable and predictable object, allowing a precise and direct target.

This would work. I knew it. We just needed to figure out how to compress something enough to do so. I needed to tell the United States as soon as I possibly could, even if it was still at the Chinese agency. This was an excellent idea.

I think I remembered seeing a bathroom on my way in. I could go there and talk to the USQDA. I could tell them I needed to urgently talk to them about an idea that China could not get their hands on whatsoever.

I decided to do this. I left the original drawing for the idea I was supposed to tell China about in my office, then left the room. I shoved my new idea into my pocket hastily and walked into the bathroom. I checked to make sure there was no one else in there and found myself in an empty room.

"Hello, anyone," I said in a whispering voice. "Anyone?"

"Yes, Mr. Barnes. What is it?"

"I have an idea. It is a weapon that could end this war forever."

"All right," the person on the other end responded. "Before you release any details on the idea, we need to get you to a secure location. Tonight, after you leave work, we will be able to talk to you. Until then, don't tell us anything. We will talk to you soon."

"I need to tell you now. It's—." As I said this, though, the Chinese director walked into the bathroom.

"Hello, Mr. Barnes. I thought I heard you talking to someone. Who was it?"

Oh no. He heard. My cover might be blown. I simply responded, "No one."

"Are you sure?" he questioned. I'm busted. There's no way I can get out of this.

"Yes. I was going to the bathroom and was just leaving . . . "

"All right." He paused. "What's that in your pocket?" No, no, NO. There's no way I could be that careless. The paper containing my idea was sticking out of my pocket.

"Nothing," I responded, trying to seem as un-flustered as possible.

"Well, then, can I see it?" he asked.

"It's nothing. It's—"

"Is there a reason I can't see it? After all, this is *my* workplace."

"It's just—"

"It's just what?" He seemed to be getting irritated. I had no idea what to do.

"It's just—"

"Give it to me." I did. I had to. I had to let him see it or I was done for. How could I let this happen? China now has access to an idea that could destroy the world if used incorrectly. He opened up the paper.

"Is this your new idea you have created for us?"

"Yes." That was the only thing I could say. "I wanted to wait to show it to you until I could have it fully developed," I added to make it sound more convincing. I couldn't believe what I had done.

"No, I love it! This is wonderful. As soon as we finish discovering how to go quantum, we will put this idea into creation. Tomorrow we should be ready! Excellent job!"

"Thank you," I said. Really, I wanted to scream. I had literally just handed over what could be the best weapon in existence to my enemy.

The director handed the paper back to me, then told me how great I had done again. I then walked out of the room.

As soon as I entered my office, I slammed my fist on the desk then punched the wall. How could I let this happen? I punched myself. The entire USQDA counted on me and I did the worst thing possible for our cause: giving the enemy my weapon of destruction.

I'm sure I would be fired for this. I have made the worst mistake possible. I finished the day distracted, flustered, and furious.

When I was done at the Chinese agency, I walked back to my apartment. My earpiece started talking. "So, about the idea that China now has . . . What was it?" he said, with what seemed like ease. He didn't sound mad. He almost sounded . . . happy. I was confused.

"I'm so sorry. I made a careless mistake," I began. "I should have waited until I was back at the apartment."

"Apologizing won't fix the problem we now have on our hands." He sounded madder now, as his emotion suddenly changed. "We need to figure out how to work from here. So, what was your idea?"

I told him.

"That is brilliant. I just wish you hadn't given it to our enemy. We need to figure out a way to stop them from producing it. We need you here. We need you in the U.S. so *we* can create it. For now, though, you will stay in China and monitor their progress with the device. We will talk to you when we have a plan."

"I'm so sorry," I said.

"I understand, but we must now figure out a way to fix the mistake. Over and out."

I fell onto my bed without eating dinner. I just caused the United States to be put in jeopardy because I couldn't put a paper completely in my pocket. What a careless fool I was! Of all the mistakes I could have made, somehow, I succeeded in performing the easiest to prevent. The U.S. was in my hands.

I dropped them.

CHAPTER 12

As soon as I entered the Chinese facility the next day, the director told me to come into his office. When we entered, he told me to sit down.

"Good morning, Mr. Barnes," he said. "I wanted to tell you something huge. We have discovered how to go quantum." *'Great. Simply great. Just what I needed.'*

"Wonderful!" I said, with the fakest excitement I could muster.

"We will begin working on your weapon idea today. I would like you to pitch it to our entire agency at nine o'clock this morning."

"All right," I responded.

It didn't seem like any time had passed until it was time to present my idea.

We all entered a room with a long table. By nine o'clock, there were around fifteen people in the room, including the Chinese director.

"I would like to introduce you all to our newest member," he said. It sounded too much like my first day at the USQDA. "He has devised a brilliant idea for the new weapon. Go ahead, Mr. Barnes."

I took a deep breath. I needed to figure out a way to not tell them the entire idea, or at least something that could stop them from making it.

I began to talk. "Well, basically it works like a miniature black hole," I began. I had to say the general idea because the director had already seen it. "What we do is shrink something to quantum size, and of course, it will retain its previous density. Assuming Albert Einstein was correct about his space-time fabric theory, and my theory is correct, this fabric could exist on a smaller scale. It would begin to suck in surrounding matter, causing mass destruction. The shrunk object doesn't necessarily have to be the density of a black hole, but it will still need to be incredibly dense. Plus, if we did make it a black hole, it would be impossible to stop. A problem with my idea is its stability. It would not be such a stable weapon." This wasn't entirely true, as my weapon would be relatively stable. "Also, we are not one hundred percent sure this space-time fabric on a smaller scale is possible." Now, that was true.

"This is brilliant, isn't it, folks?" the director said. "Does anyone have any questions for Mr. Barnes?"

"Yes, I do," one of the employees said. He was a short and rather large man, most likely in his late forties. "Why do we have to stop it and not make it a complete black hole? I'm sure it would eventually stop pulling in the surrounding matter. Why can't we just have a weapon with maximum damage?"

"Yes," another one of the scientists said. "Why stop it?"

"It wouldn't stop attracting matter," I responded. "Ever. You would not be able to stop it and it would eventually consume all of the earth, other planets, our sun, and other astronomical objects."

"Mr. Barnes has a point," the director said. "But as Mr. Wang said, we could create a weapon with unmatched damage and potential if we used your idea and made it into a full black hole."

"Sir," I began. "I don't think that is a good idea. It would destroy the earth and kill everyone in the process."

"It seems like you don't want us to create this weapon, Mr. Barnes," he said. "Is this the case? Do you not want us to have a powerful weapon? If so, tell us now so we can remove you from our agency."

Oh, man. This Chinese director had always seemed to instantly think I was on the United States' side every time I disagreed with him. He was quick to jump to conclusions, but I could see why. If I were on his side, I would be hesitant to trust me as well, as China knew I was once on the United States' side. But that doesn't make sense. Why would they allow me to still be here if they knew I wasn't on their side? Maybe the examiner realized the machine had made a mistake and just told that to the director instead of fixing the paper. I had no idea. It was so confusing

My brain was sore from thinking about why China still allowed me to be here, but my thoughts were interrupted when I remembered I was in the middle of a conversation. "I want you to have an unmatched weapon, but I—" I started.

"Wonderful," the director responded before I could finish. "Then we will begin with your idea and make it a full black hole. Thank you all for attending our meeting. Our new priority is creating a weapon using our new quantum technology to end this war. And the United States. Thank you all." He seemed to say this with such ease. Destroying another country.

People began standing up around me to leave. I had no idea what I was going to do. I needed to tell the United States about what they planned to do. I'm sure the agency could figure out how to stop this. If they couldn't, the world would perish.

***

As soon as I got back to my apartment after the day at the Chinese agency, I communicated with the USQDA. I began to tell them about the situation.

"China is planning to attack you using my invention," I told them. "They have figured out how to go quantum, or at least that's what the director said. I'm not sure when they are going to attack, though; they never said."

"Okay. What are we going to do about this?"

"We need to stop them. I could sabotage their creation."

"That could work. What we really need, though, is you here in the United States. When you get here, you can help us create your idea and use it against them. Also, we will take you out of the situation so you would not be forced to help them. They will most likely not be able to create your idea without you. Then, of course, we have the problem of them not allowing you to leave. One of our only options may be to forcefully remove you."

"But that will blow my cover!" Well, I guess they already knew I wasn't on their side.

"This is much larger than you blowing your cover! If they go through with this, it will cause mass destruction of the United States and the world."

"I understand. So, what is the plan?"

"Give me a second. Let me discuss this more with the director." He put himself on mute.

A couple of minutes later, he began to talk again. "We have a plan," he said. "We will come to pick you up as soon as possible. We should be at your apartment by two o'clock in the morning your time."

"How will you get here so fast?" I responded. It usually took twice that long to go from the U.S. to China.

"We have developed a type of jet propelled by quantum energy. That was just one of the things we worked on before you joined our agency. We will be there."

"Okay," I said. He gave some more details in the next few minutes on what would happen when the U.S. came to pick me up.

I was just hoping that China wouldn't notice the U.S. airplane landing in the middle of Beijing.

***

At around 1:50 in the morning, my earpiece sounded. "Get ready. We are almost here. We have our stealth features online so China should not see us coming. The airplane is also incredibly quiet so they should not hear us either."

I had all of my belongings ready in a single bag. I waited around 10 more minutes and was then told they were about to fly into the city. I began taking the stairs down from my apartment and eventually reached the lobby. Luckily, there was no one in the dimly lit room.

They had told me they would land close to my building. When I stepped out into the cool night air, though, I didn't see the plane. All I could see was the wide street that ran in front of the apartment building. I heard something though. Something that sounded like a loud buzz.

"Where are you guys?" I asked my earpiece. "Have you landed yet? Are you the buzzing noise I hear?"

"We are right in front of you."

"What?" I was confused. There wasn't anything in front of me. Especially an airplane. I would have to be able to see that, and all I could see was the street.

"We are in stealth mode. Just take a few, slow, careful steps out from where you are standing."

I began to walk. I slowly strode, my arms out in front of me to block impact. I had gone around three yards when I ran into something metal, although I couldn't see what it was.

Then suddenly, a door opened directly in front of me. No way . . . that couldn't be. The plane was invisible. It was invisible!

"Get in," I heard, but not from my earpiece.

I found there were steps in front of me and I quickly walked up them and shut the door behind me. Inside, I found three other people. There was Director Beck, a pilot, and the communicator I had been talking to through my earpiece during my mission. They were all sitting in plush leather chairs, and both the director and communicator had computers in front of them.

I saw many wires running along the interior of the fuselage, as well as another four chairs, not including the pilot's or co-pilot's seats (though there wasn't a co-pilot today). I assumed the wires had something to do with the invisibility.

"Hello, Mr. Barnes," the director said. "We need to get out of here." He turned to look at the pilot and he nodded. He locked the door I had shut, and the plane began to rise. Not go down a runway. Rise. This aircraft had vertical takeoff.

I guess Director Beck noticed my amazed expression. "This is a pretty neat piece of technology if I do say so myself."

"Very much so," I responded. "What is this anyway? How do you do the invisibility? And vertical takeoff? And not even have the plane make much sound?"

"We call it the Quavert. For invisibility, we use exterior cameras and screens that encompass the entire plane. The quantum engines are ultra-quiet and can change direction, allowing the plane to have a vertical takeoff then fly like a plane while in mid-air."

This was incredible! "So, this Quavert . . . do you guys have a lot of these? Are any of them weaponized?"

"We have a couple that we can use for attacks, but the others are just transports. The ones with weapons are much more expensive and much, much faster, so we—" He stopped as the pilot interrupted him.

"Sir, we seem to have a problem," he said urgently. He looked back at the director and his eyes were wide. He seemed to be gesturing that I shouldn't hear. Director Beck stood up and the pilot whispered something in his ear. I couldn't make out his words.

When Beck responded, I barely heard what he said. "Now I wish we had brought the weaponized plane," he said angrily. "Are the invisibility functions down?"

"No. They are perfectly operational." They were still in low whispers. Even though I was sitting right there with them.

"What is the problem?" I asked.

The pilot shook his head at Director Beck, but he ignored it. "Put on your seatbelt. We have a missile lock-on. It is trailing us and will catch up to us soon. It's set to detonate in three minutes."

"What?"

Everyone checked their harnesses and I made sure I was buckled in. "They must know you are gone. I bet they saw us open the door." He looked at the pilot. "Try to shake them."

"Got it," he responded. The plane began a sharp roll. Then a sharp pitch. Then both at the same time. I was becoming nauseous.

"It's still trailing us," the pilot informed after more extreme maneuvers.

"Take us lower. China won't allow the missile to detonate if it harms their people."

"Got it. We have about thirty seconds left until it detonates."

Seconds passed before the pilot spoke again. "Oh my gosh," he started. "It's . . . changing." The director showed me his screen with a live feed.

It *was* changing. The missile we had seen was transforming into something that looked like a heavy machine gun.

"We have ten seconds until the gun starts firing," the pilot said urgently. "I'm going to pitch up and do a barrel roll . . . NOW!"

At that moment, the plane lurched upwards and began to spin violently as I began to hear deafening pops, which were definitely from a machine gun. After a few more rolls, I passed out.

When I woke, minutes later, we weren't rolling anymore. We seemed to be retaining a constant altitude as well.

I looked around. Everyone seemed to be calm. "We shook it. We are out of the country's border now," the pilot said when everyone realized I was awake.

I was almost shot out of an invisible jet by China. Almost.

You can't get rid of the United States that fast.

CHAPTER 13

After that eventful plane ride, we arrived near the time of sunset in the United States. It was so weird adjusting to the time change.

I was told to go back to my original apartment. When I entered it, I found it almost identical to what it had been when I left it. Only a fine layer of dust made it different.

I set down my bag on my bed and walked into the bathroom to take a shower after the long time spent in another country. I was very tired because I had almost stayed up the entire night, though I got to sleep a bit on the plane. At least the quick plane flight on that fascinating aircraft allowed me to get back into the U.S. by dusk.

I stripped off my clothing and stepped into the refreshing, warm water of the shower. I took a long one, as there was still so much on my mind.

One of the biggest questions was why China had allowed me to stay in their country. Maybe they kept me so they could give me incorrect information. That would make sense. They kept me so they could feed the wrong things to the U.S. Man, this was like a double reverse. We were going to feed them the inaccurate information and steal theirs, and they were doing the same thing. I still had no idea, and I doubted I would ever find out.

I stepped out of the shower and dressed in my pajamas. I brushed my teeth and got into bed.

After I had fallen asleep, I had a dream. I dreamt I was still in China. The director had found my idea and I was pitching it to the entire agency. They wanted to make it into the full black hole. This time though, I didn't warn them. I continued to help them. I assisted them in making a weapon that would destroy the world. As soon as they were about to launch it, I woke up in a cold sweat. I checked the clock. It was already eleven o'clock in the morning.

I was late to work. I rushed to get dressed and didn't even worry about breakfast. I hurried out the door to the building housing the USQDA.

I walked quickly to the elevators and stepped into one. It was around 11:10 AM. I rode it downwards and finally reached the work floor. As I stepped out, I saw the director. I went over to apologize for being late.

"I overslept, sir," I began. "I apologize. That time difference messed my sleep patterns up and—"

"It is quite fine, Mr. Barnes," he interrupted. "You just finished an undercover mission in a foreign country and was almost shot out of the sky by Chinese missiles last night. I expected you to be late. Now, though, you must begin redrawing your design for a weapon. If we can create it first, we may be able to end this war."

"Yes, sir," I responded. As I walked over to my workstation, I saw John and Marisa there. They waved and hurried up to me. "Hey, Alan!" John started. "Are you okay? We heard of the attack when you tried to leave. Are you good? We wanted to contact you during your mission, but Director Beck wouldn't allow it."

"We've missed you so much," Marisa said, and I blushed.

"Glad to see you," I responded to both of them. "I need to get started on redrawing my idea. I'm supposed to get it to Director Beck so we can start making it." I paused then added, "China's got my original. It's my fault they have the idea now."

Marisa gave a smile of sympathy. "You are all right. You didn't do it on purpose. All that matters now is that you are safe." Marisa said. She turned around and walked away.

As we were walking back towards our workstation, John stopped me. "So, I've got to know, do you like Marisa, I mean *like* like?" he whispered.

"Well, I don't know. I—"

"Dude, it's obvious. Every time she talks to you, you go as red as a tomato. Like, just now, when she was talking about you, I don't think you realized how awkward you were."

"I guess I kind of do, I don't know . . ."

"Why don't you ask her out, then?" John said with a toothy grin.

"I don't know, I just . . ."

"You just what?"

"It's just, I've never . . . "

"Don't tell me you've never had a girlfriend."

"Well, I . . ." In all honesty, I had never been in a relationship. Every girl I knew was at least two years older than me because I was in such advanced classes through high school.

"Just do it," he told me. "It's not that hard. Just go up to her and say, 'Yo, you wanna go get some dinner sometime?' Then they say, 'Yeah, I'd love to.' See, it's not that hard. You can do it."

"I don't know," I said looking at the ground.

"C'mon man. Just do it."

"Okay, I might later."

"All right."

I continued walking towards my workstation and signed into my computer. I began designing my idea for Director Beck.

I tried to make it as detailed as possible. I also did the math to see how large of an object we would need to shrink to quantum size for my idea to be effective. I finished it in around an hour. Afterwards, I took my lunch break and used my computer modeling software and the 3D model printers to create a physical copy. I also printed out my digital designs on regular paper.

I began walking towards Director Beck's office. The door was open, and I stepped in. He seemed to be waiting for me. "I see you've finished your models," he said.

"Yes, sir, I have," I responded. "I made it the most detailed I could for you so we can immediately begin building. If we can jump in front of China, we will be in good hands." I handed him the papers containing my designs, as well as the 3D model. He looked at them with an approving look on his face. I continued talking, "I'm so sorry I messed up. I just gave them the ideas."

"You are all right. These ideas are wonderful. Wonderful," he said. "We will begin constructing it tomorrow. Excellent work, Mr. Barnes."

"So, you aren't mad I screwed up?" I was confused.

"Of course, I was frustrated, but we've made the best of the situation."

"Thank you," I replied, then paused. "But I feel like we should get a start on it today. We need to get going."

"Okay, then. We can get started today if you would like. I will notify you about when we will meet, most likely later this afternoon." I was still so confused why he thought it was okay I had given the idea to our enemy.

"All right, sir." I continued to stand there, contemplating telling him one more thing.

"Is there something else?" he asked.

"Well, yes."

"What is it?"

"I found something while I was in China."

"What was it?"

"I—you know, it doesn't matter."

"No really, what was it?"

"Never mind, it's fine."

"Are you sure?"

"Positive." I was about to tell him about the paper I had found in the Chinese director's desk. About my polygraph indicating I had lied. I decided to not say anything because I remembered I had been instructed to not look around. I didn't want to get in trouble.

"Okay, then," Director Beck said. "If you don't mind, I will be keeping your model."

"No, I don't mind at all."

"Thank you, Mr. Barnes. See you later today. "

"Bye." As I walked out, though, I saw the director pull something out of his pocket then reach under his desk. He did something with his hand under the desk where I couldn't see. Then I saw him reach down towards the bottom right-hand drawer.

I didn't see any more of what was going on, but I think he put my models in it.

As I continued walking away from the room, something bizarre occurred to me: the desk Director Beck used looked identical to the one the Chinese director used. It was just a different color. The style was the exact same.

If so, that meant the drawer he put my idea into was a steel locked drawer like the one I had investigated while in China.

It also meant the USQDA and the Chinese agency knew each other. And might be working together. No way. But why else would both directors have an identical desk?

They were working together. I knew it. They had to be.

I needed to see what else was inside Director Beck's drawer. It had to be something important. Something to do with our relationship with China. No doubt.

These thoughts were blazing through my head. Before I realized I was still walking, I bumped my chair at my workstation, snapping me back to reality.

John said, "You seem to be thinking about something, dude."

"Yes, just a little bit," I responded. There was no way. Director Beck was on China's side? That was impossible.

"About that idea you had?"

"Yep," I lied. I couldn't tell him what I was really thinking about. Not yet. It would put him in danger if my assumptions were correct.

I acted like I was getting back to work on the design. As I began, Marisa came up to me.

"Hey," she said.

"Hey, I replied, still intrigued about what had just occurred to me.

"So, that idea you had . . . John told me it's great. You should tell me about it sometime."

"Of course. I'd . . . I'd love to." I replied.

"Really? I mean if you . . . I mean . . . if . . . would you like to maybe like to come over tonight for dinner and tell me?" She blushed.

'Did Marisa just ask me out?' I saw John smirking behind her and concluded he had something to do with this.

"Sure, I'd love to!" I replied as coolly as I possibly could, although I couldn't believe what she had just said to me. Or what I had just found out about Beck.

"Great!" She walked away and I found my gaze transfixed in her direction.

The only problem was that I couldn't completely focus on what she had just said. I had just discovered Director Beck might not really be on our side. Or maybe the *Chinese* director was on our side, but then I wouldn't have gone on my mission to the Chinese agency because we would already have a spy.

China could be spying on us through Director Beck if he were on their side. Even more, if he was on China's side, that meant China was running the USQDA.

I needed to find out. Now. And the only way to do that would be to break into his office to look inside that drawer.

CHAPTER 14

As I left work that day, all I could think about was Director Beck. I needed to find out what was in that drawer. It could hold the secrets to his affiliation.

My only problem was actually getting *into* it. First, I would need to get into the agency undetected. Then, I would need to sneak into the director's office and open the drawer. Of course, the drawer had a lock. I would need to find the key. Also, I would need the key to the office door. Where would I find those?

Probably in Director Beck's home. This plan to get inside the office was getting increasingly more complicated. I would need some help. The perfect person might be Marisa. Tonight, at dinner, I could tell her the current situation and she might be able to help me.

By 6:30 that night, I was ready to go. I had showered, fixed my hair, and made myself look as presentable as possible.

I left the house to begin walking towards Marisa's apartment. She had given me the address earlier today after she had asked me out.

Eventually, I reached the door and knocked. A couple of seconds later, she opened it and greeted me.

"You look lovely!" I said. She had obviously prepared herself as well. She was wearing a dress and had her hair fixed in braids.

"Thank you," she responded. "Why don't you come on in?"

I walked in and she ushered me to sit down at the table. I saw steaming hot plates of food sitting there. She pulled out a chair and sat down, as did I. I couldn't believe I was on a *date*. I mean, people in high school had talked about this so casually . . . dating. This was the first one I had ever been on.

We began to talk about ourselves, our family, and many other things.

Eventually, we neared the topic of work. "I want to know all about your time in China," she said. "What was it like being a spy? And why did the United States get you out of there so fast?"

"It was stressful," I responded, then paused. "But I found something that changes everything. It could mean something horrible for the United States."

Her expression hardened. "What is it?"

"Well," I began. "Shortly after I talked to the Chinese director, I was forced to take a polygraph test, also known as a lie detector test. According to them, I passed."

"I'm sure you did. They of course wouldn't let you stay if they knew you weren't on their side."

"That's the thing. While I was in the Chinese director's office, though, I did a search through his desk drawers and found there was one that was locked. Then, I found the key. I used it on a hidden keyhole and the steel drawer—yes steel, disguised as the wood of the desk—opened. Inside, I found a single file folder named 'U.S.' Inside that folder was a piece of paper."

"What was it?" she asked, legitimately intrigued now.

"It was my polygraph results," I said. "Except not the results I was verbally given. On the paper, it said I was lying. I looked at the results of each question and I had a much larger response to the relevant questions rather than the control questions."

"Wait . . . does that mean they knew you were lying?"

"Yes."

"So, China was playing us while we were trying to play them?"

"Yes. But wait, just listen. There's more." She instantly quieted. "Director Beck's desk is identical to the one the Chinese director had. I think I even saw our director use the steel locked drawer. That's where he placed my models."

"Are you saying . . . you're saying Director Beck is on China's side?" she asked, astounded.

"Yes. Or maybe the Chinese director is on our side."

"Then you wouldn't have gone on your spy mission."

"Correct. That's why I think Director Beck is not on our side. We need to see what else is in that drawer. I bet there will be a ton of information about his relation to China and what he has lied to us about so far."

"That's impossible. There's no way." She paused. "Is there?"

"I think so."

"Does this Chinese director have a name?" she asked.

Now that I thought about it, I had never heard his name. I guess that would be better for him in the case I was a spy, which I was, so I couldn't turn him into the U.S. military.

"No, I never heard his name."

"So basically, there's an anonymous Chinese director who knows Director Beck, and they have secrets hidden in their desk about how they know each other, as well as information about their agencies?"

"Basically."

"So, we need to get inside Director Beck's drawer to see what he has been hiding?"

"Yes."

"But how do we get inside his office without him noticing? And where do we get the keys?"

"I bet they are either in his pockets or at his house most of the time."

"Then how do we get them?"

"I have no idea. Maybe we could break into his house. That's the only way we could ever get those keys. I assume when he comes home, he drops them near his door or something like that."

"But he'll notice they're gone or that some random people have entered his house. Or could we make a copy of the keys?"

"That key I saw while in China was very intricate. It would have to be a perfect copy, and I'm not sure that is possible. Stealing the keys is our best chance. We need to stop him and alert the rest of the agency before he gets to build my idea."

"And if he catches us?"

"We have to try. If not, America is as good as gone."

"Then let's do it."

***

After discussing our plan to break into the director's office, we decided it needed to wait until tomorrow night. Also, we would need John's help to do it undetected.

First, we needed to get into the director's home at around one o'clock in the morning. I would meet up with Marisa at her apartment a few minutes before that. We would walk to Director Beck's house and would need the code to his door. Assuming we had it, we would then sneak in, grab the keys, and get out without him noticing.

Next, we would head to the USQDA building. We would need John's help to hack the system. There are tons of cameras and motion sensors all around the base and inside the USQDA. John would disable them so we could enter undetected. Then, using the keys we got from the director's home, we would unlock the office door and unlock the drawer.

But then came the tricky part that we might have to play by ear: we had to return the keys without the director noticing.

We would close the drawer, leave the office, then exit the USQDA. Next, we would go back to Director Beck's house, return the keys, and return to our apartments. Another possibility might be to directly go to the Air Force or the rest of the USQDA to alert them and not even try to return the keys.

A lot of this plan was just based on our speculation of the keys being in his house and us knowing the code. If the keys weren't where we thought they were, we would have to ditch the whole plan and try to create a new one. Also, we didn't yet know the code to his house, so we would need to figure that out too.

Once I left Marisa's apartment, I walked to John's apartment and knocked on the door. He opened it and told me to come in.

"So, how was your date?" he asked.

"Good," I paused. "I need your help."

I told him the entire story, about the desks, the drawers, my polygraph results. When I finished, his mouth was open from shock.

"Director Beck is really on China's side?" he asked.

"That's what Marisa and I think. So, we created a plan to get inside that drawer to see what he's been hiding, and we need your help."

"Anything," he said.

"We need you to hack into the system to disable the security cameras, motion sensors, and so on."

A smile appeared on his face. "Oh, I can do that all right. I've been hacking since I was ten years old. Figured out how to get into our Wi-Fi without a password before second grade."

"Nice! So, we can count on you to get us in undetected?"

"Absolutely. How will I talk to you, though? I'm going to need to be in contact with you while you are executing the plan."

I thought for a moment. "I still have my earpiece. I completely forgot about it. It's still in my ear, actually." It was such a small piece of technology that I couldn't even feel it.

"I can hack into that and talk to you that way."

"That's fine. We have everything in place, except for knowing where he keeps the keys and what the code is for his door."

"I can tell you one of those."

"What?"

"I can tell you where he keeps the keys."

"How?"

"There is a hidden camera in each room, aimed towards the door. I guess it's for security purposes. I can hack into it and we can see if we can locate the keys."

"Perfect! What about the code for the door? Can you hack into it too?"

"No, it's not online. The only way I could do it is to be physically there and do some complex stuff. I have an idea, though. It's a four-digit code, right?"

"I've never used the keypad before. I've always just used my ID."

"Okay, well, it is a four-digit code. What if it's his birthday . . . four-digit code, four-digit birthday?"

"How in the world would you know his birthday?"

"We had a celebration for him. It's August 17th. So, maybe the code is 0817?"

I thought for a moment. "I think that's the best we've got. We'll try it."

"So, do you want a look at his door?"

"Absolutely." He went into his bedroom and came out with a laptop then signed in. From there, I wasn't exactly sure what he was doing. After a couple of minutes, though, John showed me his laptop and it displayed a view of his door and the peripheral surroundings.

"There are his keys," John said. I saw them. They were sitting on a small table right next to the door. "So, all you've got to do is open the door and stick your hand in to grab the keys? He probably won't notice, then, unless he hears the door open."

"That's right. Tomorrow, at around midnight you should probably get online and start doing your magic, I'd assume." He smiled again.

"Yep. I will broadcast a pre-recorded video feed of what the cameras would usually see at one in the morning, so it looks like any other night."

"Thanks so much, John. We appreciate it."

"No problem."

Now, all we had to do was break into the director's office of the most secret agency in the United States.

CHAPTER 15

The next day at work, Marisa, John, and I tried to act like we did any other day. The Quantum Research and Development Unit had begun to work on my idea. Really, we had just started on the basic parts of the weapon.

By the end of the day, I was anxious about what was to come tonight. Finally, it was time to leave the USQDA. I headed back to my apartment and changed into some more comfortable clothing that happened to be all black.

I ate dinner around 6:30. I had to wait over three more hours until I would attempt to look in that drawer. After sitting and watching television until a little after midnight, I decided to go over to John's room. I knocked on the door and I heard some shuffling from inside. He opened the door and ushered me in.

"What's up?" he asked.

"Just came over to see if everything is going well."

"Yes, it is. I have a feed of every camera you may encounter under my control. Come look over here."

I walked with him. He had a huge set-up with many computer screens. Each one was displaying two video feeds: the actual feed and the feed that would be displayed to security. Once he clicked a button, it would start displaying the pre-recorded video to security.

There was also a headset sitting next to the main computer, which I assumed he would use to contact me.

"Do you want to try out the communication with the earpiece?" he asked. "I planned on scaring you with it at like 12:40, but I guess since you're here we can give it a go."

"Wait a second . . . you were going to just randomly start talking in it, just for the fun of it?"

John smirked. "I have a little sense of humor."

I punched him playfully on the shoulder. "Okay, let's see if this works," I said.

"Then here we go. You go into my bathroom so we're pretty far apart and can see if it actually works."

"All right." I walked into his bathroom and talked. "Test, test, 1, 2, 3, test."

"I hear you," he said. "Can you hear me?"

"Yes."

"Okay, we're good." I walked back into his living room where he had the computers.

John gave me a detailed explanation of how he had hacked into the system. By the time he was finished, it was almost time to go.

"Look, it's like 12:50, you need to go," he said.

"Yep. Wish me luck."

"We've got this."

"See you soon."

"Bye"

At that, I left his room and started towards Marisa's apartment. I had dressed in all black to prevent being seen by any human eyes, though I doubted there would be any out this late at night. I strode briskly through the base and after a few minutes, I reached the door and knocked. Marisa let me in.

"Okay, are you ready?" she asked. She was also wearing all black.

"As ready as I'll ever be," I responded.

"Then let's go."

In my ear, I heard John say, "You and your girl in position?" Really? He had to already start saying that?

I laughed in my head then responded. "Dude, c'mon. We're ready."

Then Marisa asked, "What'd he say?"

"Oh, nothing. Just asking if we were ready."

"Okay. Let's head out."

We left the apartment and began to walk towards Director Beck's house. Since he was the director, he got a much larger living area than the other employees.

We walked very quickly in the dead of night. A minute or so after leaving, we saw an officer. He was patrolling the streets. We immediately crouched behind a car. Hopefully, he didn't see us.

After a couple of minutes of sitting there, we decided it would be safe to move. We continued towards our destination, both of us staying silent. Finally, we reached the director's house. At the front door, there was a keypad, just as we had planned.

Marisa whispered, "What's the code?"

"John thinks it is his birthday."

"Okay."

In my ear, John began to talk. "Get ready to enter the numbers." He paused. "Okay. Zero."

"Got it," I responded.

"Okay. Next: 8, 1, 7."

I finished entering all of the numbers, then clicked the enter button. There was a pretty loud beep then the lock clicked, and the door popped open. Marisa and I looked at each other and frowned. The lock had been so loud. If he had woken up, it was over. We both scrambled out of sight if Beck decided to look around his front door.

We waited for a few minutes. Clear. He wasn't coming to check. We gestured toward each other and went back to the door. I stuck my head through the open part of the door and looked around. I found the little table I had seen the other day. On top was the ring of keys.

But, in the distance, on the floor, I thought I saw something metal gleaming in the moonlight from the window. I looked a little closer. I noticed there seemed to be a wood plank from the floor pulled up next to whatever that metal was. I couldn't see what the metal was any better, though. I decided I just needed to get out of here.

I grabbed the keys and shut the door as quietly as possible. I don't think he woke up. On my mind, though, was that metal. What was it? Maybe it was just a belt or something. It just seemed much larger than that.

Anyway, it didn't matter. We just needed to get to his office. I put the metal out of my mind. As I decided it was nothing, John began to talk through the earpiece. "Was the code correct?" he asked. "Did you get the keys?"

"Yes. We've got them."

When we were a little further from Beck's home, Marisa asked me, "What took so long? What were you looking at in there?"

I didn't think whatever that was really mattered, so I just replied, "I don't know. I got the keys."

"Okay, then." We closed the door behind us and began to walk towards the USQDA in deafening silence. We made it to the building and entered. Next, we opened the door saying, "Special Operations."

We found the elevator and I used my ID. I had to. There was no other way for us to enter the headquarters. It would have been much better if we would have used someone else's so no one would know it was us who were the people who happened to be entering the USQDA in the dead of night.

We rode the elevator down and stepped out. We started towards the office and reached the door.

"Which key is it?" Marisa asked.

THE QUANTUM STATE

"I'm not sure. We can just try all of them."

"Okay."

We tried each of the keys, but none of them worked. Finally, we reached the final key and inserted it. It turned and unlocked the door. Marisa and I let out our breaths. For a second, we thought none of them would let us in.

We entered the room and shut the door behind us, but only so that it was still ajar. We went to the desk. It *was* identical to the Chinese director's desk, just like I had thought.

I reached underneath for the latch. I found it. I inserted a key that seemed like it would fit, and it did. I turned the key and the drawer popped open. It was a steel drawer like I had expected.

When I opened the drawer, I found a few different things.

The first was, of course, my models. The second was my polygraph results. It was identical to the results I had seen in China. Then, I saw the paper I had been forced to give to the Chinese director with my original idea that I had so carelessly not shoved in my pocket well enough. Except it was not an original. It was a scanned copy. All of this evidence proved Director Beck was absolutely on China's side.

Then, the final thing I found was a note. It was just random letters:

uljdce gd zamzyqgngd gc if ihpnwceel lmhnnq ilxnz qw ecyxw fijjb fcnu dm qajk ixwq ey vshqem sj iufd ifafw

"What is that?" Marisa asked.

"Looks like a code," I said, then continued. "John, you there?"

"Yes. What did you find?"

"Beck's on China's side. We found my actual polygraph results, my models, including a scanned copy of the one I was forced to give to the Chinese director, and something that looks like some type of code."

"What are the letters?" he asked.

"Oh, there are over one hundred."

"What are they?"

I began to give him the letters. Once I was finished, he asked, "Is there a key?"

"Nope. Just the letters."

"All right. I bet it's a Vigenère cipher. You have to have a key to crack it unless you want to try the million words in the English language, and it might not even be one of those. Most likely it's not. If we can get a key, though, it's possible to decode."

"Okay. We need to get out of here, crack the code, and go to the rest of the USQDA. We need to get out of here fast. We should go straight to the Air Force."

"That might be a clever idea," a familiar man's voice said near the door. "But you should have left a couple of minutes ago."

It was Director Beck. With a pistol in his hand.

CHAPTER 16

Marisa and I were petrified.

"I have a system that alerts me if that latch is opened," he said. "But now I will need you to come with me." He put on a sly, chilling smile. "I knew my brother shouldn't have let you stay in his office unattended." What was he talking about? His brother? When was I—then I remembered: In China when I originally checked out the Chinese director's desk, he left me unattended. Did that mean . . .

"Wait, the Chinese director is your brother?" I asked.

"You finally figured it out. Of course Calvin is my brother," he said in a mocking, sarcastic voice. So that was the Chinese director's name. Not very Chinese.

"And the attack on the Quavert back from China?"

"Simulated! Ha! And, let me make this clear: Don't try any funny business." He gestured towards his firearm and pointed it at Marisa. The look on her face was pure fear. She seemed to be in shock.

He told us to come with him, and we did, although we had no idea where he was taking us. We approached the elevators and he told us to get in. Were we going to the surface? He inserted his card and stepped in with us.

Then, unexpectedly, the elevator lurched downwards, and we began to lower even further than we were right now.

We seemed to descend forever until we stopped. The doors opened and we found a massive, sparkling white room filled with computers. It almost looked like the NASA mission control center. There was a door to our left and our right. We seemed to be heading towards the one on the left.

"So, do you like my . . . second office?" he asked, rhetorically, with a sly smile. "But, you two will follow me through this door." He opened the one on the left side and forced us through it. At that point, I contemplated the idea of fighting back. Marisa was in front of me, and if I could get on top of Director Beck before he could shoot, I could grab the gun.

I didn't want to risk Marisa getting hurt, though. It was just too large of a risk.

On the other side of the door, I found a hallway with at least ten different doors, five on either side.

"Now, this is where you will be staying." He opened the door and prodded me with his pistol.

"Wait," he said as his phone began to ring. He pulled me back and put me into a half-nelson with his free hand holding the gun to my forehead. "I think you may have someone who wants to talk to you." He held up the phone to my ear.

"Alan, HELP!" It was my mother. "There are people in our house. We're hiding and they have almost found—" I heard Dylan yell and the call ended.

"How did you get my phone?" I asked, not knowing if I should believe that was my real family or not.

"The USQDA can do whatever they want," he responded. "But, I would recommend you do everything I say, or this pistol might need to be used on someone other than you or Palmer's skull. Now, in." At that moment—I'm not sure if it was rage or a sudden burst of risk and energy—I decided I had to defend myself. Before I walked into the room he was instructing me to go into, I turned around incredibly fast and punched him as hard as I could in the face, hoping it would knock him clean out.

As I did this, I heard Marisa say, "No!" but it was too late. He had staggered backward but it wasn't enough to knock him out. In Beck's momentary pause, Marisa dove for the gun as fast as she could. It didn't work. Before she could grab it, Beck was back on his feet with the gun in his hand. He fired it at Marisa and it nearly hit her. He got a better hold on the weapon and pointed it at me before Marisa could do anything else. Everything stopped. Marisa and I stopped fighting against him. It was just us and him, him with a gun, pointing it straight at me.

He seemed winded, but not too exhausted. Then, after the momentary silence, Beck moved his hand, not to the left as to hurt Marisa, but down. He pulled the trigger.

Excruciating pain erupted all around my foot. It was the worst pain I had ever felt in my life.

"You need to calm down," Beck said coolly as though nothing had happened, although he still was breathing heavily. "Oh, and don't worry, that shot won't kill you," he added. "It will give us enough time to torture you before we do that."

I could barely hear him through the screaming pain of my foot.

He forced me into a room and I crumpled to the ground, feeling as though my life was ending. If I didn't do something, it would. I needed to think. The lessons from my father were beginning to emerge in my head. I needed to calm down, take a deep breath, and think. The times people needed to think most were usually the times they thought least. That needed to not happen to me. Nevertheless, it was agonizing to formulate anything through all this pain. But I tried. I tried harder than I ever had in my life to do something. Harder than the times I competed and won at academic contests of people years older than me. Harder than the time when I had studied for the ACT for hours upon end. I tried to conjure my thoughts, make access to my brain. And I succeeded.

I took a deep breath and put the excruciating pain on a back burner. I used my brain. 'What was the first thing I needed to do?' I needed to stop the bleeding. I didn't remember any main veins or arteries in my foot that could make me bleed this much, but he had hit *something* important. So how would I stop it? I took off my shirt so I could use it to help stop the loss of blood. I rolled up my pants and began to use the skills I had learned back in high school. Outside of school, I had taken a first-aid class.

I had my foot wrapped up. 'What did I need to do now?' Pressure. The wound needed pressure. I applied as much as I possibly could to help stop the bleeding. After a couple of minutes, it did begin to slow. Then, after a bit longer, I felt it begin to stop. There was no way I would remove the shirt, even if it was wet with blood. That was one of the number one rules about treating a major wound: apply pressure and never remove the fabric or whatever else you are using to stop the blood.

Now that I had my bleeding stopped, what did I need to do next? I didn't know if Beck was telling me the truth or not—if the shot would kill me. Since the loss of blood had ceased, I now had time. Time to figure out what to do. I needed to get out of here and to a hospital. I looked around the room.

I realized there was a single bottle of water sitting on the floor with a lone wooden chair in the center of the room. That was it. The rest of the room was just empty. No windows, no food, no bed. Just the water and chair. The room was pitch black, except for a tiny red dot on the ceiling—a camera—and a streak of light in the crack of the door.

I needed to drink water. I had lost so much blood I needed fluids. I slowly moved over to the water and opened it using one hand. My foot still was searing pain, and I thought my nerves might just stop working. That is kind of what I hoped. With no nerves in my foot, that meant no more pain. I drank around one-third of the bottle before I stopped myself. I would need to save it for later, assuming—no, hoping—I would have a "later." I needed to have optimism, just like Beck had once told me. I needed optimism.

But that was hard to find right now. I was stuck in a pitch-black room, held captive by someone I used to trust, had a gunshot wound in my foot, had no way to contact the outside world, put my parents and brother in danger, had no food, and only had a small bottle of water, enough to last a few days.

I had to figure a way out. Or I would die.

***

The following hours felt like an eternity. I was fortunate that the shot had not penetrated a vein or artery. If so, I would be dead. It still hurt like heck, though. It was nothing like I had ever felt before.

But I needed to figure out how to get proper medical care. And how to get out of here.

I had been thinking about what to do. There's no way I could do anything without help, but I could at least try. After all, I was an engineer.

All there was for me to work with was a chair and a bottle of water. What could I possibly do? First, of course, I needed to get out of the way of the camera. It was placed in the corner so it could see the entire room, but I knew there was always a blind spot. Right underneath the camera always was unable to be seen. I grabbed my water and scooted the best I could underneath it. My foot was still killing me, but I had to do something. I had to deal with the pain.

It took me at least a couple of minutes to move a few feet. I then began thinking of a way to get out of here. I analyzed the door. There was no door handle on this side, and based on the technology down here, I suspected the door had an electromagnetic lock.

What could I use to get through that? With a chair and some water?

Then, it occurred to me: if it were an electromagnetic lock, water would mess up the electricity. But then where were the wires? They were most likely in the wall.

I began to move again, this time towards the door. In the crack between it and the wall, I thought I saw some type of metal, probably the lock.

My only chance of survival would be to try and make that lock open. If I could fry the wires, I could escape. I decided I would need to pour my precious water there. As I attempted to get up, my foot cried out in pain. I couldn't reach it from the ground. I tried again and made sure all my weight was off of my foot. I was able to get to the door.

I opened my water again and tried to get some onto the lock and the area around it. I mean, even if I drank the water, I would die anyway. I had to try.

I heard a crackling noise, but it didn't look like anything had happened. I tried pushing on the door. Again, nothing happened, except for the pain in my foot spiking.

As I was about to give up hope of escaping and living, I pushed with every ounce of strength I could muster, and I felt the door move as my foot shrieked out in pain. I pushed again, trying my hardest to block out the pain, and it opened.

I couldn't believe that had actually worked. After briefly having a feeling of relief, I realized the camera would know I was gone. It would see the door opening and closing.

I rushed out of my cell as fast as I could with an unusable foot, still with searing pain, and went to Marisa's cell door with the water in hand. I banged on the door as loud as I could without alerting Beck. I had to make sure no one heard me but her. She came to the door and realized I was there. I splashed water on the lock and began to pull, although I didn't feel like I was doing such a respectable job because my foot just spiked in pain again. She mirrored my actions by pushing from the other side. We got the door to open and she rushed out of her cell.

Before saying anything, she came up to me, wrapped her arms around me, then kissed me as I fell to the ground. The overwhelming pain in my foot seemed to dissipate and all I could focus on was in front of me. It was like nothing I had imagined. This—my first kiss—came out of nowhere. Was she even being genuine? Or was she just doing it because we had almost died. She kissed me passionately on the lips, so only a true kiss would be like that. I was surprised. I could manage my searing pain, but I couldn't comprehend what was happening right now. It wasn't exactly in the surroundings I would have ideally dreamt of, but it was astounding nevertheless.

As we pulled apart after what had seemed like forever, we both looked at each other, unsure of what had just happened. That moment of relief, to say the least, was an escape from our circumstances—that we were prisoners on the run—well, not me, as I couldn't exactly run with one foot.

"Oh my goodness! Are you all right?" she asked.

"I'm not dead," I whispered hoarsely, as my foot threatened to make me pass out. I wished I could have said more. I wish I could have just acknowledged the kiss. But I couldn't. I could only deal with the pain for so long. And that "so long" was beginning to wear off—and so was the shirt I used to stop the bleeding. It had stopped working. Fresh blood was streaming down my skin.

"You need to get that foot taken care of," she said when she realized it was bleeding again.

I gave a nod. I couldn't say much through the amount of pain I was experiencing.

"You need a wheelchair or something you can use to move." I nodded. "We need to get out of here. Beck will be here any time now. Here, I'll help you walk. Put your weight on me."

I did what she said and we began to move, though not effectively at all. Before we could make it further than a few paces, we heard footsteps behind us.

"Run!" she yelled.

But I couldn't. Not with this defective foot.

We attempted to move as fast as we could, almost operating like people would in a three-legged race. I wish that were the situation we were in. My foot felt like it was on fire. I had to keep going though. I had to. If I didn't, I would die.

The pain was incomprehensible. I could barely hear the gunshots behind us. One whizzed past my head just as we turned at the end of the hallway, opposite the door that led into the hall with the cells. Apparently, there was much more to this complex.

We continued to move as fast as we could and eventually found ourselves in another, much shorter hallway with a single door at the end. Although we had seen many doors before this one, there was a label on it saying, "Exit." If we could just get to that door, we might be able to escape.

But I didn't think I could make it that far. I felt as though I was about to pass out. I was about to *make* myself pass out so I could just stop the pain. No.

No! I couldn't do that. That would end all hopes of Marisa ever getting away. And I would die. I had to keep going.

We were almost to the door when Beck appeared behind us. We kept running—or at least moving.

"You didn't think you could get away that fast, did you?" He fired his pistol and nearly hit us again.

We didn't stop. We went through the door and slammed it behind us, finding a long staircase. He wasn't following us, or at least it seemed. But why would he do that? He could burst through at any moment and kill us for good.

"That must lead to the surface!" Marisa said.

"How are we supposed to stop Beck from coming in here?" I asked urgently.

She looked near the door handle then turned a lock. How didn't I see that? I wondered if I was delusional from the pain. Moving that far so fast was excruciating.

All I could do was look at the stairs and hold my mouth open in shock. Marisa seemed to understand my expression.

"I'll help you." The door began to sound. Beck was pounding on it. He seemed to be out of his mind.

We quickly began to climb the stairs. After several seconds, we had only made it onto the first step. Hopefully, the lock would hold.

Once we got into the hang of it, it took us around six seconds for us to climb a stair. It took every bit of energy I could gather.

We continued going up the never-ending stairs. The pounding on the door eventually subsided.

After a few more minutes, we made it to the top. There, we found another door. So many doors in this place.

Marisa opened it with excitement. As we did this, I slipped. I fell down the stairs. My foot erupted in pain, along with the rest of my body.

For a moment, I just lay there, in excruciating pain. In the next, I hear a scuffle up above me. It sounded like fighting. Before I could listen any longer, I passed out from the unbearable pain.

CHAPTER 17

I had no idea how long I was out. All I know is that Marisa was standing over me when I woke up. I was still at the bottom of the staircase, but there were no more sounds of fighting.

"Alan, are you okay?" she asked.

"Beck . . ." I croaked. I had to figure out what we needed to do next.

"He's up there." She gestured up the staircase. "I had to take him out."

"How?"

"Well, let's just say I got a good hit on a place we shouldn't talk about." She gave a quick smirk. Usually, I would have laughed, but I couldn't even remember what it felt like to be uninjured. The wound hurt so much.

"Then, I got some good punches to his face before he could react," she continued. "And now he's knocked out." She showed me his gun and his ID badge she had taken from him. "We need to get out of here."

"How . . ." I could barely make out the words.

"Well, that's not really an exit. Behind that door is just an empty room. I have no idea how he got into it. There must be some secret door or staircase or something. I'll figure out a way out."

Then I remembered. "My . . . family."

"I don't know where they are," she began in a somber tone. "We'll find them. I promise. But we need to get you out of here and to a hospital."

I didn't even attempt to stand up.

"Just stay here. I'll get you something. We need to get you to the hospital as soon as possible."

She left, and in around two minutes she returned with a rolling desk chair. "I found this in his office—well, complex. If we can get you in it, I can push you around."

I tried my hardest to be helpful while she attempted to lift me into the chair. After a couple of minutes of struggling, we finally were able to get me into the chair.

My foot was still killing me, but at least I didn't have to walk anymore.

"Where are we going to exit?" she asked me. "I don't think we should use the main exit because when we go back up to the USQDA, they will not know what's going on. Plus, they might be on Beck's side. Even if we get up to the ground level, the Air Force might not even be on our side." I just nodded. I attempted to pull myself together and use my brain. But my foot was hurting worse than before. Worse than ever.

"We should look around for a secondary entrance or exit," she continued. "There has to be one that his coworkers from China use. I mean, they won't just let those guys on the base, unless, of course, the Air Force is on Beck's side." She paused. "Then I guess we have to look for a door down here. Any other way means the Air Force isn't on our side and will go after us as soon as we use the main elevators."

I nodded again. My foot was hurting like nothing I had ever experienced before. I needed medical care. But I also needed to find my family. I was unable to do that right now though. I needed to get to a hospital.

After a few minutes (or hours, I had no idea of how much time had passed as all I could process was my pain) of looking around the complex, we were back into that initial room with the computers. I bet there was tons of information stored on there, but none of that was any use if I didn't live through this.

We ignored the potential information on the computers and continued to look around. On the wall near the elevator was a map of this whole area. It showed this main room connected to the hallway with the cells, as well as many more areas, all of which seemed to be laboratories. This place was huge.

Then, we noticed on the map there was the exit we had been looking for. It was behind the other door that we hadn't gone through when Beck brought us down here.

We decided to cautiously go through it. Marisa opened the door and pushed me past the doorway. We were in another hallway, this one dimly lit. We walked briskly through until we reached a huge open area. It had to be at least the size of a football field.

I looked around and realized that in the center of the floor was one of those planes. Like the one that picked me up from China—a Quavert—but this one was weaponized.

"Oh my goodness . . ." Marisa said. I gave her the best smile I could in this situation.

We continued towards the aircraft and found the door open. It even had a ramp. Marisa pushed me up, then came up behind me. She did a look-over on what we had here.

"How am I supposed to fly this?" she asked. I shook my head, expressing I had no idea. "And how do I start this?"

She just stood there for a few moments, pacing slowly. As she was turning around to go the other way, the Quavert powered on. We both jumped as we felt the machine come to life. The buttons on the dashboard lit up, and the main screen powered on.

Marisa looked down at where she had just come from. "Ahh, there's a hidden ID scanner. The badge must have rubbed the pad when I turned around."

She then began to investigate the controls. She clicked a button and the door slid shut. She clicked another button, but nothing seemed to happen.

"Invisibility," she said, turning to look at me with an amused face. "Now, we just need to figure out how to get out of here. The problem is that I'm not a pilot."

Instantaneously, an automated voice sounded through the speakers embedded in the ship. "Enable fully-automated pilot?" On the screen, the same question popped up with the option to say yes or no. I guess this aircraft was listening to us.

Marisa clicked, "yes" on the screen, then looked to see what had happened. It said that the auto-pilot had been enabled. She seemed to click something else on the screen, and the Quavert began to talk again.

"Welcome, Timothy Beck. Where would you like to go today? Either enter a destination on display or say where you want to be taken."

Marisa responded, "The nearest hospital."

"Access denied. Voice authentication failed. Confirm using security questions?" It must have noticed that Marisa did not have the same voice as Beck. I guess this plane knew more than we thought it did.

"Yes," she responded.

"Loading encryption and response mechanisms." A couple of seconds later, it continued. "Here is the question: What is the name of your brother?"

Marisa looked confused. She didn't remember.

But I did. When Beck had caught us, he let his brother's name slip. "Calvin," I responded, as confidently as I could, with as much energy as I could conjure. My never-ending pain made it hard to do anything.

"Response accepted. Initiating flight mode and locating the nearest hospital." Marisa turned around to me with a look of delight. "Nearest major hospital found. It is located in Las Vegas, Nevada. It will take approximately eight minutes to destination. Vertical take-off commissioning in less than ten seconds. Please secure yourself into your seats."

Marisa came over to me and tried to help me into a seat. After a couple of tries—and more excruciating pain—we got me into one and secured myself to it.

She got into the seat next to me, and we heard some type of door above us opening. There must be an opening ceiling on that huge hangar where this plane was kept. After a few more seconds, I realized we were outside and flying. I had no idea how they kept that opening ceiling concealed, nor could I even think about it. My foot was hurting the worst it had so far since Beck shot me. It felt like hot knives were being jabbed into my skin. Then before I knew it, I felt reality slipping away and I passed out yet again.

***

When I awoke, I was on a stretcher, being pushed quickly through a hospital. Marisa was nowhere to be seen.

"He's awake." One of the people pushing me had noticed my eyes opening.

"Put him under," another one of them said.

Then, again, after a couple of seconds, I was out of it and falling into a terrorizing dream.

I was back in my cell in Beck's underground complex and was about to die from dehydration. Suddenly, my door opened.

"Get up," Beck said. I couldn't. He repeated himself. "Get up." When I didn't, he came over to me and forced me up onto my feet. I was too weak to do anything but feel pain.

He led me into the hallway, and I saw Marisa, my mom, my dad, and Dylan standing in a line, all held captive by members of the USQDA I had previously trusted. They each had a pistol pressed against their head as Beck just smiled.

He clapped his hands. Less than a second later, the person I recognized as the Research and Development Manager pulled the trigger, and Marisa dropped to the ground. Beck clapped again, but before my mother was shot, she released a couple of words: "I'm sorry." Then she fell. Then was my dad, then after him was Dylan. By now, I was screaming and crying. Beck himself pointed a gun at me and pulled the trigger.

***

I was stuck in this dream for what seemed forever until I began to see blinding white lights. *'Am I dead? Is this what it feels like to die?'* The pain in my foot had gone away, so I assumed I was dead.

But in the next moment, I saw a person I didn't expect (assuming I was dead). It was a nurse. I *was* alive. I was in a hospital.

As I attempted to sit up, I realized I had just been in surgery. The nurse began to talk to me then started asking post-surgery triage questions.

"Your surgery went very well," the nurse said. "The entire bullet has been removed from your foot. You should be able to walk very soon. But first, I must ask you some questions. What is your pain level on a scale of one to ten?"

I thought about it and responded, "Three." I still had some pain in my foot, but it was so, *so* much less than it had been before.

"Is the pain you are experiencing specifically in your foot?"

"Yes." The questions continued like this.

Then, one of the last questions she asked was not just about my health. "Do you remember any information that would be useful in the immediate search for the culprit?"

"No, I don't." I had to say that. There was just so much that could go wrong if I said yes. If other people got involved, Beck would just kill my family. He would also hurry up the process of destroying the United States.

After questioning me, the nurse asked me if I was hungry. When I was talking to the nurse, I had no idea if I was making sense or not. In my own mind, I seemed to be.

She came back with a plate of steaming hot food. I gobbled it down, though I was still experiencing effects from the anesthesia. I couldn't believe it had only been six hours ago when Beck had found us in his office. It felt like ages.

After finishing my meal, I fell asleep. I had no idea for how long, but when I awoke, the sun was shining very brightly through my window. I assumed it was around midday. My foot was still hurting and throbbing, but it was nothing compared to what I had experienced before.

Then in a few more minutes, the nurse came back into my room and asked me some more questions. I guess she decided I was completely rational by now because she decided to tell me something.

"If you are feeling well enough, we would like you to meet with someone today to describe what happened to give you this injury." She gestured towards my foot. "Just let me know when you are ready."

That made sense. Except, for some reason, I felt the police department wanted the information as soon as possible. Before I could think about anything else, though, I needed to know where Marisa was. I asked the nurse.

"You may see her later today." She seemed to be avoiding my question.

"What about my fam—" I stopped myself, remembering that I shouldn't let slip about anything that had happened. If so, China and Beck could strike the U.S. before their planned date (if they had one) and the U.S. military wouldn't be able to do anything to stop them. I needed to keep it a secret and get out of here before that meeting today so I wouldn't be forced to tell them about the current circumstances. I needed to find my family and Marisa then stop China before they could destroy the United States.

How I would do that . . . I had no idea.

CHAPTER 18

"Alan? Are you there?" John's voice burst into my ear. He must have just gotten off work because it was around six o'clock in the evening. I had completely forgotten about my earpiece.

"Yeah, I'm here."

"I'm so glad you're here! I thought you had died! What happened? I tracked you to a hospital. Why are you there?" Even though he had so many questions, I was so glad to hear his voice.

"Well, Beck is definitely not on our side," I responded quietly to ensure no one would hear me. "He's got my family. He also shot me in the foot then locked me up in his secret office, well, complex. It's underneath the USQDA. Marisa and I were able to escape, and she took down Beck. We explored some more and found the exit I guess he uses for the Chinese so they can come into his complex undetected. Then, we—"

"Are you okay, dear?" My nurse had just come into my room. I guess she had heard me talking to John, even though I was talking very quietly.

"Absolutely fine."

She looked at me with a face of disbelief. "Alright. Let me know if you need anything." At that, she left the room.

"So, keep going. What did you do next?"

"We found this huge underground hangar. It had a weaponized Quavert in it. When we got inside it, Marisa tried to figure out how to get to a hospital. When she mentioned that she couldn't pilot an aircraft, this automated—"

Another nurse had come in this time. "Mr. Barnes, are you alright? You seem to be talking to yourself."

"No, I am not talking." I was getting stingy now. *'Could I just finish my story?'* "And I would appreciate it if you left me alone in my private room." She walked out without another word. Great, I was on her bad side too.

"Okay, keep going."

"Okay, this automated system on the plane asked if she wanted to enable auto-pilot. When she said yes, it basically told her she wasn't Beck based on her voice. It then asked the security question, 'What is your brother's name?' Earlier, Beck had let it slip that his brother was the Chinese director and that his name was Calvin. So, the plane brought us here, but I've been out since the plane took off, so I'm not sure what happened. I just know I had surgery."

"That's crazy." He paused. "So, how do we stop him? And what's the plan to rescue your family?"

"First, I need to get out of here. I'm supposed to have a meeting this afternoon about what happened. I can't be telling the world what happened. If so, Beck and the Chinese agency will destroy the United States as soon as possible so the military can't react. Remember, they still have that original weapon we designed first. The one that works like a nuclear bomb. They could still use that. Plus, if I say anything, he will kill my family—if he hasn't already." Those words made my heart sink. They couldn't be dead. They just couldn't.

"You know, he's not going to hurt your family. He'll continue, maybe, to use them against you, though. Like right now, he's going to try to draw you in to try to save them. He might just be waiting for you so he can get you then, so you can't tell anyone. He knows if he hurts any one of them you will tell the world, which works out badly for both of you. He'll keep them alive so he can catch you when you come to retrieve them. The one way he would hurt them is if you tell anyone. Until then, they have much more value alive than dead to him."

John's little conversation gave me mixed emotions. He was telling me my family was safe—or at least as safe as they could be while captive. That made me feel good. But he was also telling me that Beck might use them against me. That made me feel horrible. After all, I was the one who joined the USQDA, which was what led to all this. If I would have just said 'no thank you,' I wouldn't have put my family in danger. I would still be a student at MIT.

"What about escaping the hospital?" Escaping a hospital—so weird to think about.

"I think you should tell them you don't feel up to the meeting. That gives you an extra 24 hours to figure out what to do."

"Okay. Where do you think Marisa is?"

"Honestly?"

"Yeah."

"She's probably in jail. She's a prime suspect for your bullet wound. She's going to be held there until that meeting, I bet." So, I put Marisa in danger too, just by joining the USQDA. I put the entire world at risk.

"What about my family? Where are they?"

"I have no idea. I did want to bring something else up, though."

"What?"

"Remember that code? The one you gave to me from Beck's office?"

"Did you crack it?"

"That's the thing. My computer has tried every word in the dictionary and is moving on to random letter combinations. It hasn't cracked it yet."

"What do you think is in that message?"

"Something especially important. I mean, if it weren't, they wouldn't take the time to encode it."

"True."

"I'll keep working, see if I can crack it. You need to get some rest."

"Thanks so much, John."

"No problem."

I then remembered something I wanted to ask. "Hey, wait. What are they saying about me and Marisa at the USQDA? Has anything changed?"

"Beck is just saying you guys have been let go. He won't give any other information."

"Are you guys still working on my idea?"

"Yeah. We are making a lot of progress. We're working every day of the week, including Sunday. The weapon may be ready in a couple of weeks or less." This was an issue.

"Okay. I'll talk to you later," I said.

"See you. Get some rest. Bye."

"Bye."

***

Later that day, the nurse came in to remind me of the meeting. I had told her I didn't feel up to it. Luckily, it was the first nurse I had seen after my surgery, not the one I had been rude to earlier.

I needed to figure out how to get out of here and rescue Marisa. From there, I would need to stop China.

But, how would I do that? How could I escape from my hospital room? I mean, I just began recovering from an emergency surgery.

Then, how would I find Marisa? We had no way to communicate. Plus, if she were in jail, I couldn't break in there. *Breaking into jail?* Man, this whole plan was so ironic.

Maybe, just maybe, I should wait until the meeting. There, she and I could figure out something together. I wasn't strong as of right now with my foot in recovery. But, if both of us were to try to escape at the same time, we might be able to make it to the Quavert.

Then, I had an even better plan. If we did wait until the meeting, we could tell the police a fake name or something. We could say Marisa was in shock, so she did not see the guy. We could tell them a fake place it happened, just so we could get out of there and to the aircraft. Once we made it to the Quavert, it was smooth sailing from there—at least smooth sailing away from the police.

Later that night, I was eating dinner and thinking about exactly what I would do. I finished my pile of green beans and set my plate to the side. A few minutes later, I fell into a dreamless sleep.

I awoke the next morning at around ten o'clock. Soon after, the nurse came into the room, offering me breakfast. She also reminded me I needed to attend the meeting.

"The police request you attend a meeting with them today for more details on the shooting," she said.

"What time?" I asked.

"As soon as possible. If you are ready now, they will be here in a couple of minutes."

"Yes, please, I'm ready." I wanted to get my plan in action ASAP.

"Wonderful. They should be here very soon."

"They?" I was curious to find out who else would be there.

"Yes, they. I'm not sure who all will be there, but I think there's going to be the case detective and a few others." I hoped she was talking about Marisa.

The nurse left the room, leaving me in my bed. After a couple of minutes, just like she said, a few people knocked lightly on my door and made their way in. Marisa was not among them.

The first was a man who had dark brown hair that came down a bit past his ears. He seemed to be in his mid-forties and was carrying a pad of paper in one hand and a briefcase in the other. The other was a police officer.

"Hello, Mr. Barnes," the one with the long hair said. "My name is Charles. I am the detective on this case. I hope you are feeling better compared to yesterday."

"Yes, sir, I am. How did you know my name?"

"We found your records after we confirmed your identity using your ID. I am glad you are feeling better. As I'm sure you have guessed, I am here to find out exactly what happened to result in this injury." He gestured towards my foot. "Tell me exactly what happened yesterday morning when you were delivered to this hospital. The bullet wound seemed to have been there for hours before. Did this delay between the time of the injury and time you were brought here have anything to do with the location in which you had been shot?"

I needed to keep my answers consistent that I did not know much about what happened. "I'm not sure, sir."

"Do you know where you were at the time of the shot?"

"I don't remember. Everything was so crazy afterward."

"What do you mean by 'crazy'?"

"I just mean that my foot hurt horribly."

"Do you remember what your attacker looked like?"

"I have no idea."

"Was the injury self-inflicted?"

"No, sir."

"Do you have any other information that could be useful in determining the subject?"

"I'm not sure, sir." The interrogator seemed to be getting frustrated.

"Was the suspect, Marisa Palmer, involved in any way?" To stay with my current trend of not knowing anything, this would be a tough question to answer.

"I'm not sure, sir. I believe, though, she was the one to deliver me to the hospital. She and I have been friends for a long time. I highly doubt she did it."

"Do you believe the shot may have been an accident?"

"I don't know. It's either that or some random person was the culprit."

"Are you saying that your friend, Marisa, is most likely the offender?"

"No, no. That's the least of what I'm saying. I mean it's either her or someone random, and the random person is much, much more likely to have committed the crime."

"Would it be helpful for you and Marisa to be interrogated together so we can find out exactly what happened between the two of you? This might allow us to piece together the entire story."

"I think that might be a good idea." I tried to fake being frustrated, but really, inside I was relieved. I had made it so Marisa and I could possibly communicate and figure out a way to get out together. I continued, "I really want you to catch my attacker for the safety of myself and others. It's just I don't remember anything, and I wish I did."

"Do not worry, Alan." His expression seemed to soften. "We have seen many cases where the person affected is like this. We will call Ms. Palmer to come to meet with us here for joint questioning." He stood up to talk to the police officer and said something into his radio.

Around ten minutes later, Marisa and another police officer entered the room.

"Mr. Barnes has requested that you be part of this interrogation," Charles said to Marisa. "He seems to not remember much of what the cause of his injury was and believes if you both tell the story at the same time, we may be able to piece together the entire event. Now, please sit." The police officer that had brought Marisa here left the room.

"So," Charles continued, "Let's get straight into some questions. Marisa, were you or were you not the cause of Alan's injury?"

"I was not," she responded.

"Alan, do you agree with this?"

"Yes, sir," I said.

"Ms. Palmer, do you have any clue to what may help find the attacker?"

"No, sir." Marisa seemed to have caught on to how I was doing this when I said that I agreed, and she was pretending like we didn't know anything. "When I found Alan, he had the bullet wound in his foot. I immediately rushed him to the hospital."

"When you arrived at the emergency room, you had come in a silver SUV. Is this registered under your name?"

"Yes, sir."

"When we verify the ownership of the vehicle, will we find the information you have told us to be true?"

"Yes, sir."

"I have one more question. How did Marisa know Alan was injured if she was not at the scene of the crime? Alan does not remember much from directly after his injury. How would you have been able to find out he had been shot?"

As I was about to speak up, Marisa did instead. "He called me."

"He called you?" he said, disbelievingly. "Why would he call *you* and not an ambulance?"

"I'm not sure. He didn't seem to be . . . with it."

"Why did you not call authorities as soon as you found out about this injury?"

Marisa looked like she didn't know what to say. "I'm not sure. I guess I wasn't thinking straight either. I must have been too worried about him."

"But you were able to drive a car?" These questions were getting increasingly more difficult. Since the story we were telling these people was not true, it was hard to keep a consistent storyline going the entire time. I had no idea how this question could be answered.

"I'm not sure, sir," she responded. That's probably the best either of us could have done.

"Where did you go when you drove the car, Ms. Palmer? You had to have a destination in mind."

"I . . . I don't know."

"There seems to be a lot of missing information in this story. I feel like there's something going on here. For now, I want Ms. Palmer to continue to be detained at the—"

I suddenly decided to speak up. "Sir, I know she didn't do it, and she says she didn't, so why can't we all just let it be?"

Charles gave a sad smile. "We must have valid evidence, and, unfortunately, your word is not enough."

"Why not? I was the person shot. I am the one with the injury! Don't you think I want to catch the person the most?" I was yelling now. "I know she didn't do it, and you just won't believe me! I tell you; I should be the most valid source here." Charles looked legitimately surprised at my little outburst.

"I'm sorry, but it is the law that—"

"Change the law. This is completely and entirely unfair and I—"

"Alright" he yelled loudly, obviously angered. "She may return to her home, but as soon as we find anything against her, she returns to me." He pointed a finger at himself. "Also, you must wear this." He opened his briefcase and pulled out what looked like a black plastic armband.

"This is a tracking device. Please take this pad of paper and pencil." He handed it to her. "Write your name on it."

She did, looking slightly confused. "Hold out your right arm. We will put this on your dominant arm to reduce tampering. And, be warned, we will know exactly where you are, one hundred percent of the time. We will also know if you tamper with the device or remove it from yourself." As he installed it on her forearm, Marisa gasped and her eyes became wide.

"What are you doing to her?" I asked, angrily.

"We are putting on the tracker."

"Why did it hurt her? It did hurt you, right?" Marisa looked at me and gave a slight nod. "Why?"

"We are putting on the tracker."

"You haven't answered my question. Why did it hurt?"

"I may have put it on too tight! I don't know!" He stood up with his briefcase and paper. "You both are making it very hard to work on this case," he said as he was walking out. "And be available. We will be contacting you frequently about this case."

Before he left, though, I heard him say something else to the police officer leaving with him.

"Hard to get valid information out of these two. Also, ridiculously hard to find records from the last couple of months. Couldn't even get in contact with Barnes's parents. The police were at their house and the parents weren't there either. It's almost as though we have another case on our hands. I hate stuff like this." Then he shut the door behind himself leaving only Marisa and me in the room.

I didn't like this man, Charles, very much.

CHAPTER 19

"Are you alright?" I asked her.

"Yes. You?"

"Much better than before my surgery. How did you get me here anyway?"

"Well, apparently there's a ground vehicle connected to Quaverts. The plane just lands itself and there's an option to deploy the vehicle. When I did that, it then gave me some more options in regards to whom I wanted the car registered. Apparently, you can do it to any name you want, and the Quavert inputs it in the government's system. That's why if they were to check to see whose car it was, it shows up under my name."

"That's amazing. Where is the plane now?"

"It's still hovering in the air."

"What?"

"It's solar-powered. It can drop us off, turn invisible, then go back into midair. If it needs to, it can move out of the way of another incoming flying object."

"Really?"

"Yeah!"

"Any other functions you've discovered?"

"Not yet, but this plane, and I don't know if we can even really call it a plane, I'm sure, has many more features that only the designers and pilots are aware of. I mean, there's so much capability with that aircraft."

"So, what's the plan? When am I going to get out of here?"

"I feel like we should let you recover a bit here. Our biggest problem is this tracker." She held up her arm. "We need to figure out a way to disable it then escape on the Quavert. Do you think John could do it? He might be able to hack into it and disable it. How would we talk to him, though? We don't— oh, wait, your earpiece. You still have it right?"

"Yep. I've talked to him once. He reminded me about the code . . . and some other stuff."

"Has he cracked it yet?"

"Nope. He said his computer finished the entire dictionary and is now moving on to random letter combinations. It must be really important, or it wouldn't be encoded. I mean, it was already in a locked steel drawer."

"You're right. We need to crack it as soon as possible."

"Then, we also have my family. We've got to get them. We don't even know where they are, though."

"I think we should talk to John. He's still at the USQDA. He might know more of what's going on."

"Okay. Let me try calling for him. I don't know if this is even going to work."

Hesitantly, I whispered "John?" I hoped the earpiece would pick up my voice.

Instantly, a message played. "Hey Alan," it was John's voice. "I'm at work right now. I can talk to you later, most likely a little after six o'clock. Hope you're feeling better. Bye."

"What did he say?" Marisa asked.

"I just heard a message saying he was at work. He said I should be able to contact him a little after six o'clock."

"Well, try contacting him then. I feel like you should stay here the entire time they expect you to so you can recover. Also, it will be easier to escape once you are officially released from the hospital."

"What about my family? I need to find them!"

"You need to spend some time recovering. You can help a lot more once you can operate correctly."

"But I need to find them now!"

"I know you want to, but we need to wait."

"No!"

"I'm sorry for this, but I won't help you unless you stay here for today and tomorrow, then leave on the 23rd like you are supposed to."

"Why not?" I was getting mad now. She was basically telling me she would not help save my family.

"I've already told you; you need to recover."

"Fine."

"Fine." She left the room.

***

The next two days I was in anguish, not because my foot hurt, but because I knew my family was in danger. Marisa had left me in my room, and I had no idea where she had gone. I guess there was no way I could help my family without her help.

Luckily, I still had John. I had tried contacting him right at six o'clock, but that same message came up again. I tried a couple of minutes later, and he answered.

"Hey, Alan."

"What's up?"

"We are almost finished with the weapon. Probably less than a week before it's ready."

"Did you crack the code?"

"No. My computer has tried everything up to eight-letter random combinations and has made it to . . . let's see . . . not even past the c's. We've got nothing so far. What's the plan for you?"

"Marisa and I are going to leave on the morning of the 23rd when I'm released from the hospital. She says she won't help me unless I stay until I've fully healed."

"No convincing her?"

"Nope. I tried."

"Okay. Well, then what's the plan once you get out?"

"We've got to get to the Quavert. Then, we've got to find my family and stop China from proceeding with their quantum weapon. Any idea where my family is?"

"I have no idea. If I were a bettin' man, though, I would think they are in Beck's complex somewhere. Maybe in one of the cells. Remember, they have much more value alive than dead, so don't worry."

"We still need to find them!"

"I know, I know, but that would be the first place I'd look."

"How do we get past everyone?"

"Dude, I don't know. At least we have a few days to play with it."

"And for Beck to play with my parents and brother!"

"I'm so sorry about your family. Just wait where you are. I'll figure something out."

"Everyone seems to think that's the best idea, but I'm not so sure."

"Just wait. I'll contact you if I figure something out."

"Why is it that I shouldn't go now?"

"You need to be able to fully function. Right now, you are still recovering from a bullet wound."

"So, you won't help me either?"

"I just want you to help yourself so you can help others. Imagine an airplane. They always remind you that in the case of an emergency, you should put on your own oxygen mask then put one on others. If you don't put yours on first, you can't help anyone else."

"I've got enough oxygen."

"You need more."

I didn't respond. It was like they didn't care. They didn't care that my family was in the clutches of someone so dangerous and out of their mind. I needed to get to them even sooner. I had to.

The next morning, I decided I needed to make an escape attempt, one day earlier than what Marisa and John wanted me to. Then again, what could Beck do to them in one day?

The answer was a lot. Too much. I mean, it wasn't John or Marisa's families. It was mine. They didn't have the attachment I did. Really my only option was to rescue them now.

The problem was that I had no one on my side. It was crucial that I do this, though. My family was in danger.

I planned to leave the hospital in the middle of the night. I would leave my room, find the elevators, and then go down and out of the hospital. Then a huge problem occurred to me: I had no idea where the Quavert was located. That made the plan virtually impossible. I guess I had to have Marisa with me.

Ever since second grade, I hated group projects. You always get stuck with someone who doesn't want to work, or they are demanding but have no idea what to do. In this case, I was stuck with a bit of both, I felt.

So, even though *I* wanted to save my family, I couldn't because other people were prohibiting me from doing it.

Now I had to wait. Wait another full day until Marisa or John would help me.

For the rest of the day, I just lay there, thinking about what I would do tomorrow. The day seemed to pass as slowly as it possibly could.

At six o'clock that night, I remembered that I needed to ask John to disable that tracker. I said his name.

"You still at the hospital?" he asked.

"Yeah, not that willingly though. I need you to do something if it is possible. Marisa has a tracker on her arm. Is there a way to disable this?"

"I'm going to need some more information than that. If you can get me the serial number and some other information on it, I should be able to disable it. Can she just take it off with a knife or something?"

"She could, but then they would know it's off her."

"So . . ."

"So?"

"If I disable it, they are going to know too. It might just be easier to cut it off. They aren't going to find you."

"I guess. Where are you with the code?"

"I think we're in the d's or the e's."

"No results so far?"

"Nope. Just random results. We did have one that spelled part of a phrase I shouldn't repeat. My computer alerted me to it because it thought it was the code."

"How excited did you get?"

"Bro, I dropped my PB&J because of it." I laughed for the first time in a while.

"Well, tell me if you find anything."

"Will do, buckaroo."

"Bye."

A few hours later, it was finally time for me to go to sleep. I did and had a rather restless night. I woke up earlier the next morning, at half-past seven. I was supposed to be released from the hospital before noon.

Later that morning, the nurse came into my room bringing breakfast. She told me once I was finished and a friend or family member was here, I could leave. I don't think she understood why I became so sad after she said that. My family was imprisoned, and it was all because of me. There should be no reason they shouldn't be able to come and pick me up right now (unless of course, you realize it would take hours to get here). Really, they shouldn't have to even come to the hospital. If I wouldn't have joined the USQDA, I would still be at MIT and we would still be talking.

Marisa was at the hospital by around 9:30. She came into my room and asked how I was feeling.

"I feel ready to get out of here," I responded.

"Did you ask John about the tracker?" she asked in a low whisper.

"Yes. He said to just cut it off. As soon as we get to the Quavert, take a knife or something and do it."

"Could he not disable it?"

"He said it would just be easier to remove it. He told me they will know if he disables it anyway. There's no reason to go through the trouble. Once we get into the Quavert and fly away, there will be no finding us."

"True. So, when we leave and get the Quavert—"

"How do we get it?"

"Get what?"

"The Quavert. How do we get to it or get it to come to us if it's just hovering in the sky?"

"I think we just kind of wave the ID badge in the air. It's supposed to notice it and come down. Or, you can park the car and click a button, I think."

"Then let's go."

"Grab your crutches."

"Got it." I got out of bed, keeping all my weight on my good foot. I put the crutches under my arms and began to move. Marisa opened the door for me, and we left the room.

On our way out, we stopped by the counter and officially checked out. They gave me information about my payments. They told me, due to the cause of my injury, that the police department would be contacting me about how we would approach the costs. If they can find the person who shot me, they would force them to pay for the medical procedure. If not, we would talk about it later.

We walked out of the ground-level doors and into the cool, refreshing air. Marisa walked in front, guiding me to the car. Over the last few days, the staff at the hospital had shown me how to use the crutches so I was almost able to stay up to speed with Marisa.

When we reached the car, she used Beck's ID to unlock the car by placing it near the door handle. She opened the drivers' side then walked over to open the passenger side for me. We both got in and she turned the key in the ignition.

We drove a few minutes to a closed supermarket's parking lot which was luckily empty; we would need that space to enter the Quavert.

When we parked, Marisa clicked a button on the dashboard.

"You have to turn off surrounding cameras, so they don't see you enter," she said, motioning at the button.

"It's funny. No one mentioned that when they picked me up from China. It was all part of the plan to get my idea then get rid of me."

She didn't respond to what I had said but, instead, continued preparing so we could board the aircraft.

"Now, when I click this button, the Quavert should come down to us and land right here. The car will automatically move out of the way, I'm pretty sure. Here we go." She clicked the button, but nothing seemed to happen. She clicked it again. Nothing.

"What's going on?" I asked.

"I'm not sure." She looked at the screen in the car. It said, "Signed in as Timothy Beck."

Also, on the screen, it had an option named "Quavert," except it was greyed out. We couldn't click it.

"Does that mean . . ." I couldn't face it. Is that what that meant?

Marisa nodded, devastated. "I think . . . I think Beck took away our access."

"So we can't get the plane?"

"I don't think we can."

"It's gone?"

She didn't respond, but instead just looked at me.

Now, I had no way to get to my family. Or a way to stop China. I needed that plane. But it was gone.

It was gone.

CHAPTER 20

"What are we going to do now?" I had no idea. We were stuck. We couldn't do anything.

"I don't know," she responded. "We need to move."

"Why?" I was devastated. I had to have a way to get to Nevada. Or at least somewhere.

"Beck knows where we are. I'm sure he does. He's the one who disabled the plane. I bet he can track this car also."

"The police know, too. They probably don't expect anything, though, since we're just in a parking lot. We need a new car."

"How are we going to get to one? Plus, if they want to, they could track our phones. I don't think there's any way to avoid being tracked by Beck. So, a better thing to think about is *where* we should go now. Any ideas?"

She shook her head.

"We need to talk to John—"

As I said that, his message played, telling me that he isn't able to talk right now.

"Are you okay?" Marisa asked me, noticing I had stopped.

"Yeah, I'm fine. His message just played when I said his name. Anyway, we need to see if he's cracked the code."

"Where do we go after that? Better question: what do we do after that?"

"I don't know. We can't go back to the USQDA, of course. Our only option would be to get a jump on creating our own weapon that we will later use against China's laboratory or ours. We just need to make sure your family is out of there before we were to bomb it."

"How are we supposed to get them?"

"I'm not sure yet. But we need to get out of here first. Beck might be here soon."

"Okay. Let's go." She pressed on the gas pedal and we left.

"So, where are we going? And what about my family?" I asked after we were back on the main road.

"We need to give it time. If the Chinese agency is going to blow up the United States, they are going to want to get out of here. That means Beck will want to get out of here. But, wait . . . whose side is the rest of the USQDA on? If they are on our side, we could really use their help. If not, we need to tell John. It's possible they all knew they were working together, and we didn't. I say, they are going to want to leave, so once they do, we make our move to rescue them. Until then, we work on a weapon."

"Wait . . . what you were saying . . . could John be on China's side? What if he's—what if he's tricking us?"

She stopped moving and looked at me, formulating a response in her head. "I trust him. I don't think he would ever do that. Anyway, he's the only chance we've got to crack the code."

"I guess. But where do we go now?"

"I don't know. Is there a place—"

"It's got to be somewhere where we don't have to tell anyone. If we do, and Beck finds out, he'll kill my family."

She didn't say anything for a moment. "Do you want me to tell you something?"

What could she want to tell me? "Sure. What?"

"We need help. We can't do this alone."

"We can't do it with anyone else either!"

"How are you and I going to break into a complex underneath the United States Quantum Defense Agency, which happens to be located under the most secretive military base in the world?"

She was right. I didn't want to admit it, but she was right. "Where do you suggest we go?" I asked.

"I'm not sure. You have any ideas?"

I thought. Where could we go? Then it came to me. "I've got it."

"What?"

"MIT. Phylus Boctrum. He could help us."

"What?"

"He was my professor at the one class I attended. He teaches quantum physics. He might still be on our side. Plus, he's got plenty of laboratory space."

"Perfect, but how will we know if he's on our side or not? He could just lie to us."

"We could run a polygraph on him."

"How?"

"I'm sure there's one somewhere at the university. Probably some student with a project that made one at some time. I feel like that's our best option. It's really our only option."

"Then we need to get there. We need two plane tickets to Boston."

I pulled out my phone (which I somehow still had, even through all of this) and began looking for tickets. Here we go; a little over $700 for us both to get there. I told her about the price.

"How are we going to pay for it?" I asked, thinking. "Wait a second . . . My dad is a pilot for this airline. I get free tickets on standby, and standby isn't a problem because there are so many flights going in and out of Las Vegas."

"Great! How do you get on the standby list?"

"Usually, my dad does it, but I might be able to talk to one of the representatives about it."

"What about my ticket?"

"I've got a hundred bucks in my pocket. I always keep cash on me." I did. I always liked to have money just in case something came up. This wouldn't have been what I expected to come up, but it works.

"Thanks, but I don't know if we're going to need that, though. I've got a bank card, but the only problem is that I don't have it with me."

"Do you know your card number?"

"I think so. Can we use it?"

"If I can enter it into my phone, I can use it to buy the ticket. Do you have enough to buy it just with your card?" That made me feel like an idiot. *'I just asked my girlfriend if she had enough money to pay for it herself.'* Well, I guess she was my girlfriend. I was so new to this stuff that I didn't even know if we were really together. After that kiss, though, I doubted there was any way we *wouldn't* be together. *'I guess we'd have to figure that out later.'* "I mean, just so we can do it all electronically," I added so it didn't sound so weird and awkward.

"Yes. You can buy my ticket online and then talk to someone at the counter for yours. Or, I can just buy yours, too."

"No, don't worry about it. I can probably just figure out a way to get myself a free one."

"But what happens if I get on the flight and you don't because of your standby?" That could be a problem.

"It'll be fine," I responded. I didn't want to make her pay for my ticket. Then again, she had a very valid point about the standby. This was a matter of life or death.

"Just let me buy it."

"Are you sure?"

"Yes."

"Thank you." I went ahead and purchased two tickets on the website using the card number she had given me.

"The flight leaves at 1:15 today so we have a while." I checked the time. "It's ten o'clock right now, so we have to wait a while."

"All right. Are we renting a car when we get to Boston?"

"We kind of have to. How else are we going to get to MIT?"

"Good point. At least we have a few hours to think of exactly what we are going to do."

"There is one thing we need to do, though."

"What?"

"Your tracker. We need to get it off of you."

"When is the best time to do it?"

"Before we get to the airport. If we take it off at the airport, they will know we are there. If we take it off before, it'll take them a while to find us, and we should already be gone."

"Okay. Why don't you pull over into another parking lot and we'll work on it?"

"I've got a pocket knife, so we can use that."

"Got it." After a few minutes, we were in another parking lot.

"So, we need to just pry it off, right?" I asked her.

"Yes, but the goal is to not cut my hand off in the process," she responded half-seriously.

"I'll do my best. Stay still."

I took the knife and opened it. I found there was a little crack in the plastic where the two sides of the band would connect, which meant there was some type of latch system right there. I began, very carefully, to put the knife in the crevasse. I moved it slowly across but was stopped by what seemed like a piece of plastic. I pushed harder, but as I did, Marisa winced in pain, but I knew I had not nicked her with the knife.

"Are you okay?" She took a deep breath, then nodded. I continued.

After a minute of working on it, I was finally able to break through whatever that was. We were able to take it off but when we did, we were surprised to find what was on her arm.

In the middle of the plastic armband was a needle that had been inserted into her skin. I looked closer. Next to it, it said, "NoTamper." That must have been to prevent what we were doing right now. By trying to move the tracker around on her arm, its needle would drag along her flesh, destroying it. '*Was that even legal?*' It would be so ironic if the police got sued.

When I looked at her arm, I saw where the needle had poked into her skin. It was bright red and bleeding, but I assume that was from the tampering we had just done.

"That must have been why it hurt when he put it on you," I said. "He injected that needle into your skin!"

"That must be why it's been hurting the last couple of days."

"Well, I'm glad we got that blasted thing off. Now, we need to destroy it. Give me a second." I got out of the car and positioned the already broken armband underneath the car's wheel so it would be run over and crushed when we drove off.

"Okay, we're good," I told her.

"Then let's go."

We drove off, and as we did, we felt the car lurch over the plastic. Good. The armband was destroyed.

We made it to the airport after around fifteen minutes and parked our car. We wouldn't have to pay until we got the car back, so that was good.

We stepped out of the vehicle and through the large doors of the

Las Vegas airport. We made our way to security and waited in the long line. It wasn't any easier with crutches. Nevertheless, Marisa and I talked like old friends as though we weren't about to attempt to stop a weapon from destroying the world.

As we finally made it near the front of the line, we took off our shoes and I put my phone in a bucket for it to go through the x-ray machine.

I left my crutches behind and stepped into the machine that scanned people. As I did, there was a beeping noise and they asked me to step out. I guess I had forgotten to take off something.

They took me over to the side. "Please put one of your arms out," the guard asked me. "You can use the other to support yourself on the crutch.

He started using his metal detector wand and began checking my arms then my chest. He went down my body to my legs. So far, it had not alerted him to anything. Then, he did a quick swipe across my head and the wand beeped. He next did a much slower and detailed check. I realized it was beeping at my earpiece. He finally pinpointed where it was coming from but didn't know what it was.

"Do you have any type of hearing device installed in your ear?"

"I believe so, sir."

"What is it?"

"Just a communicator."

"What?"

"I just have a communicator in my ear." I put my finger in it and pulled it out to show it to him.

"What is it for?"

"Talking to other people."

"Who?"

"Just a friend."

"Why would you have this in your ear? Why don't you just use your phone?"

"I don't know. I just prefer it this way."

"We will be checking your bag. You may pass."

"I have no bag."

"Just yourself?"

"Yes, sir."

"All right. Put that *thing* back into your ear and walk this way." He pointed towards the side past the scanners and towards the gates.

"Thank you, sir."

When I made it back to Marisa after picking up my phone from the bin, she was eager to know what had happened.

"It was just my earpiece," I told her. "It set off the alarm."

"Did they confiscate it?"

"No."

"Good. Without that, we would be in trouble. Let's find our gate." She paused. "Actually, first, we should get you some new clothes."

I looked down at myself. I was still wearing the clothes from the hospital. Luckily, it wasn't a gown, but some old, baggy clothing.

"Let me see," she continued as she walked over to a map. "There's got to be some type of clothing store somewhere in this airport." She paused while looking at it. "Here we go. There's one near our gate. We can go there and get you some new stuff."

"All right."

We walked through the airport and eventually into the store. Inside, we found a suitable selection of t-shirts and shorts. I went to go look at them. I found my size shirt then looked at the cargo shorts and found some that worked.

I took them to the counter to buy them as I pulled out my hundred dollars to pay. As I did, Marisa offered to pay, but I went ahead and used my money anyway. They took it then returned my change, which happened to be a very minimal amount. The store was pretty expensive.

"Got it?" Marisa asked as I left the store.

"Yep," I responded.

"There should be a restroom right down that way. You should go change in there. I'll be right behind you."

I went to the bathroom and put on the new clothes. I decided it would be better just to throw away my old stuff.

I walked out and Marisa was waiting for me. "You look good."

"Thanks."

We found our gate and checked the time. We still had a couple of hours. During that time, we talked. Just talked. She told me about her family, and I told her about mine. While we sat there, we did not talk about anything to do with Beck, China, the USQDA, or anything else like that. It was nice to just have a friend.

Finally, the plane was boarding, and we came back to what we were facing. What we were about to do. We got on and it took off going down a runway, of course. It was underwhelming to be riding on a regular airplane after riding in a Quavert.

After a few hours and one stop in Cleveland, we made it to Boston around dinnertime. We disembarked the plane.

"So, what do we do now?"

"We need to rent a car. Luckily, MIT is only fifteen minutes from here."

"Okay."

We made our way down to the rental car area and found the cheapest one we could. As we were walking towards the correct one, we remembered John.

"We need to see if John has cracked the code yet," Marisa said.

"Oh, yes. Here, I'll check in." I paused. "John."

When I said this, he didn't answer. This time, though, a new message played. I listened while Marisa stared intently.

"I've got it, Alan, I've got it. The key is USQDA. The translation is as follows: attack on Washington D.C. on September 26th at 8:45 AM with—" After this, I heard what sounded like a door slammed open and someone yelling. After a few more seconds there was just a buzzing noise as the message recording dissipated. What was this? What was this yelling in the background?

"What did he say?" Marisa asked inquisitively.

"He got the message," I said slowly, still frightened about what I had just heard at the end of the recording. "There's an attack on Washington D.C. on September—" I paused, trying to remember all the details. "September 26th at 8:45 AM . . . then he stopped. It sounded like he was . . . like he was being kidnapped. I still have buzzing in my ear from the message."

"What?" she said with her eyes wide.

"I think they've got John. They know he's not on their side (they might not know if he's on our side either), but they took him. He's probably with my family. Beck's using them as bait."

"Bait for what?"

"Me."

"And there's an attack on D.C.?"

"Yes. We need to get to Boctrum. Now."

For the first time in forever, I believed I needed help. We needed someone else. This thing was becoming a much more pressing issue.

I didn't know if pressing was even the right word.

Crushing was better.

CHAPTER 21

We spent the next fifteen minutes driving in light traffic to the MIT campus. We needed to get there fast. We had to start creating some type of weapon to use against China.

Once we finally entered the campus, I directed Marisa in the general direction of Dr. Boctrum's classroom. I didn't really remember where his room was, but I felt if we got close, I could remember how to get there.

I told Marisa to stop and we exited our car as I attempted to navigate to my only college class. Marisa was right behind me as we slowly made our way along the sidewalks with my crutches. If I would have just turned down the USQDA offer, I would be doing this every day for college without crutches. Also, my family and best friend would be where they belong.

'If I would have just turned it down.'

Then, another voice inside of me emerged. 'If you would have turned it down, your family would be safe, but the entire world would be at risk. All of the tens of billions of people on the earth.'

It seemed as though an argument was occurring in my head. 'If you wouldn't have accepted the job, you wouldn't have been able to give China the weapon of destruction.'

The next voice responded. 'If you had turned it down, no one would know the true alliance of the United States Quantum Defense Agency. They were bound to do some type of attack.'

I ended the argument between myself. I needed to focus on getting us to Boctrum.

While Marisa and I were walking through the campus, she mentioned something helpful and time-saving. We needed all the time in the world right now. "We don't have time to do a polygraph. If Boctrum is on Beck's side, he would be gone by now. If he is on what he thought was the USQDA's side, then he'll still be here. Boctrum is our only chance." She paused. "Do you know where you are going?"

"Kind of." I had some idea.

After almost ten minutes (and a wrong turn), we finally found Dr. Boctrum's building. We walked up to the door and I reached out to pull the handle. It didn't open. We tried again. It didn't budge.

It must require a student or professor ID. I didn't have mine anymore.

We knocked on the door for what seemed like hours, but no one came.

"Do you think we could go to another building and try to get in?" Marisa asked me.

"I don't think so. No one is going to walk all the way over here to just let us in."

We knocked a little longer and still, no one came.

As we were about to give up hope, we saw someone—another professor—walking along the sidewalk behind us. She seemed to be looking at us like we weren't supposed to be here. I guess that was fair. Why would two students be pounding on a random building's door when they should have an ID badge.

"Can I help you two?" she asked us.

"We need to speak to Professor Boctrum. It is urgent."

"What is the subject of the matter?"

"Something from class," I responded, thinking of that off the top of my head.

"Could this not be put into an email?"

"No, ma'am, it couldn't."

"If it really is so urgent, I can take you to him."

"Thank you so much."

As she was about to unlock the door, she stopped. "Why do you not have an identification badge? As a student, you should have one. If you lost yours, you were instructed to contact the administration office for a replacement."

What were we supposed to say to this? Marisa spoke up. "We are former students here. We must really talk to Dr. Boctrum, though." Was this going to work?

"Why do you need to talk to him? And you two look very young to be *former* students."

"Ma'am, we really need to talk to him."

She seemed to have a disapproving look on her face. "I will call him on his phone."

She took her cell phone out of her pocket, then a few seconds later held it up to her ear. "Phylus, there are two students out here that are demanding that they see you. Would you mind coming out here to talk to them" She paused, listening. "Okay. They will be waiting right outside the doors."

The professor walked away. In around a minute, Dr. Boctrum emerged through the door. "How may I—" He stopped when he recognized exactly who we were.

"We need to talk," I said.

He gave a nod and gestured for us to walk through the door with a concerned look on his face. Once we were in his office, he asked, "Now, why are you here, Mr. Barnes? And who is this?"

"My name is Marisa Palmer," Marisa responded.

"Alan, is she . . . is she part of the . . ." He raised his eyebrows, attempting to ask if she was with the USQDA. He obviously didn't know.

"Yes, she's part of the USQDA. Well, kind of."

"What brings you here? Why are you not at the agency?"

"We need your help." From there, I told him the entire story. About Beck, about my weapon, about China, about the planned attack, about everything, including my family. I decided there was no way I could rescue them without help. He acted like he had no idea about anything I was saying. Hopefully, it wasn't an act.

When we were finished, he seemed shocked. "So, Beck isn't on our side," he said, "Your family is in prison in his underground complex, there's an attack on the United States in three days, and we need to figure out how to stop it?"

"That's right," I replied.

"What . . . what about the rest of the USQDA? Do they know about Beck?"

"We aren't even sure if they are on our side," I started. "Plus, there's more. Today, we attempted to contact John, who is the only other person we know is on our side, and we think they took him, too. We think he and my family are most likely in Beck's complex, as I said earlier."

"We need to tell the president. Right now."

"That's right," Marisa said. "He knows about this agency too. I forgot about that."

"What about my family? If someone within the USQDA found out that we had told anyone, they will just kill my family and bomb the U.S. as fast as possible."

"They are going to bomb the United States anyway," Dr. Boctrum began. "We need as much help as we can get. Without him, we can't do anything."

I knew he was right. I didn't want to admit it.

"I . . . I . . ." I began, "I guess you are right. It's just I have to keep my family safe."

"I understand," Dr. Boctrum said, "You will do anything to help them.

I understand you."

I'm not sure what made me so mad. It was as though a monster had emerged inside of me. He was saying he *understood*? How could he understand? Before I knew it, I was yelling. "You *understand*? How could *anyone* understand? My family is being held captive in a frickin' underground complex that happens to even be underneath the most secret government agency in the world. They also happen to be captured by the most dangerous and ruthless person I have ever met. How could you understand?"

I stopped. I was breathing hard. Boctrum, on the other hand, seemed to be unmoved by my outburst. I looked at him and he began to talk.

"As a boy, my father was held as a Prisoner of War. He had been deployed to an active war zone. For months, he stayed prisoner. The worst part for me was having to go to bed every night with that on my mind. All I could think about was him being tortured while I was over here with a warm place to sleep and a pillow under my head. Like you, I constantly told myself different reasons that he couldn't have died." He took a deep breath. "Then, once the U.S. won the war, they sent in a Navy Seal team to rescue him. When they got there, they found him. Alive. Not well by any means." He took another deep breath and I could almost feel the memories rushing back to his head. "They were able to remove him from the hostile environment and bring him back to the U.S. Here, he spent time in a hospital bed, recovering from all the injuries they had inflicted on him. But he recovered. My father lived through that. And so did I."

He stopped talking. I now felt so guilty for yelling at him. He did indeed know how I felt.

"I . . . I'm sorry. I shouldn't have—"

"I get it. I had a few outbursts like you just had during the time he was imprisoned. Now, a difference between me and you during our situations is that *you* can help. You can make a difference if your family is released. And I feel like the best way for you to do that is to get as much help as possible."

Marisa spoke up. "I agree with Dr. Boctrum. You need to tell the president. He has the power we need to help us defeat China. I mean, he is the chief in command."

"Okay. Let's do it."

"But, wait," Marisa started. "Why do we need to use a new quantum weapon? Why don't we just use a regular explosive?" She made a good case.

"That's a good point," I said. "That would have a much larger radius of damage." I was thinking. "But is that necessarily a good thing? Even if we destroy their headquarters, a full nuclear war may break out if we use a larger bomb. They may think we are just bombing Beijing, especially if their leader doesn't know about their agency. It would also cause many more casualties."

"I agree with that," Dr. Boctrum responded. "Except if we can't finish creating a quantum weapon first, I feel like we should still bomb it with a standard explosive. I mean, if what you say is true and the weapon will be so powerful it could destroy the world, we need to do everything possible to stop it, even if it resulted in catastrophic damage and loss of life. We will all die if they launch the weapon they are intending."

"I think you're right."

"But what do we plan on creating?"

"The idea I had that Calvin Beck stole . . . we can use it, only not at full scale. Once we use it, we can stop it. It should even be precise enough that we could only destroy that building."

"Do you still have your plans? Not on paper, but in your head?"

"Yes, sir."

"I'm not 'sir' anymore to you. I am your colleague, your coworker. Please call me Phylus."

"Okay, s—" I almost called him sir again.

"We need to get the president here and brief him. We would go there, but since we only have three days to create a new, technologically superior weapon, we need all the time we can get. Why don't you two start drawing up the plans while I call the president?"

He pulled out his phone, tapped the screen a couple of times, then brought it up to his ear.

"The president is on speed dial?" I asked him, astounded.

He nodded with a smile on his face, and Marisa and I went to a desk to get started. We grabbed some blank paper from his desk then found a pencil. As we began drawing, we heard Phylus talking to the president.

"We need you here. We have an urgent matter of national security. You need to be here tonight." He paused, apparently listening. "Yes, it involves China. I do not feel like we should discuss any more over the phone." He paused again. "See you tonight."

"He's boarding Air Force One right now," he told us. "He should be here in less than ninety minutes. He's coming undercover once he gets off of the plane."

"Got it."

We continued to draw up plans. Phylus was right there by us as we created them. We explained all of the details of how it would work. He seemed to be amazed at the idea. I was very proud on the inside, but I continued to work.

After about thirty minutes of explaining and drawing, we had an extremely detailed version of my idea. We also realized we hadn't eaten yet and were getting hungry. Phylus seemed to read our minds.

"Do you guys need some food?" he asked us. We both nodded. "I'll be right back, then."

He returned in around ten minutes with two plates of food, most likely from the cafeteria. We gobbled them down as we waited for the president of the United States of America to personally come to talk to us.

For thirty minutes, we sat, discussing my idea and how we could make it work. We didn't have nearly as high-tech labs as there were at the USQDA, but we should have enough to make it work.

The hardest part of attempting to create the weapon here is that we didn't have the designs for the mechanism that makes something go quantum. Luckily, Marisa and I remembered them very well. It basically worked like a compressor. The object is so airtight, it can compress the air inside (and the object) so much, it can get the object to go into a quantum size.

Now, coming back to a regular size is the hard part. We would have to somehow take that compression and release it. This should cause the object shrunk to return to its previous size, or so we hoped.

We continued to talk like this until Phylus got a call. He answered, then listened. "All right," he responded, then hung up.

"The president is almost at this building. I need to unlock the door for him. Stay here and I'll be right back."

He left the room, and Marisa and I just stayed quiet in the anticipation of meeting the leader of this country. A few minutes later, Phylus came back with the president and a couple of men from the Secret Service. Marisa and I stood up to go and shake his hand.

"Hello," he said to both of us as he held out his hand. I reached out first and returned the greeting. Marisa did the same.

"Dr. Boctrum says there is something that must be discussed," he said firmly.

"Yes, Mr. President," I responded. Up until now, I hadn't realized that Marisa was never the one to speak. It must be because I always start talking first and never give her a chance. I decided I would attempt to make sure she got to talk from here on out.

"Why don't you sit down, sir?" Marisa said to the president. "This is a long story."

Never in my life would I have expected to sit down with the president of the United States of America. Phylus went to his desk and was about to roll his chair over for the president, but he just waved him off and sat down at a desk beside Marisa and me.

"The USQDA is not what you think it is," I began. "Beck is not on your side. His brother even runs the Chinese agency." After this, I explained what we found inside the desk, how we were captured, how we escaped to the hospital, then left the hospital and flew here, how my family and John were imprisoned, and finally the encoded message about the attack.

The president immediately had questions to ask. "Why did we not know about Beck's real alliance?"

"I'm not sure, sir. I don't think anyone knew but China." I paused. "That might not even be true. We can't be sure if the rest of the USQDA is on our side or not. I would think not because John was taken. That might mean the only people who *thought* they were helping the U.S. were Marisa, John, and me."

"How do we know *you* are on our side?" he asked.

"You have to trust us." Marisa was talking this time. "We wouldn't just bring you this brilliant idea if you were our enemy. We must stop China from destroying the very planet we know and love."

"Okay then. More about this attack. You said it's supposed to be in D.C. on the 26th at 8:45 AM—three days. You said the way to stop it is to bomb the Chinese base?"

"Yes, sir. We need to do this before they launch the attack."

"Then, about your family . . . you believe they are in the USQDA base?"

"Yes."

"How long have they been there?"

"Four days." Saying that made me sick to my stomach. "I didn't tell anyone because I didn't want Beck to hurt them."

A look of empathy appeared on the president's face. "I understand. We will do anything for our families."

"Yes, sir. There is one more bit of speculation I have about the attack."

"Anything, anything."

"Beck and his men are going to want to leave the country before they bomb it. That means either he's going to leave guards there . . . or kill them." I could barely say that. If I said it, it felt like it would be destined to happen.

"Then we need to rescue them. Assuming Beck wants to leave for China, the thing we should do is eliminate his destination. That means we can have all of the enemies in one location. I think you are forgetting the power of the United States military. If we were able to storm the base, we would be able to save them."

"So, sir, you are suggesting we bomb China's base then storm our own?"

"Yes."

"What bomb do you plan on dropping on China?"

"Any explosive to eliminate the base."

"It's just . . . I've had an even better idea. We do not want to engage in a full nuclear war with China, correct? You of all people would know that."

"Absolutely."

"So, we definitely only want to destroy the one building? If you drop a nuclear bomb in the middle of Beijing, a full out nuclear war will emerge. And no one wants that." The president nodded. "So, we will want to use this new quantum weapon we are designing. We can make it only destroy that single building. And when I say destroy, I mean flatten."

"I like this idea. But what if you can't finish it in time? If the attack is on the twenty-sixth at 8:45, and it's the twenty-third at," he checked his watch, "a little past eight o'clock, we've got . . ." He paused to do the math in his head. "We've got slightly over sixty hours until the attack."

After he said this, one of the Secret Service members interrupted. "Mr. President, if that is the amount of time until the attack, and it is launched from China, it will most likely be in Beijing's time. They are approximately twelve hours ahead, meaning the attack is really in forty-eight hours."

"That's right. It is in forty-eight hours, then. Let's say they will leave twelve hours before, which means we need to invade our own base and bomb the other in thirty-six hours. If we don't get to our base before they leave, then I'm not sure we will be able to catch them. That means we must be ready in less than thirty-six hours. Even if that means using a nuclear bomb. Like you explained to me, this weapon they have their hands on will destroy the world if it is not stopped. I would rather have a chance at survival than none at all."

Everyone in the room became quiet.

"Just to confirm, Mr. President, you want us to continue creating the device. Then, once we finish, you will take it and use it on China? We will also invade our own base before everyone is able to leave? Correct?"

He nodded.

So, we had less than two days to save my family or they would die, as would the United States of America if we didn't stop this attack. The world would cease to exist if we didn't.

I literally felt the weight of the world on my shoulders.

CHAPTER 22

That night, we continued to discuss the details of exactly what would happen to stop this attack. Everything would need to happen simultaneously. We would have a fighter pilot drop the explosive on the Chinese base soon after we infiltrated the U.S. base. The president left around nine o'clock at night to go back to the White House, where we assumed he would work for hours longer on what he would do to stop this.

Once he left, Phylus, Marisa, and I worked on the weapon into the depths of the night. Designing, building, molding, and more. I told the president we would have it done, but the process was intense.

By the time we were beginning to tire, the sun was already beginning to come up. We had been working in one of MIT's industrial labs (which, luckily, had everything we needed) all night to create the weapon.

So far, we had finished creating the compression chamber and had begun working on the mechanism that created the compression. The chamber was a two-foot cube with an open top. Once we put the largest and most dense object we could find or make inside, we would put on the lid, bond the two together, then give it to the military. They would put on the airplane that would drop it.

The only problem was its weight. It would be very heavy once we put the object (whatever material we decided to use later) on the inside. We would need to find a way to move it. We had a hydraulic lift here, but it could only go up and down. It couldn't carry the finished product outside. I wasn't even sure if we could carry the chamber and the insert separately. They were both so cumbersome. We would worry about that later, though.

The compression chamber we created was formed by a new element, Tripentoctium, that was recently added to the periodic table. Unlike many others, this incredibly heavy element *is* very stable. Other elements that have many protons in the nucleus are usually very unstable. Another one of its qualities is its physical strength. It can contain substantial amounts of pressure with only a thin, solid layer of the element. For us, we used a thick layer of it so it can hold the immense amount of pressure that will be produced in the process. Luckily, MIT had everything we needed and massive amounts of the material, as they had taken an interest in it as well. This was particularly good since we needed so much of it.

This new element was the inspiration that started the USQDA a few years ago. Scientists had discovered its strange properties, including a perfect melting point for its purposes, and I guess this somehow made it back to someone who convinced the president to start the agency.

I guess Phylus had noticed me zoning out for a second. I mean, we had traveled across the country, talked with the president, and begun building a bomb all within twenty-four hours. "Why don't you two go and get some sleep?" he suggested. "I can get you a vacant dorm room."

Marisa and I looked at each other and nodded. "Thank you," she said.

I was getting exhausted. It wasn't necessarily a physical weariness but, rather, a mental one. "We'll take a break for a few hours then we'll be back here if that's okay with you," I said, then yawned.

"I have a class this morning so I will meet you here after that. It should end around eleven o'clock."

"Got it."

I grabbed my crutches and he led us out of the lab and out of the building. I hadn't really even noticed any pain in my foot. That hospital must have been one that had experimental technology. Scientists had recently developed a line of surgical technology that cuts down on recovery time greatly.

Across the street from the building from which we had just emerged were some dorm rooms, and he led us up to one. He took out his ring of keys and inserted one into the door handle.

"There are a couple of beds in here. Make yourself at home." He opened the door and we found ourselves in just a standard dorm room.

"Thank you," we both said.

"No problem. Get some sleep."

When we entered, we both went straight to a bed. I didn't even get under the blankets. I did set a timer on my watch for a few hours, though. After a few moments, I fell asleep.

***

We awoke to the beeping of my watch. I attempted to turn it off even though I was still in a sleepy state. I finally pushed the button and got out of bed. Marisa did the same.

"Well, let's go," I said.

"Let's get this thing finished."

We walked out the door and started towards the lab. The hardest part of creating this would be testing—or the lack thereof. We didn't have time to test it, nor could we test it without having to create another compression box as we could not get the explosion to repeat itself once it was completed.

We got to the lab and began to work on creating the mechanism that compressed the inside of the box. The goal was to make something incredibly dense. That was it. It didn't have to be some super complicated device. It just had to make the object inside very, very dense.

We had been working on it for a few hours before Phylus showed up again. As he said, he was there by eleven o'clock. "How's it going?" he asked us when he got there.

"We're doing really well," Marisa said.

"We've got the internal part of the compressor finished," I added. "Now we need to stick it in the cylindrical hole right here and bond it."

We only needed a few more hours. The weapon would either work or not work. There was no in-between or reason to spend extra time doing testing that wouldn't matter in the long run.

"Good. Let's get it installed and bonded then," Phylus said. "What are we using for its fuel?"

"We've got a lithium-ion battery," Marisa responded.

"Will that be powerful enough?"

"We did the math. With the current wattage, it should have just enough energy to run the compressor long enough to get the object to go quantum."

"How are we going to stop it from pulling in everything around it?"

I hadn't thought about that much. We all sat there for a second with looks of concentration on our faces. I had no idea how we would do that.

Then, suddenly, Marisa had a sharp intake of breath and immediately went for the pad of notebook paper sitting near us. She began writing what looked like numbers lightning fast.

"Mar—" I began, but all I received in return was a wave from her left hand telling me to be quiet.

After a little while longer of Phylus and I just sitting there, she dropped the pencil. "I've got it. I just did the math. Once the object goes quantum, it will stay compressed for just long enough so it deals damage to only a radius of the building. It will only destroy that one structure. Before it can do anything else, the release of quantum energy will destroy the compression chamber, causing the object that was quantum for the ever-slightest moment to return to its previous state because the compression chamber will be blown apart. After all of this, all that will be left is a huge clump of something that used to be a building. Everything around where the explosion occurred should remain standing."

This was amazing. If she was right, this would absolutely work. If not, then we were in trouble. "How did you—" I began.

"Look at it. Check it too. Make sure I'm right." She handed me the pad of paper where she had done the calculations.

Phylus and I leaned over to review the work. Everything seemed to be correct. He nodded as did I. "That's right," I said.

A look of pride appeared on her face, along with a subtle smirk. "Now, all we've got to do is get this compressor installed," she said.

"How long do you think until it's ready?" Phylus asked.

"A couple of hours," I responded. "Our only problem is that it's so heavy. We need a machine to move both the compression chamber and the steel insert."

We decided to use steel because we didn't have vast amounts of platinum or lead, so it was the best available option. MIT also had tons of steel, which was very convenient. The government would most likely replace the materials we were using. If not, there would be some confused people wondering why all their steel was gone, as well as all of the Tripentoctium we used for the chamber.

"We can figure that out in a bit," Phylus said. "We need to get the compressor installed. I'll let the president know we're almost finished. He'll have a team come and pick it up with some type of machine to get it ready for the jet. Let's hold off, though, on the steel. The machine they bring might not be able to carry the final product all at once."

"Got it."

We began to install the compressor. It wasn't too difficult. We just had to put it through the cylindrical hole in the box, then bond it using melted Tripentoctium.

I wondered what the world would be like without element 358. None of this would be possible; that's a fact. But what would it be like if no one had discovered what it could do? The USQDA wouldn't have been started. And my family wouldn't be in danger.

Then, I also had to remember that the U.S. was in a cold war with China. For years. Or at least as long as I could remember. With Tripentoctium, we had the opportunity to end this war. Without it, we would be stuck with nuclear weapons.

My thoughts raced while we finished installing the compressor. By lunch, we were finished. All we needed to do was install the steel then attach the final side of the cube. Phylus had called the president earlier today, and he, or a team of his, was supposed to be here in approximately thirty minutes.

Phylus brought us lunch, again from the cafeteria. By the time we were finished eating, Phylus received a phone call.

"Yes, sir," he said. "It is ready. We will need help moving it. Once the steel is installed, it will weigh thousands of pounds." He paused, listening. "Yes, I know. I'm glad it doesn't weigh too much for the airplane." He paused again, this time for a very long time.

"Thank you, Mr. President," he concluded, then hung up the phone. He looked at us. "We've got a plan. We will need to get the final product onto a truck. From there, we will drive it thirty minutes to the Hanscom Air Force Base where the president will meet us. Then, it will be loaded onto a stealth bomber which will drop the bomb on that specific Beijing building. Sound like a plan?"

"Yes," I said. "But how are we going to get the weapon on and off of the truck? It's way too heavy."

"The vehicle they are sending has a special type of hydraulic lift attached. It should be here in no later than forty-five minutes. It can get under the object then load it onto the truck. It can hold enough weight that this is no problem."

"So, we can go ahead and install the steel? It will be much easier to do that here because we already have the bonding equipment set up."

"Yep," he said. "The lift can move around on the floor. It can come in here and get the finished product. We can go ahead and install the steel into the compression chamber."

"Let's go, then." We had taken basically all of the steel from storage earlier and molded it together to form one large cube to fit inside the chamber.

It was already on a lift in the laboratory. The chamber was on another one. We needed to figure out how to get the block of steel inside the chamber. I asked Phylus and Marisa just that.

"There might be a way we can get the steel above then drop it into the chamber," Phylus said.

"I don't think so," Marisa responded. "If that much weight drops into it, it could damage the structure of the chamber."

"Can we turn the chamber onto its side? If we do that, we can just have the machine push the steel into the chamber."

"That might work," I said. "But how are we going to turn it onto its side? It's way too heavy."

"I think we can. Watch this." Phylus went over to the machine holding the chamber and clicked a button and entered something on the screen. This lift was very advanced.

At that moment, the lift slowly went all the way down to the ground. Then, its platform began to tilt. It almost acted like a slide for the chamber. It continued to tilt until the angle was too much for the object and it slid down. The only difference between earlier and now was that it was now on its side—and on the floor.

"How's that?" he asked us.

"Perfect," we responded.

"I'm going to do something similar to the steel. I should be able to lower the lift then move the platform so that it is right next to the cube's opening. Then, we'll do the same thing we just did, but instead of flipping it, the goal will be to get it inside the chamber. The machine should be able to push it into the opening. It's going to be close."

"It's our only chance," I said. "Do it." Marisa nodded.

Phylus adjusted the settings as he had before, and the machine began to do its job. When it neared the ground, the platform began to move towards the box. It was raised just enough that it could make it over the bottom—which was really the side. It was just like if you took a cardboard box and turned it ninety degrees so its side would be on the ground. It had to make it over the raised part.

The lift began to move horizontally towards the inside of the chamber. It was able to do it. It fit the steel perfectly inside of the chamber, then removed the lift platform so we had the steel installed into the chamber. It did not even damage the compressor we had installed earlier.

Everything was perfect. All we needed to do now was install the cover over the open side and we would be finished.

"Yes!" I said as we were all congratulating each other.

Then, suddenly, we saw the door of the lab open and a professor walked through. She seemed to have no idea what was going on here. "Boctrum?" she said. "What are you doing here?" She paused and looked at the ground at our device. "And what is this?"

Phylus didn't seem to know what to say. "It's just a class project," he said, acting confidently as though nothing was out of the ordinary. "These two students are working on it and I am here to see their progress." I would have believed him.

The woman didn't seem too convinced. "Why are you making such a large model with such . . ." her mouth fell open as she realized what we had done. "With all of the university's materials?"

"I can explain," he said.

"Good," she said. "The campus directors will love to hear."

She stormed out of the lab, leaving us, our weapon, and an uncertain future of saving the world.

CHAPTER 23

"What do we do now?" Marisa asked us.

"I have no idea," I responded. "We can't just leave this here, but there's no way to get out of here ourselves."

"The president's crew should almost be here," Phylus told us. "They aren't going to know what to do if I don't meet them at the door. This lab is supposed to be closed anyway. I put a sign on the door so no one would interrupt us."

"I don't know what to do," I said. "I feel like our only option is to stay here. I mean, I guess we could leave, but then everyone will be after us. And they'll have the weapon."

The conversation continued like this, and we decided to stay. It was too big of a risk to leave. That would mean MIT was left with an object they knew nothing about that could destroy almost anything.

Less than ten minutes later, the professor was back with a group of people including the campus police. We tried to look as innocent as possible.

"Boctrum?" one of the men said who had just entered the room. He was the dean of the college. "What are you doing here? What is this? And who are these two?" He gestured to us.

"We are working," Phylus responded. "Working on a lifesaving project." I don't think the dean took that as literally as it was intended.

"Why have you used so many materials? You look like you've used every ounce of steel and Tripentoctium. Why?"

"As I said, this is a huge project."

"One that needs the entire campus's store of materials?"

"Yes, sir."

"Well, if it is so important, why don't you tell me all about it. I would love to know what could be so important that we should use all of the steel and—"

A group of eight people had just walked into the room. They were all wearing suits. "We'll take it from here," one of them said as they stormed into the room like they owned the place.

"What allows you to tell me to get off my own campus?" the dean responded.

The man in the suit looked at him with a tinge of annoyance. "Does this help?" He got out a badge and showed it to him. It was the Secret Service.

"Why . . . why are . . ." he seemed to be at a loss for words. Being all tough earlier wasn't so easy now that he knew who these people really were.

"Oh, I know you may have many questions, but I need you to leave this building. Now."

"How can you tell me—"

"I hope you realize that the *entire* Federal Bureau of Investigation *could* be here if we asked them to. So, I will ask you one more time. Leave immediately."

Everyone listened. One by one, they all walked out of the laboratory, each of them with a look of disgust on their face. The dean was the last to leave, and he seemed to be infuriated.

Once they all left, one of the Secret Service members spoke to us. "Is it ready?"

"We must bond this piece to it, then it will be one hundred percent finished."

"How long will this take?"

Phylus looked at us. "Maybe twenty minutes," I said. When the agent frowned, I said, "Possibly even ten."

He nodded. "Do it. We need to get this to Hanscom Air Force base as soon as possible."

Phylus, Marisa, and I began to work. Luckily, the lid of the contraption was light enough that we could use a roller cart to move it around. Still, 'not heavy' on this project was hundreds and hundreds of pounds.

In about fifteen minutes, we were finished. We had the lid bonded with the rest of the chamber. It was finished.

"Thank you very much," the agent said. "We can take this and load it." He turned to another one of the agents. "Go ahead and bring the hydraulic lift cart in here, please."

The man jogged off and returned in a minute with the cart. It was rolling of its own accord in front of him while he walked behind it. "Here we go," he said. "Let's go ahead and load this on here." He clicked a button and it lowered down until its front was level with the ground. It somehow moved underneath the explosive, then began to slowly lift. Eventually, it was a few feet in the air and entirely on the platform.

The agent, who appeared to be the boss, began to talk. "We've got it. We will now go load it onto our truck and take it over to Hanscom. You need to come so you can explain how it works."

It was simple, but if they wanted us to go, that was fine. "Alright," we said, then walked out with them and the explosive. The cart wasn't moving as fast as it was when it had come in empty but was still moving at a decent speed.

When we reached the truck, the head agent opened up the door on the back of the vehicle. He told us to get in. By the time we had walked up the stairs, the people still outside of the truck had already loaded the weapon. I guess there was some type of special place where the hydraulic lift had to go.

Once they were inside and sitting on one of the benches which were on either side of the truck, we began to move. No one said anything. It was silent.

After a bit of time riding, we hit a bump in the road, and I saw something fall from an agent's pocket and hit the ground. Since we were moving, it slid across the floor of the truck down in front of me. As I looked down to pick it up, I realized it was his badge. *'An official Secret Service badge.'* I never thought in my life I would hold one of these.

I had studied a lot about the Service—how they worked, what they did, and what their badge looked like.

What their badge looked like.

I stared at it and examined the golden bald eagle on the top of the badge. Usually, the eagle pointed left but, instead, was pointing right. Why? Was it a mistake? Was it a coincidence? Was it intentional? The United States would only print a correct version of the badge. Why would it be incorrect?

Then, looking even closer at the badge, I realized the logo in the center of the badge was also changed, although it would be incredibly hard to notice if that wasn't exactly what you were looking for. Luckily, that was what I was looking for. It usually had a fancy version of "U.S.," but here it had five stars—one large one and four small ones.

I had seen that symbol before. Definitely not on aSecret Service badge. I had seen it somewhere . . . but where?

Then it occurred to me.

China's flag.

That was where I had seen this. Did that mean . . . did that mean this wasn't the real Secret Service? Did that mean they were actually from China?

I was still pondering these thoughts when I realized I needed to give the badge back to the agent—my original intention. I handed it back to him. Something was going on here. Something I didn't like.

I needed to figure out how to get out of here. I bet we weren't going to Hanscom if it wasn't really the government who had come to pick us up.

But how could I do that? It was me versus eight other adults. Marisa didn't even know what I was thinking.

Was I safer being in this car and going where they were taking me, or was I safer attempting to escape? If I were going to escape, how would I do it? The only exit was the door on the back. If I was able to get it open very quickly and jump out, I might have a chance.

But I couldn't just leave Marisa. And, as I was not nearest to the door, someone would probably stop me before I could get out. What was I going to do?

Suddenly, my thoughts were jolted outside of this truck as I heard something from outside. Police sirens. Not just a couple, but a lot.

Everyone in the truck seemed to tense. Marisa didn't know what was going on, but everyone else did. Including me. The police were coming. They realized that wasn't the real Secret Service that had taken us away.

We felt the vehicle speed up. Fast. Previously, we were probably going seventy miles an hour. Now, we were at least going one hundred miles an hour. Marisa seemed to sense something was wrong too. She heard the sirens and felt the sudden acceleration.

Then, suddenly, the truck stopped and skidded a good way before the driver pressed on the brake. I didn't know exactly what technique they used, but it was obvious the police had been able to force the driver to stop the car.

We all knew now that it was Marisa, me, and the police versus the eight other men in this truck. The person who seemed to be the lead agent put on a sly smile. "So, this is how it is. The boss said to bring you two alive, but I might be able to make a compromise." He opened up his jacket revealing a small handgun. "Make any wrong move, and I pull the trigger."

The police would be forcing entry into the truck any time now. It was hopeless. There was no way the police could help us before the men could shoot us.

Outside of the truck, the police were beginning to talk on their megaphone. "Any person in the back of this truck, open up the door now."

No one made a move.

"Open up the door. This is your final warning."

They did do something this time. The lead Secret Service imposter grabbed Marisa, put her in an inescapable headlock, then took the pistol hidden in his jacket, and put it against her head. Before I could react, one of the other men grabbed me and did the same thing.

At that moment, we heard a loud crack from outside and the door busted open. At least fifteen police officers were standing there, all with their guns out and pointed towards the inside.

They yelled, "Hands in the air!" as soon as the door was open before they even observed what was going on in the back of the truck. They didn't realize there were two people about to be killed.

"Let me make this clear." It was the man who had Marisa. "If anyone of y'all makes any move to shoot that lil' pistol of yours, I'll make a move to shoot mine. So y'all best listen to me."

This was the scariest event I had ever been in. It had been the closest to death I had ever experienced. Escaping from Beck's complex we even had a better chance of living. Here, all this man had to do was pull his index finger less than an inch and it was all over.

"Sir, I need you to stay calm. We can figure this out."

"Then let us go on our way!"

"Where are you going?"

"Why should I tell you?" He spat out of the truck onto the ground and stuck his middle finger out at them.

"It is not an order for you to answer that." He continued with a cool tone. "Why doesn't everybody step out of the truck? Come out here and stand on the ground."

"Put your frickin' pistols away and I will."

Instead of putting them away, the police just stepped back. Then, the guy who had Marisa nodded and everyone began to filter out of the truck. As I walked out, my captor tightened his arm around my head. It was really starting to hurt now and the pistol against my head would leave a permanent mark. I was sure of it.

We were all out of the truck. No one had their hands up.

"Now," the police said. "Why don't you release these two and we can talk this out."

"How 'bout no?"

The police did not say anything. It was obvious why in a moment. In one quick second, every one of the eight men fell to the ground. They just fell.

Marisa and I ran as fast as we could to the police. We made sure to keep our hands in the air to show we weren't a threat. Once we were to the side with the police cars, most of the police officers were already over by the fake Secret Service members, handcuffing them and beginning to search their clothing. Marisa addressed one of the police officers. "What just happened?"

"Keep your hands in the air," he said in a much gentler tone than he had used with the imposters. "That there is something we call a long-range taser. It basically works like a sniper but fires a type of energy that stuns them."

"Thank you so much, sir," I said.

"This is our job. We got a call from Dr. Phylus Boctrum of the Massachusetts Institute of Technology saying some imposters had abducted you. I guess you had arrangements to be picked up with someone else." He paused. "Who was it?"

Before we could answer, one of the police officers near the imposters signaled for the officer we were talking to. "Stay here," he told us as he started toward the man by the fake Secret Service members.

From where we were, Marisa and I could barely make out the conversation between them.

"Look what I found in his pocket," the investigator said to the man who had just talked to us. "It looks like a Secret Service badge." We saw puzzled looks on their faces. "Why were they threatening to commit a murder?"

"Were they legitimate?"

"We can test these badges thoroughly, but they look genuine."

"May I see it?"

The man already investigating the badge nodded then pulled something out of his pocket. "Here are some gloves." Then, once the other man had put on the gloves, the investigator handed it to him.

He stared at it for a second. "That's not real."

"What?"

"Look at the eagle. Its head is in the wrong direction. Then look at the center emblem. It's wrong. I'm not sure what it is, but it's incorrect. It looks like stars."

The investigator nodded then took back the badge. He then walked to each of his fellow investigators who were searching the other imposters and stopped them, then told them about his findings. Each of them nodded and he would move onto the next person. The initial investigator was now walking back to meet us.

"We have just discovered something. The badges these men have are fake Secret Service badges. Did you know this?"

"Yes, sir," I started. "That was how I figured out they were not exactly who we thought they were. Well, that was before they put us at gunpoint. One of the badges had dropped out of a man's pocket and I noticed something incorrect about it. Then we heard the sirens behind us, and you know what happened from there."

"Who did you think those men were?"

"We thought they were the . . . we thought they were the real Secret Service."

"Why would you be with the Secret Service?"

"We . . . uh . . ."

"You what?"

"We . . . um—"

Before the officer could say anything else, I saw something behind me. I turned to get a better look and saw a group of black cars approaching us. Many of the other officers seemed to notice this, as they all had begun to walk away from the imposters and towards the new cars with their guns out.

The cars stopped around fifty yards away. No one exited. Then, suddenly, every radio in the vicinity began the same message. It was a man's voice, authoritative and distinct.

"This is from the group of dark vehicles that have just approached you. We are the Secret Service of the United States of America. Please come to the window of any one of the cars so we may present our identification. That is an order."

The officers looked among each other with looks of disgust and surprise on their faces. "Who is he to tell us what to do?" one of them said.

"How did he get into the system and contact our radios?" another one of them said.

The chief of police who had come with the rest of the officers pulled out his megaphone as he gestured for everyone to walk with him towards the car. Then, he pointed towards a few select officers and told them to stay with the imposters.

"Everyone within any one of the approached vehicles, exit the car with your hands raised."

As soon as he said this, the doors of every one of the cars opened and they all emerged with their hands above their head. The officers began to approach them. When they reached them, the chief, through his megaphone, said, "Who are you?"

"We are the Secret Service. I need your squadron here to get out of the way for us. We have business to attend to here. You have done brilliantly so far, but I am afraid we can do much more."

"We have just encountered a group of fake Secret Service agents. How do we know you aren't just more of them? From our perspective, that is the most plausible possibility."

"I realize that, Chief, but we must assess the situation and perform some actions that are, sadly, not your call."

"Let me see the badges."

The so-called Secret Service agent began to walk towards the police, holding out his badge. After a couple of seconds, the chief looked around and nodded. "So, what exactly do you need us to do?"

"I need you to leave the premises. Now."

"How do we know you are legitimate? We just witnessed a case of imposters! How do we know you aren't just posing to be real and had it planned with this other group," he said as he pointed towards the handcuffed men on the ground by the truck, "so that you would seem like the real ones?"

"This is why."

"What is why—" he stopped as he saw three helicopters approaching. Three helicopters with the presidential seal on them.

Everyone was quiet as the helicopters approached where we were standing. Finally, they landed, and out of the chopper that had landed on the left, emerged the president of the United States of America, surrounded by what seemed like legitimate Secret Service members.

The police chief seemed to be at a loss for words as the president and the Secret Service members approached him. Only until the president himself was feet away from the officer did he seem to be able to speak. "What are—"

"I see we have had a slight mishap with some imposters taking the role of my Secret Service members. I am here to tell you that these Secret Service members here," he pointed to the men to whom the chief had just spoken, "are genuine. Now, I would greatly appreciate it if you were to let Mr. Barnes and Ms. Palmer come with me. They are needed for causes that do not concern you. I also need you to please retreat to your vehicles with the imposters. We have some business to attend to."

Then, at that, the police chief put his megaphone up to his lips and said, "I need all officers to return to your vehicles immediately. Bring the imposters with you to your car." He walked away, looking astounded at what he had just experienced.

The president walked over to Marisa and me. "Where is the weapon? I understand you have it finished?"

"Yes, sir," I started. "I handed it over to the fake Secret Service members. They did something with it after we had gotten into the truck."

"I believe there is some type of compartment on the exterior of the truck that contains the weapon," Marisa said. "I'm pretty sure that's where they loaded it."

The real Secret Service agents who had shown up were now right by the president. "I need everyone to search for any type of storage compartment on this vehicle. Ms. Palmer says that is where they loaded it."

After a few minutes of searching, someone had stopped to get everyone's attention. "Over here, Mr. President!" he began. "I found some type of compartment, except it's locked."

"Then pry it open, please," he responded.

"Yes, sir." The man went back to his car then soon returned with a crowbar. He attempted to use it to force it to open. "It won't budge."

"Let someone else try." He nodded then handed the bar to the person standing next to him.

"I can't get it either," he said after attempting to pry it.

"We need the key," the other said.

"Where is that?"

"I have no idea."

We had to get into that compartment. If we didn't, we'd be stuck to our only available option: nuclear.

CHAPTER 24

"Mr. President," one of the agents said. "We need a key."

"Have you attempted to pry it open?"

"Yes, sir."

"What about cutting it?"

"We can't risk damaging the weapon."

"Then find the key!"

"Yes, sir." The agent walked over to his coworkers and told them what the president had said. "I need everyone to search for a key."

"Sir," Marisa began after he had finished talking. "What if those imposters still have it? Maybe the police missed it in their shakedown."

He nodded. He said, "I bet that is correct," then walked over to where the police cars were still waiting. They had already loaded the imposters.

From here, we could see him talking to the police chief. Moments later, he got out of his car and we could see him talking into his radio. Then, we saw movement in the cars. All of the imposters were beginning to be unloaded. Once they were on the ground, they were being searched yet again, but this time, I assumed, specifically for the key.

After a few minutes, we saw the Secret Service agent walking back towards us with something shiny in his hand. "I've got it," he said when we were close enough to hear. He continued to walk towards the locked compartment and inserted the key into the hole and turned it.

It opened.

Inside was the weapon Marisa, Phylus, and I had created, still on top of the hydraulic lift. The agents looked around at each other then one stepped forward. He clicked a few buttons on the screen and the lift began to move away from the truck. Then, after a few more seconds, it was standing alone in the middle of the highway. The agent then clicked a final button and began to navigate the lift to one of the vehicles then loaded it.

All of the Secret Service agents headed back to their vehicles except the ones specifically guarding the president.

More cops arrived on the scene, replacing the Secret Service vehicles that had just departed. I couldn't imagine what everyone was thinking. There was a truck, obviously the vehicle they had stopped, black Secret Service cars, three helicopters, which all happened to have the presidential seal on them, and the president himself, standing surrounded by his Secret Service.

Then, the president began to make his way towards Marisa and me who were standing there, waiting for instructions on what to do. Neither of us had said a word to each other about what had just happened yet. It was just so crazy.

Once the president was near us, he began to speak. "Thank you," he said. "I cannot imagine what would have happened if China had gotten their hands on the weapon. Now, as you both have been the masterminds on this entire operation, I feel like you have earned the privilege to come back with me. You can come with me to Hanscom and explain how it works and why it will."

"Thank you, sir," I said. It still seemed weird to be having a conversation face-to-face with the president of the United States of America, even though I had already done so the previous day.

"Yes," Marisa began, "thank you so much for coming here. Without you, China could have gotten away with it, and Alan and I would be dead."

The president nodded. "Follow me. You may ride in my helicopter."

As we walked with him, surrounded by Secret Service agents, we eventually reached the helicopter we would be riding in.

"I assure you," the president said, "that this is the real Secret Service."

He smiled quickly then told us to board the chopper as he stepped in. Once we were settled in our seats, the rotary blades began to spin, and we started to lift off of the ground.

The president was the first to speak once we were in the air. "So, I take it that you finished creating the weapon?"

"Yes, sir," I responded.

"Good. We have around nineteen hours until we must bomb China, infiltrate our own base, and rescue your family. This is the plan. Now, I would like to know more about this weapon you have created. How does it work? And how do you know it will work?"

Both Marisa and I explained in detail how the device worked. When we were finished, the president had a satisfied smile on his face. "Good," he said. "We will be using that for the attack against China's headquarters. Now, since you have told me all of that, I shall explain our plan to rescue your family, Mr. Barnes." One of the Secret Service members looked hesitantly at the president, but he ignored him.

"Sir," I began before he started telling us the plan. "I think you may be forgetting someone. John Ross has also been taken captive by Beck."

"Ah, yes," he responded. "We will include him in our rescue mission for your mother, father, and brother."

"Thank you, sir,"

He nodded then continued. "The plan is such: We will have the FBI, along with SWAT teams, infiltrate the base. Once we are in, we will begin the search and rescue. More about that later. What concerns us now is the attack on China with your device. Hours before we do the infiltration, we will have a jet take off from Hickam Air Force Base in Hawaii. Right now, we are moving the weapon from here to California then to Hawaii as fast as possible. We should have it there in a few hours, most likely by five o'clock tonight. Then, we will take it to Okinawa, and it should be there before nine o'clock. It will then go from Okinawa to Beijing on a stealth bomber, and, once given the order, should drop the bomb within ninety minutes. Does that sound like a plan?"

"Absolutely, sir."

"Now, once we land, the plane will be about to leave for California. Your device works like any standard explosive, correct?" He paused. "Except you have no idea the standard for the United States military." He sighed. "How did you design it to know when to detonate?"

"It has a timer, controlled by a remote. It can be programmed to explode at any time. If the pilot clicks a button as soon as he releases it from the aircraft, we have programmed it to explode when it can have the most effective impact. Once that button is clicked, based on the pilot's current altitude, it will be put on a timer, using the algorithm we created, so it knows when to explode."

"And you did all of that in less than twenty-four hours?"

"Yes, sir."

"I greatly appreciate your service to this country. Now, back to the device. Where is the remote located?"

"It's attached to the weapon. It can be removed and installed temporarily onto the pilot's control panel," Marisa said.

"Wonderful, wonderful," he responded. By this time, we were about to land at Hanscom. The helicopter began to lose altitude and, after a few more seconds, landed on the ground. Everyone in the chopper stood up to leave, so Marisa and I followed what they were doing.

"I need both of you," the president said, pointing at Marisa and myself as we stepped down the steps of the helicopter, "to come with me."

"Yes, sir."

We followed him, surrounded by Secret Service agents, into a building, then into a room. It had a long table with chairs surrounding it. "Sit down."

As we did, he began speaking. "I have sensed that you want something. You want to come with us on the rescue mission. Is this correct?"

It seemed Marisa deliberately allowed me to answer the question first. "Yes, sir, I do." I had been thinking about that. I wanted to go. I needed to help fix the problem I created.

"I do not believe that is the wisest choice at this time," he responded. "I do not believe you should go with the rest of the teams."

"Why not?" If he was telling me I couldn't go, I was about to throw a fit.

"I feel it is too dangerous to have an underage person without the proper training and prerequisites to attend this mission."

"Sir, I need to come. I need to help." Was I really arguing with the president of the United States of America?

"What can you assist us with? There is nothing you will be able to do. There is no reason to put yourself in danger when we already have groups willing to do that." He just realized the mistake he had made in that last sentence. So had I.

"Are you saying I am worth more than a member of the FBI? You are saying, because we already have people going out there to the battlefield, we shouldn't do anything because they have it covered?"

"No, I—"

"It's my family they are rescuing out there. If anything, *I* should be the one to go!" I took a deep breath, hoping he wouldn't react the way I expected.

Before he could speak, Marisa spoke up. "I agree with Alan," she said gently. She had been quiet this entire time. "I will also go."

"You're going to need my help to find my family anyway," I said.

The president sighed, then said. "You make a valid point. If you insist, you may go." He paused. "Now that this is settled, I need to tell you the rest of the plan. As you know, there is an FBI station in Las Vegas. That is where we will get most of the people coming on this mission. Since we will want some to remain at that station, we will also be transferring some from Boston. As of right now, they have an excess of agents in the station. We need to leave Las Vegas with the correct number of people precisely forty minutes before the bomb is dropped on Beijing. It will take approximately thirty-five minutes to get there, and it is much better if we make it to the U.S. base first, rather than to the Chinese base first. If we make it to China first, the USQDA could evacuate. If we make it to the USQDA first, the building in China can't just go away, and it would be more unexpected."

"Yes, sir," we both said simultaneously.

"You two need to get to the Boston FBI station. You will be loaned the proper gear and you will fly to Las Vegas. Are you sure you want to go through with this?"

"Absolutely, sir." What I thought about saying, but didn't was 'What's the point of life if you have no one to share it with?'

"Then I will have one of my Secret Service agents take you there now."

I nodded, and Marisa said, "Thank you so much, Mr. President." I didn't feel like I was in the best position to say goodbye. After all, I had just had a heated argument with him.

He stood up and walked to one of the people standing next to him, then whispered in his ear. "Come with me," the agent said after the president had finished.

As we were walking out, the president stopped us. "I am sorry, Mr. Barnes, about your family. We will rescue them."

"Thank you, sir," I responded.

"Also, I am not sure what we would have done without you. Both of you. Your help has prevented a deadly attack on the United States of America." We both nodded and walked out of the room.

After we had closed the door behind us, a man wearing an FBI uniform came up to us. He looked very official. "I heard what you said in there," he told us. "I don't think you realize how much that means to me—to all of us. Realizing that we aren't just taken for granted. I really appreciate it."

"Absolutely, sir," I said. "You put your life on the line every day. I can bear to do it this once." He smiled and turned to walk in the direction he had come from.

"Let's keep going," the agent said. We continued to walk and emerged outside. He led us towards a helicopter. "We will be flying again," he told us. Once we were at the chopper, the door opened for us and we climbed in. Inside, we noticed another person was waiting there, most likely another Secret Service member.

"Strap in," he told us. The agent who had walked us here—the pilot—went to his chair and powered on the chopper. Soon after, we lifted off.

It was a short ride to the FBI station—less than ten minutes. When we got there, we landed on a designated helicopter pad and exited the chopper. The Secret Service agent who had accompanied us also stepped out.

"Follow me," he said.

Once we were a good distance away from the helicopter, it lifted again.

"Where's he going?" I asked the agent.

"Back to Hanscom. I will be staying with you."

We followed the agent through the FBI station and eventually inside a building. As soon as we entered the doors, we met a person, dressed in a suit, standing right in front of us. He looked just like an agent from the USQDA—well, dressed like him at least. Luckily, he wasn't one. Or at least I didn't think so.

"These two will be going on the infiltration mission today," the Secret Service agent said. "They need gear."

"Who are they?" the other man asked. I assumed he was the FBI director at this station.

"They are past USQDA members who found out the truth of their operations. Also, they're the ones who created the weapon that will be dropped on China today." This Secret Service member seemed to be legitimately proud of us. The FBI one, not so much. He still had a stern look on his face.

"May I talk to you for a second, Peter?" the director said. So, that was his name—or last name.

"Sure."

They walked a few paces away from us and began to talk in low voices. After about thirty seconds of what looked like bickering, Peter said something that made the director fall quiet. The two officials walked back over to us.

"I see the president has explicitly permitted you to go on this mission. I guess I cannot argue with that. Come with me."

"Thank you, Mr. Peter," Marisa said as we walked off.

"No problem. Stay safe and God bless."

We took a short, silent walk with the director through the FBI station. Even after what I had seen in movies, this workplace was frantic. I guess it was the preparation for the mission happening today. Once we were past all of the people working, we eventually reached a door labeled "Equipment." The director reached out to open it then instructed us to walk in.

Inside, we found a variety of gear and weapons. "You will need to find a suit that fits you. Since they are made for . . . adults . . . it may be difficult. Just find the one that fits best. Also, you will not be allowed a firearm. You do not have the proper training. Do not worry, though. The most elite groups will surround you. Your mission is to guide us to the location of the captives. This is a rescue. It will work." His mood from earlier seemed to change. He was now much less irritable and more optimistic.

Maybe it was him finding out the situation of my family and who I was.

Or maybe it was because he knew that if this didn't work, my family and my best friend would be killed.

CHAPTER 25

Marisa and I were luckily able to find something that looked like it would fit us. With my very small appearance, I doubted it would, though. As we walked out with our new suits, the FBI director pointed in the direction of a pair of restrooms.

"You can go change in there," he said. "When you are finished, come back here and I will give you a helmet and boots. Don't worry about putting on the bulletproof vest yet. That can come right before you leave. It is rather heavy."

"Thank you, sir."

We both walked to the bathrooms, then each entered the appropriate door. After a couple of minutes of struggle, I was finally able to put on the uniform. It was *so* awkward. I didn't know how these people managed to wear these *all* day.

I walked out of the restroom with the vest, along with my previous clothes, in my arms. Marisa wasn't there yet.

"Does it fit?" the FBI director asked.

"Yes, sir." It fit better than I expected. Even though it was uncomfortable, it fit pretty well.

"Let's wait just a bit longer for your friend. Then we can find you guys some helmets and shoes."

"All right."

We both stood there, silent, waiting for Marisa to finish. About a minute later, she was out, also carrying her vest and old clothes.

"Come with me, you two," he said.

We walked with him back into the equipment room and over to the helmets. "These are the smaller ones." He gestured to the left side of the row of helmets. "Try them on and see which one works best. Then, when you are finished with that, please try on some boots."

The FBI director needed to leave, so he sent one of his agents in to monitor us while we finished up. It took a bit for us to find the best option, but we eventually did.

For the next hour or so, we attended a meeting to explain exactly what was going to happen with everyone at the FBI. We explained the exact situation and what needed to be done. Once we were finished, and people were asking questions, Marisa and I were asked something that posed an exceptionally large problem.

"So, how are we supposed to get to these captives?" one of the FBI members who was going on the mission today asked. "Where are they located within the building?"

"They are in an underground complex below the USQDA," Marisa said. "Beck had a secret area down there where he managed his alliance with China. It has a hallway with jail cells, and that is where we think they are."

"How are we supposed to get down there? I assume we don't have access to the elevator."

"We used to," I said. "We had Beck's ID card and were able to use his Quavert—" I saw confused looks on the faces of the members. "A Quavert is an aircraft powered by quantum energy. Anyway, we were able to escape with the Quavert using his badge. That's how we made it to the hospital." I gestured towards my foot. "Beck shot me."

"Are you going to be able to make it on today's mission without crutches?"

"I haven't been using them for a couple of days now, so I should be good."

"You were telling us about the ID badge. Will we be able to use it?"

"I don't think so. I think they disabled it. We weren't able to use it to get from Vegas to here. We had to buy plane tickets."

"Is there a way to even get into the USQDA without an identification badge?"

I thought about it. "There has to be," I said. "In the case of a fire—or an excess of quantum radiation, I'd assume—they would need emergency stairs that let out somewhere. If they required some type of technological access, and the system failed, it would be impossible to leave."

"Wait . . ." Marisa began to talk. "Remember when we were trying to exit, but we just found that dead-end at the top of the staircase?" She looked at me with her eyebrows raised, obviously asking if I remembered.

"Yeah, I do."

"Somehow Beck got in there. The room at the top of the staircase . . . What if there is a secret door up there? There is no way Beck could have gotten in there any other way. That means there's got to be an exit somewhere. And all passages are two-way. What if he just used that exit inversely. Instead of leaving that way, he came in that way."

That had to be correct. How else would he have gotten in? "You're right. During that time we were making it up the stairs, I wonder if he was going to where the real exit let out and then came down it."

Everyone else around us looked confused. "We are talking about when we escaped from Beck," I said. "We think there's an emergency exit and we know where the entrance is. If we use it inversely and go in from where it is supposed to let out, it should take us to the room above the stairs."

"We just need to hope the real exit is above the ground," Marisa said. "And that it doesn't lead to the USQDA above. That wouldn't make sense anyway. They've already got an elevator for that. It has to lead up to the surface."

"Now our question is *where* on the surface," the director said.

"It could be in his house," Marisa said. "That would be the most reasonable place to put it. Especially if the Air Force personnel at that base are not with China. It would be best to keep it hidden."

Then I had a thought. When I was getting the keys from Beck's house to get into his desk, I saw something. Something that could change the course of our plans.

When I looked inside his house, I remembered seeing something. There was that mysterious metal on his floor.

What if that was the hatch to get into his complex?

It had to be. Where else would a secret passageway lead to but the leader's house?

I guess I had zoned out in thought because when I returned to reality everyone around me was talking. "I've got it," I said. Nobody heard me.

"I've got it!" I said, much louder this time. Everyone stopped talking. "It *is* in his home. When Marisa and I stole his keys from his house to look in his desk drawer to see his true alliance, I saw something metal on his floor. I remember there was a wooden floor plank that was dismantled and that there was something that looked like a hatch. It didn't occur to me at the time that it looked like a hatch, but now that I think about it, that's exactly what it was. That has to be it."

"How can you be sure?" the FBI director asked.

"I know it. I just do. This is it. Anyway, it's our only lead."

"Ms. Palmer, do you agree with this?"

"Yes, I do."

"Then let's do it."

***

Soon after this meeting, we boarded a military transport aircraft along with many FBI members from Boston. It took off from the runway at Hanscom at 2:30 PM. We would be headed to Las Vegas and would stay there until the bomber was forty minutes away from the target in Beijing.

On the way, we were able to have some food. I was starving as I hadn't eaten all day. The sandwich they gave me wasn't the best, but it was better than nothing.

We finally reached Las Vegas by around 6:30 PM. Before we had gotten there, Marisa had asked me quietly, "Why didn't you mention anything about that hatch in Beck's house before?"

"I don't know," I responded. "It just didn't seem like something I needed to tell anyone."

"Why not? It was obviously something."

"I just didn't think it was important."

"Okay. Do you remember where it was on the floor? You said you saw a wooden panel sitting next to it. That means it's probably hidden under the floor."

"I feel like it was on the right side of the living room. I'll recognize it more if I can see the room."

"I hope so."

Once we landed, we were instructed to exit the plane. We stepped out onto the Air Force base in Las Vegas. "Everyone, follow me," one of the people outside of the plane told us. We all walked with him and he led us into a building. It was a large room with many chairs and a projector. He went ahead and turned it on.

"As you all know, the goal of this mission is to infiltrate the United States Quantum Defense Agency. In the process, we need to rescue four captives: John Ross, Dylan Barnes, Nicole Barnes, and Eric Barnes. Alan and Marisa will be accompanying the Bravo team—the group who is attempting to make the rescue." I looked around and attempted to locate this team. When I saw them, they looked like the most skilled people in the room. "This team's primary goal is to infiltrate Beck's underground complex while rescuing the captives."

"Now, for the rest of you, Alpha team, I want you to infiltrate that base. Forcefully. You will enter the building that has access to the USQDA, labeled "SO-1." Your primary mission will be to infiltrate the USQDA rather than Beck's complex. Anyone that is found in the agency shall be arrested and handcuffed. Be warned, all members you may find have the potential to be hostile and violent. The use of deadly force is authorized for this mission. Once you have taken control of the base, make sure there is no one left. It is vitally important that we clear the entire facility. Also, as of right now, the Air Force at Homey Airport—commonly known as Area 51—is supposed to assist us. As soon as we get there, they should begin to fight beside us." He paused, taking a breath after all of this explanation. "I have one more bit of information that is particularly important. We are going to have a jet take off from Okinawa as soon as possible with the weapon once the weapon is delivered by the airplane in flight right now. Once the jet to Beijing is precisely forty minutes away, we will transport you all with a helicopter to the USQDA. Now, are there any questions?"

One of the men on the Bravo team began to talk. "Will the Las Vegas FBI be here soon?" he asked.

"Yes, sir. They will be here momentarily. I should have waited to share all the details of the operation until they were here." A small chuckle was let out by most people who had just received instructions. "Now that you have been briefed, you may exit the building. Go through that door," he gestured towards it, "and there will be someone waiting for you."

We walked out of the room and found the person waiting. For the rest of the day, we stayed at the base. The Las Vegas FBI had shown up minutes after us, and the person who had briefed us said the same thing a second time for them.

The anticipation I was feeling was unexplainable. '*I was going on a mission, into the place I used to trust, to save my family and stop the world from being destroyed.*'

Although it was hours, it felt like days, weeks, or years since we had gotten here. So much had happened! The man who had shown me out of the briefing room brought me to another room where I could sit down and wait for what was to come. As I sat down, Marisa came over to me.

"Don't worry," she said. "This is going to work. I know it will."

"How can I not worry?" I replied. "We're invading a base with the Federal Bureau of Investigation. We're dropping a *quantum* bomb on China. We're attempting to stop the world as we know it from perishing!"

"As you said, we're invading the USQDA with the *FBI*, we *are* dropping a bomb on China, and we *will* stop them." Her voice was so gentle. "There's no doubt in my mind that this will work."

"Really?"

"I try to stay optimistic. Tell yourself it is going to work. Just take a deep breath and relax."

I did what she said. I did feel a little more at ease. Then I remembered. That was what Beck had told me about my mission to China. "Optimism, Mr. Barnes. Have optimism." That is what he had said to me. Then look at what happened.

She noticed my apprehension return after a slight moment of ease. "Just stay calm. When you are panicked, you can't think straight. When you are calm, you can make wiser decisions."

"My dad always told me that. I guess all those high-intensity situations *were* for something other than annoying my group in group projects. This probably wasn't the situation I had in mind, though, when I would need those skills. I was thinking more like, I don't know . . . when you're about to save the world?"

She smiled. "He trained you well, I'm sure of it. We can do this. I mean, what's the use of having those skills if you're never going to use them."

"I guess. It's just that all this is my fault. *I'm* the one who accepted the job offer. If I would have just said no, I wouldn't be here."

"Exactly. You wouldn't be here. And I would still be at the USQDA.

And no one would know about the real Beck."

"I—" I began as the FBI director walked into the room, then stopped.

"Everyone," he said, "I need you to come with me and begin to board these helicopters. We need to be ready as soon as we get the word that the pilot is forty minutes away from Beijing. He seems to be around sixty minutes away right now. Let's *move!*'

We walked with the director and everyone else going on the mission outside of the building. Once we emerged into the night air, we found three choppers waiting for us. And these were not just little helicopters. They were huge—over 50 feet long!

"Everybody on. I need the Bravo team over here."

Marisa and I made our way to where he had pointed, along with the other five highly skilled men, who would help us.

"You know your job," the director said. "Board this helicopter. You are the most elite here. Don't let me down."

"Yes, sir," one of them said, and I assumed he was the commander. But, as my dad said, you should never assume anyone is anything or will do anything. Especially when you're a pilot. One wrong assumption could be fatal.

It was the same for us today—one wrong move could be deadly. The only problem was that there were more deadly moves available for *us* to make rather than him.

A lot more.

CHAPTER 26

Numbers were running through my head like wildfire. They seemed like the only thing that could help me wrap my mind around what was about to happen.

We waited about twenty minutes until we lifted off. The ride took thirty-six minutes. Zero words were spoken during this time by the people coming to infiltrate the base. Around sixty-five people were coming with us today. Five of them were coming with us to rescue my family along with John.

'*Alan. Stop.*' I had to just calm down. Like with driving a car, a nervous driver was a dangerous driver.

But how could I? I was about to invade a quantum research agency with the FBI to prevent the world from being destroyed.

And there were not many FBI members coming with us. It was because the Air Force was *supposed* to join the fight once we got there. What if they didn't?

I needed to stop worrying and focus on the task at hand. I needed to remind myself exactly what I would be doing.

As soon as we landed, we were going to check Beck's house for an entrance. We expected there to be a hatch in there that would lead down to the complex. If that idea failed, we would have to improvise. Most likely, we would go back to the rest of the team and figure it out from there.

After the seemingly long and definitely nerve-wracking trip, we could begin to see the base—Area 51, as everyone called it. It looked like a standard day down there. The people of the Air Force were going about their daily duties, aircraft were visible within the base, and nothing seemed to be happening with the USQDA.

Not yet at least.

We were now close enough that everyone would see us for sure. No shots were fired at us yet. Then, as we made it obvious we were not going to land on the helicopter pad, the people below us looked up at us and began to run out of the way.

The pilot of our helicopter instantly began a sharp descent, as did the other two pilots.

"Get ready," he yelled. "I'm going to land for the smallest amount of time, and I need everyone off. I will lift off immediately afterward. We have less than ten seconds until everyone needs to get off." He paused for a few seconds, still in his descent. "Three, two, one, go!"

We were hovering inches above the ground as everyone on the helicopter ran out. The chopper was empty in mere seconds. We saw our aircraft fly away once we were out.

Then, running towards us, was the Air Force.

Once they reached us, one of the commanders yelled, "Let's go!" There was a sudden commotion, and everyone began to run. In the process, though, we heard pops from a gun. Someone was shooting at us. Or we were shooting at them.

"Come on!" the commander of our rescue team said. "Alan! Lead us to his house! Stay low!"

We began to part from the main group as the fight began. Guns were now firing in all directions as we stayed low and out of sight of the opposing group.

As we continued running, we began to hear different noises. Not something like I had heard before. Except in sci-fi movies.

Even though I was running through an active war zone, my stomach dropped out of my body. That noise I heard was a weapon . . . but not one we had expected.

'Of course.' The United States Quantum Defense Agency. What else would they have made before John, Marisa, and I were here? The answer was simple. Firearms.

Now I realized. *'Everything they had told us was a lie.'* They had not just been researching during those four years. They must have been preparing to take down the United States. Not just with a bomb, but with more. An army's worth of quantum firearms.

But why? Why would they want to take down the U.S.? And why did they recruit me?

"What is that shooting?" Marisa yelled as we were running.

"I don't know!" he replied, yelling over the noise as everyone continued to follow me.

After scrambling past the fighting, we made it to Beck's house. Behind us, we continued to hear the sounds of those new weapons. We could also hear more sounds that occurred on a battlefield. People were falling, grenades were exploding, and RPGs were being shot. But we had more people. The Air Force had joined the fight and was on our side.

Only, no amount of people on our side would matter if the enemy had more firepower.

"This is the place," I yelled. Three of the men came up to the door and flung their bodies at it. It fell open as the hinges broke off of the wall.

We walked in and found his house. Nothing out of the ordinary.

"I don't see anything," one of the men said.

"It's under the floor," I responded. "Check every plank of wood. Some must come off." I pointed towards the area I remembered seeing the metal when I was here the first time. "Check there first."

We all began stomping and pushing the wood with our boots. "Anything?" I asked.

"Nothing!" one of them said back. "We need to speed this up!"

"Wait, I found something." Marisa was standing over a spot on the ground that looked no different from the rest. "It's loose." She got onto her hands and knees and began to feel around. "Got it!" She held a piece of wood in her hand. Beneath the plank of wood Marissa held was something metal. Part of a hatch was visible.

The other men in the group came over and got the rest of the planks out of the floor, then opened the hatch, revealing a circular hole with around a three-foot diameter. It had a ladder mounted to its side.

"Everyone in!" the commander yelled.

We all began to make our way down the hole, being incredibly careful when placing our feet on the next bar. If we fell, the people beneath us would also fall, and we would die. It was still at least thirty feet to the bottom.

We continued climbing into the earth. Finally, we hit the bottom.

"This is the bottom," the commander said, much quieter than before. He was the one who had gone first, so he made it to the bottom first. "I see the door. Come on."

We each eventually hit the floor.

"I want everyone to take out their weapons," he said in a low voice. "Alan, Marisa. Stay behind us." He reached for the door and slowly pulled it open, revealing a dark room with an old can light mounted in the ceiling, emitting an eerie glow.

We all walked into the room and one of the men turned on a flashlight to get better light coverage. Behind us, the side of the door in the room was the exact same color and texture as the wall.

In front of us, we saw another door, but this one was not hidden. The commander slowly went to open it. The rest of the group still had their weapons aimed and ready to fire.

He pulled it open, exposing Beck's long staircase leading up to the hidden exit. The stairs didn't even ascend high enough to make it to the surface, so there had to be that ladder too.

That confirmed one thing. This was definitely the room at the top of the stairs. Marisa was right. The commander made sure to not completely close the door so that we would be able to reopen it to leave if necessary.

The reason Marisa hadn't seen the door inside the room, leading to the ladder, was because it looked the same as its surroundings. She also didn't exactly have time to focus on where Beck could have used as an entrance while she was fighting him.

"Everyone walk directly behind me down the stairs. Do not touch anything. There could be traps," the commander told us.

We all slowly descended the stairs. The silence was killing me. All I could think about was what it had been like to escape and attempt to climb these stairs with a foot that had just been shot.

We finally made it to the bottom, finding yet another door. The commander opened it and it revealed the hallway leading up to the door labeled "Exit"—the one we had just come through.

The team formed a protective circle around both Marisa and me. They all had their weapons at the ready and were slowly moving down the hallway.

We turned at the end and found doors, but not the cells.

"Are these it?" the commander asked me.

"No. Keep walking," I responded.

He did as I said and gestured for the rest of the team to follow him. As we neared the end of the hallway, we arrived at a fork in the path.

"Do you remember the way?" he asked quietly.

"Left," Marisa responded. "Then, I believe we turn right, and we should be at the cells. I'm not one hundred percent sure."

"Let's do it."

We did just as Marisa had said. So far, we had not encountered any obstacles as we turned into the hallway with the cells.

But that didn't make sense. Beck would know I would be coming. Why wouldn't he be ready? I already knew he was capable of doing that.

Then, as though my thoughts were transferred within the surrounding atmosphere, I began to feel like an electrical current was flowing through my body. I tried to turn my head. I couldn't.

I tried to take a step. I attempted to lift my arm. I couldn't.

I couldn't move a muscle. Literally.

Electricity. I was being electrocuted. But not that much. If it were a lot, I would be dead or unconscious. That didn't mean it didn't feel excruciating.

Then, there was a loud noise coming from the ceiling and I found a device like a helmet on my head.

Once it had secured around my head, the door on the opposite side of the hallway creaked open. The man coming through it was someone who had haunted my dreams, possibly killed my family, and was about to destroy the world.

"Beck," I attempted to form in my mouth, along with a couple of other words, but nothing came out. I had lost control of all my movements.

"Hello," he said. "Is this a little . . . shocking?" He laughed and put on his evil smile. "You are only at around eight milliamps. Why don't we crank it up a bit?" He paused, pretending to think. "Well, then I wouldn't have anyone to talk to. I guess other than your family, Alan."

I wanted to run at him. I wanted to rip him apart limb by limb and punch him until I broke every bone in his face.

"You know," he continued. "I really liked you until you began to speculate. Speculate my true intentions. You *were* a great worker." He paused. "It's a shame all this has had to happen to you. So, I've come to a conclusion. I want you back. I need your young, brilliant mind to help continue my discoveries."

That was why he had recruited me. He needed a young mind. That must have been why he sent me to China. All of it was a set-up to get my ideas. Did that mean . . .

Did that mean John and Marisa were part of the plan? No, no. That was impossible. They had obviously been on my side the entire time. Or were they?

Could they have been working for Beck? Just another one of his minions?

My question couldn't have been answered any clearer. Beck pulled a device out of his back pocket. It looked like a small tablet. He clicked something, but I wasn't able to tell if anything had happened. It wasn't until she was walking freely in front of me that I realized I was right, yet again.

Marisa was walking, unscathed in front of me, her demeanor changed from a helpful, brilliant (and likable), young woman to a full out liar and manipulator.

But this was impossible! I knew she had been on my side this entire time. Or at least I thought. There was no way she could be on Beck's side.

Then again, why was she walking unharmed towards him? Maybe the reason she had been so keen to help us was because she was, in fact, on Beck's side.

He clicked something on his remote after Marisa was standing next to him with a sly smile on her face. "I only wish I could have seen the look on your face for this rather large reveal," he said, then clicked something on his remote. The electricity surging through my body concluded and the grasp on my head was removed.

Everyone that had been paralyzed by the electricity was now let loose. We were all free from the binding that had held us.

As soon as the electricity had let us go, none of the team hesitated to open fire. My eardrums were no match to the power and sound of the firearms. Then it stopped. After a few rounds, no shots had collided with him or Marisa. In fact, every bullet was laying on the ground around a foot in front of him.

The team ceased fire. It was as though there was an invisible barrier between us and him . . . and Marisa. I still couldn't make myself believe she was not on our side.

In fact, there had to be a barrier between us and him. I mean, why else would all the shots be laying on the floor in front of him. "You didn't think it would be that easy, did you?" he asked. "That I would just let you waltz in here and take my captives? Little Marisa here helped me get you all here." Then, in my utter amazement, she smiled. That same smile she did the first day I had seen her. But it was all a trick. All a trick to get me here. All a huge act to kill me and my family once my job was done.

And what was my job? To blindly create the weapon to destroy the United States of America.

Then that got me thinking. He seemed relaxed right now. Shouldn't he be worried that there was a quantum bomb heading straight for China?

"Now," Beck continued. "Before I kill you all, does anyone have any questions? I would hate to leave you all on a hook as I end your life."

If I was going to die, I needed to figure out what was going to happen to the rest of the world.

As though a switch of confidence was turned on, I formed my question. "The bomb is on the way to China. It has probably annihilated the building by now. Why are you here? Shouldn't you be evacuated before we destroy the agency? My weapon has no use for you anymore." I paused, then added, realizing that I was at the fringe of death. I needed to hold on a little longer so I could figure something out. "My idea can only be built by me. I'm the only one who can help you. So why would you kill me? You need me."

"Oh, foolish boy," Beck responded. "You expected I would allow the bomb to make it to China? Of course not. It's on the way to the U.S. And I have made a couple of slight improvements. Let's just say I have some military contacts. I won't need your ideas anymore as you have already given me exactly what I needed. Sincerely, I thank you. You have given me the gift of a lifetime."

I didn't respond. But how could he do that? Before I could finish my thoughts, Beck spoke again. "Well, oh well. No more questions. Let's get on with it now. Before I do this though, I want everyone to listen to something." He quieted, then continued. "Do you hear those sounds up there?"

I could barely hear the sounds of the battle. Even though I could still hear the quantum weapons firing. "Do you hear that?" he asked, then took a deep breath. "Years of arduous work finally on the job. It is so satisfying to hear your ideas really . . . making a difference. Even more, making *history*." He smiled cunningly. "As for you, Alan, you may not get to see the results of your work, but the world will be sure to know who did it."

He took another deep breath. "Now, it has come to the time where I will complete the task I have been working towards for a while now. It is finally time to kill you. It's very unfortunate that you brought a few other men with you, as they will need to perish also."

He pulled the controller out of his back pocket. As if the next moment happened in slow motion, I could see Beck's finger about to touch the screen. That would mean death once he clicked the button. But then, John's cell door busted open and I saw him with his chair in his hands.

In an act of surprise, Beck clicked something on his device by what looked like an accident. Then, John swung the chair at Beck's head as hard as he possibly could and he fell to the ground. Then, as he realized the fact that Marisa was not on his side, he swung the chair as her as well. She dodged the hit and was now reaching for Beck's pistol which had clattered onto the ground after his fall.

The commander now rushed towards the barrier and attempted to hit it with his shoulder to break it. It didn't budge. It didn't even seem to be cracked from the bullets which we had shot at it earlier.

That meant there was no possible way to help stop the battle between John and Marisa, as they were still fighting. Luckily, Marisa had not gotten hold of the gun yet. Finally, though, John was able to get a perfect shot with the chair on her head and she fell backward.

He rushed to pick up the gun and the device Beck had used. He examined it, then clicked a button. I heard a *whooshing* noise and saw the barrier retreat into the floor.

As I stepped forward, as soon as the barrier had been completely taken down, I felt a surge of electricity in my body similar to the one I had felt earlier erupting from my right leg. Only this one was worse.

I was able to stand just long enough to see a door opening from John's side and my mother, father, and brother walking out into the hallway next to him.

CHAPTER 27

I felt like I was falling into a pit of darkness. I believed my life might have just ended. But I did my job. I rescued my family and friend from Timothy Beck and stopped the world from being destroyed. Well, maybe.

Then, just as suddenly it had come on, I was out of the darkness and back to my world. Or what I thought was my world.

I looked around and found I was inside a building. Long fluorescent lights were attached to the ceiling. Just the ceiling itself showed I was in a relatively small room. I looked down. I was dressed as a highly accomplished military official. On my chest were numerous awards and honors, along with the title "General Barnes." Why was I a general? Where was I? Was this a dream or reality?

Before I could focus anymore on where I was or why I was here, I realized there were other people in the room with me. We were all sitting down at a table, then one of the men spoke. "The president is secure," he said. I looked more around and realized there was a chair missing at the end of the table. It still had a nameplate in front of it that said, "President." Why did he need to be secure? The man continued. "A nuclear strike is being prepared for launch. The president will just need to give the verification and we will launch."

"How much time do we have?" another one of them asked.

"Seven minutes. We were just alerted. We already have the Air Force attempting to terminate it and anti-aircraft systems are active."

What was going on? What was all this frantic talk about?

"The Pentagon has been evacuated," another one of them said. "They are all in the underground complex down here."

I was in an underground complex. I tried to form the question, "What is going on?" but the words did not come out. I tried it again. They wouldn't work. I couldn't speak or even move my mouth.

I tried to stand up. I couldn't. It seemed the only thing I could do was look around and move my head.

One of the people around the table's phone rang. He picked it up quickly. "Hello." He listened intently. "You say what?" He listened some more. "What's the expected radius?" He listened. "You're kidding." He paused and took a deep breath. "Do anything possible to stop it," he said, then hung up.

"We have just received the information," he began, "that whatever aircraft traveling with this weapon cannot be caught. It flies faster than any missile that can be launched at it. And the expected impact radius is over the size of Washington."

Frantic conversation broke out and there were many phone calls made over the next few minutes. Then, everything stopped. It was as though time itself had stopped. There was a noise louder than anything I had ever heard and the entire building shook. Everyone in the room was pitch quiet as the lights went off.

A couple of seconds later, a generator went into action and the lights turned back on. Sitting on the table in front of us, I had just noticed, was a camera feed of the exterior. It had just appeared out of what seemed like thin air. I disregarded this and looked at it. It was just grey fuzz now. One of the people around me went to the laptop and clicked the rewind button and it went back around fifteen seconds.

It was night. I examined the feed some more and realized the building I could see was the Pentagon. Then, suddenly, there was a bright light and a rush of mist, then the camera lost its feed.

A bomb was dropped on the Pentagon. Where was I? Who was I? What had happened? What was that?

Just after we had seen that, an alarm sounded. Red flashing lights appeared on the walls and a blaring siren sounded throughout the building. All of the men cussed and immediately ran out of the room. I ran with them, though I had no idea how. I wasn't the one controlling my legs. They were running of their own accord.

"Everybody!" They were yelling. "Evacuate. Now!"

Evacuate the shelter? Why?

My question could not have been answered clearer. At that precise moment, there was a deafening boom and the ceiling fell.

It didn't just fall, though. It caved in. Everyone down here would die—no, was already dead.

Right after the mounds of concrete and steel had fallen on me, it was as though a switch had been flipped, my eyes opened to dim lights, revealing a ceiling. I attempted to look around, but I couldn't really even move with all the machines hooked up to me. I had a mask on with oxygen, tubes going in and out who-knows-where, and I heard a series of electronic noises around me.

Then, the door of the room burst open and someone walked in with an overjoyed expression. "Mr. Barnes," she said excitedly. "I'm so happy you are awake. I'll alert the rest."

The rest? What was she talking about?

And what was all this stuff on my body? I used my free right hand and ripped all of the tubes off of me. Once I finished that, I grabbed the mask and threw it off, then looked around. I was in a hospital.

A couple of minutes later, the woman returned with a man. A doctor.

"Mr. Barnes," he began. "I'm glad to see you're awake. How are you feeling?" He did not seem concerned that I had ripped off all of the medical equipment.

What was going on? It was like everyone was so surprised I had just woken up. What happened to me? "What's going on?" I asked.

"I'll explain in a bit. Your family will be here momentarily."

"The Pentagon. Is it still there?"

The man looked confused. "Of course it is," he said slowly. "Why would it not be there?"

"It's just I—I saw it be destroyed. Everyone in the bunkers died too."

"I don't know what you are talking about. There's nothing wrong with the Pentagon."

"My family's alive?"

"Yes, they are." The man seemed less concerned about *what* I was talking about than *why* I was talking about it. He obviously didn't know what had happened. Instead, he seemed worried that I was saying these things, not that they had happened.

The doctor left the room. What was going on here? How did I get here? I was just in D.C.. Then before that, I was in Nevada. I had so many questions.

A couple of minutes later, the door opened, and a group of people walked in: Dylan, John, my mom, and my dad.

Before I knew it, my mom was running towards me, with her arms out. "Alan, you're alive!" She was saying this with fresh new tears on her face. She continued to hug me the hardest she had in forever. I embraced this moment, still confused about what was going on. Maybe what had just happened was a dream. Just a dream about the Pentagon being hit.

After she finally let go, Dylan came up. "I'm so glad you're awake. I thought you were gone." We shared a hug.

Next up was my father. "Alan . . ." He came towards me and hugged me. "I'm so sorry about everything." He was also crying. "I—"

"I forgive you."

"I'm so sorry," my mother said. "I shouldn't have reacted the way I did when you called. I'm so sorr—"

"You are good. I forgive you."

Then, after waiting for my family to finish, John came over to me and gave me a high five and a handshake. "Good seein' you," he said. "I'm glad you're back." He then returned to where he was standing previously.

They all smiled back at me, staring, until I said, "Can anyone tell me what's going on? Why is everyone so surprised I'm awake?"

The room faded to quiet and their smiles slightly fell. When no one responded right away, I was going to ask again, but my brother began to speak.

"Well, the reason we're so happy is that you're awake."

"I go to sleep all the time. What's so different about this time?"

"We, uh, didn't think you would make it out of this." He took a deep breath, spared a glance at my parents, and they nodded. "You have kind of been in a—"

"In a what?"

"In a coma."

"For how long?" Instead of telling me, he reached inside his pocket and pulled out his phone, then handed it to me. I looked at the date: November 2nd.

November 2nd? I had been in a coma for over a month. Everyone's smiles in the room faded, including mine.

"I didn't know how to tell you," Dylan said.

"No, it's fine. Just weird to think about. It was just like a night's sleep for me."

"Did you dream?"

"Yeah, I think so."

"About what?"

"Well, I, um . . ." How could I tell them? They had no idea the extent to which everything was happening.

"What?"

"I kind of need to talk to John about this. It's, uh, about the USQDA, you know." My family shot glances at each other and began to make their way towards the door. John seemed surprised that I needed to talk to him so badly. "Thanks, guys," I said as they stepped out of the room and closed the door.

"So, what is it?" John asked.

"The dream?"

"Yeah."

"Well, it didn't seem to last a month, but it was very real. When I woke up I thought it had happened."

"What was it?"

"Well, to start, I was dressed as a super highly accomplished military official. Like, you know the guys with all of the medals hanging on their uniform and everything?"

"Yes."

"Okay. I also had a nametag that said, "General Barnes." Basically, I was a U.S. general in my dream."

"Okay. Keep going."

"I was in this underground bunker below the Pentagon. Apparently, there was a bombing aircraft heading straight towards us from China. It had just come onto our radars and we were trying to figure out a way to stop it. We had already tried sending jets after it and other anti-aircraft systems, but this airplane was too fast. Then it made it to D.C. And dropped the bomb. As soon as we heard the rumble of the blast, the lights went off and a generator kicked on right after. I also saw a camera feed of the bomb dropping on the Pentagon.

As soon as I had finished watching it, there were these sirens that went off. The other military officials started yelling for us to evacuate, but before we could do anything, the roof collapsed and everyone inside died. Then, my eyes opened, and I was here." I gestured to my surroundings.

"Well, none of that happened in real life," John responded.

"Okay . . . well, if that didn't happen, what really happened?"

"So, you and those FBI guys were coming down to save me and your family, correct?"

"Yes."

"Right. Thank you. You found the hatch in Beck's house and made your way down through his complex, which was where we were. When you guys made it down there, Beck had already known you were coming. So, he set up the electricity so that once you stepped to a certain point, it would activate and electrocute you."

"How do you know all this?"

"Dude, that man is crazy. I'm not going to say he's not brilliant, because he is, but he's absolutely insane. He was literally explaining the entire plan to himself, out loud. Then there's more that makes him even crazier, like he couldn't think for the future, but I'll explain that in a moment. Now back to the story."

I nodded and he continued. "So, we're at the point where you were just electrocuted, all right. He just made some small talk before he attempted to kill you. That's all that was. Just something to get you all fired up. Then, I'm not sure exactly what happened, but it sounded like Marisa came over to Beck's side. Literally."

This was the part I wanted to hear most. I needed to see what he knew about Marisa going to the other side. Or finally revealing herself that she had been on his side the whole time.

"Why did she do it?" I asked. "I guess she had tricked us the entire time."

"Not quite. I'll explain that in a bit. Let me finish this main story."

"Okay, but hurry."

"Once Marisa and Beck were both on that side of the glass, I heard all of the FBI people open fire. And hit the barrier. He talked about that before you had shown up, how he would do that. Then, I heard you talk, asking why he wasn't worried about the bomb heading straight towards China. He told you that it was actually going towards D.C. And that was true. The plane was heading towards D.C. And, remember in your dream how there was no way to take down the plane because it was too quick?"

"Yes."

"That happened in real life. The plane was a Quavert. A weaponized one. That's why no one could catch it. The quantum energy had created too much power for anything to catch it. They didn't even go invisible. They used every bit of power they could to go as fast as they could."

"Then how did you stop it?"

"Once I had gotten out of my cell and hit Beck and Marisa, I picked up that controller Beck had used. This was one of the things I told you about that was so insane and he didn't think through very well. He had every little control for everything you could think of that had to do with the USQDA. That included disabling all of the quantum firearms on the battlefield above us and turning around the plane."

"Really?"

"Yeah. It also had the regulator control for the weapon you and Marisa designed. I doubt it could have had any larger impact than what you designed it for, but still, I was able to turn down the regulator to the preset labeled "standard." He had it at max. And, spoiler alert, your invention worked perfectly. Just the one building was destroyed and flattened like a pancake." He smiled and I felt a sense of pride emerge through my body.

"So, you were able to turn around the plane, turn down the regulator, and destroy the Chinese headquarters with that single remote control?"

"Yes. It's crazy. I don't think Beck ever anticipated someone else would get their hands on it."

"You were also able to end all the fighting above us?"

"Yes. All those weapons were also linked to the control. Beck had complete power over everything."

"A dictatorship never works out very well, does it?"

"No, it does not."

"Then, what happened after I . . . went down?"

"I was able to free your family with that same remote. It was able to open and close the cell doors."

I was still trying to comprehend all that he was telling me. "How did you get out when you did? And why? Why then and not earlier?"

"Well, I used the only thing I had access to. My water. I was able to—"

Then, both of us said the exact same thing at the exact same time. "Fry the electromagnetic lock." We were both surprised that the other knew that.

"How did you know that?" he asked me.

"I think you're forgetting that I escaped once with Marisa."

"Oh, yeah, that's right."

"But why didn't you get out earlier? You had been there for days. If you knew how to get out, why didn't you?"

He didn't answer immediately but eventually spoke. "I figured there was no reason for me to leave. What good was it going to do? If I were going to escape, I needed to take your family with me, and I wasn't sure how I would do that. If I were the only one who got out, Beck would just kill me. Don't worry. I spent *plenty* of time weighing the options. Not like I had anything else to do."

"Thank you so much. But, after I was . . . asleep, we'll call it . . . what happened?"

"Well, I took down the barrier and the FBI guys just tasered the two of them to keep them unconscious. They carried the two of them out of there and went up the elevator from his complex to the main part of the USQDA. We went up some more and eventually found ourselves at the surface. When we got there, we found that we had indeed won. We lost a lot of our men, but we won. I'm really glad I disabled the weapons when I did, though. If I hadn't, they may have wiped out all of our people before we could have stopped their guns."

"This is all crazy. I don't know what we would have done without you, John."

He smiled, then spoke again. "There are a few more things I need to tell you about. I'll go through these really quickly." He paused. "First, the presidential election is coming up and we'll have a new president who won't know how to manage what's on their hands. Second, the thing on his hands is the problem caused by dropping the bomb on the one building. I'm not even sure if China knew about the base and they just think it was a random attack. The new president will need to know how to manage any treaties coming his way. Third, the world is now questioning what type of weapon that was. And lastly . . ." he paused. "You asked about Marisa earlier, right?"

"Yes."

"I think I know what happened to her. This is the thing I really needed to tell you. The most important thing by far you could learn today, even after everything else."

"What?"

"The Quantum-Brain Interaction Unit didn't just know how to erase memories. They knew how to change them."

CHAPTER 28

"What?" How did they know how to change memories? That was impossible.

"I was waiting to find a good time to tell you. They—"

"What do you mean by changing memories? Like just adding whatever they wanted?"

"Basically."

"How did you find out?"

"I, well . . ."

"How?"

"They used it on me."

I couldn't respond, even after my burst of energy. The QBIU had used it on him? What did that even mean?

"I found out before I was imprisoned. Really, right before I gave you the code. Remember?" I nodded my head. "Do you think it was a coincidence I was taken right after I was able to give you a code? Huh?"

"I, uh . . ."

"It wasn't. The reason I was imprisoned was because Beck found out the modification had worn off."

I took a deep breath, trying to formulate all of this information. I needed an answer. "What did he change?" I asked.

"My allyship."

"Do you mean . . . do you mean he turned you to his side?"

"Yes." I immediately scooted further away from him. *'What if he was still on Beck's side?'*

"For how long?" John stared at the ground. He didn't answer. "For how long?" I asked, more forcefully.

"Since before you came to the USQDA."

"No, you couldn't have." I took a deep breath of astonishment. "You . . . you were my friend."

"I'm so sorry, Alan. I didn't know what I was doing. Literally. I had no idea what he was doing to me. I had no idea anything was wrong until after it wore off."

"What wore off?"

"The modification. It didn't wear off until after you had told me the code. Then, the only reason I was able to tell you the decrypted message was because my brain cells had reverted to their previous state. Beck didn't expect that. He thought it was permanent for us. Not temporary."

"Us?"

"He did the same thing to Marisa. Hers wore off around the same time as mine. So, when I gave you my message, she probably knew the whole story of what had happened."

"Why didn't she say anything?"

"Would you have said anything? If you knew Timothy Beck had modified your memory and you thought he would do it again?"

"I guess not. Then why was she on Beck's side when I came down to his complex?"

"I . . . I don't know. That's the part that didn't make sense. The only thing I know for certain is that he indeed did use the modification on us."

"Then, how do I know you are on my side?"

John looked sadly into the distance when he heard my question. "I don't know how to prove it to you. I knew you'd ask that. I thought the most I could try to do was tell you the truth. Or at least what I believe to be the truth. What if Beck got a hold of me and implanted a fake memory again that made me say all that? Dude, I don't know. I feel like my whole life is in question. I don't know what to believe."

He looked convincing, but he was right. What if Beck had done as he said? Implanted a fake memory? "What about Boctrum? Is he really on our side?"

"He works at MIT, correct?"

"Yes."

"I don't know. I mean, what's so special about him? Isn't he just like the rest of the USQDA? We don't know if they are on our side or not."

"He's the one who helped Marisa and me build the weapon they used on China."

"Oh. I see. I would think so. Since Marisa and I had our memories changed at the same time, that would mean her's had worn off by the time you were at MIT. I would think Boctrum would have done something to stop her if he were on Beck's side. Or, he could have been like you and been oblivious to the whole operation."

"Hey!"

"Sorry, but it's true. You had no idea."

"I guess. But why me?" John looked like he was holding something back. "Why me?" I repeated.

Again, he signed. "I'm not sure how to explain this. Marisa and I were . . . we were supposed to be you."

"What?"

"We were supposed to be the ones to create the weapon you did. Did you ever find it odd that we were the only young people there? When Marisa and I couldn't invent anything, Beck decided to use us to get someone else to create it for us. You. He modified our memories to get you to create what you did so he could use it against the U.S. At one point, if you would believe it, we were in the same spot as you. Having no idea what was being orchestrated behind the scenes . . ."

"Why does Beck hate the U.S. so much?"

"I don't know, but he does."

"Where is he now, anyway?"

"In prison. With Marisa."

"Why is she there if she's actually on our side?"

"She's on Beck's side right now. I don't know how or why, but she is. She'll be in prison as long as she's like that, and maybe even longer. Everyone thinks she's on his side."

"Do we have any idea who is really on our side, then? What if Beck's men change the new president's memory or something. We would have no idea."

"I'm not sure."

"So, what do we do now? What are the next steps?"

"Well, as of right now, all of the people at the battle are in prison with Beck. He might still have contacts outside of the USQDA, but we haven't found anyone else."

"What about Boctrum? Is he in prison?"

"No. He's still teaching at MIT. There's no evidence against him. He was actually acknowledged by the president for helping you two create the weapon."

"Do you want a crazy conspiracy?"

"I guess . . ."

"What if Beck had his memory modified? What if there's someone even above this entire operation?"

"I don't know . . . That's pretty far fetched."

"It's possible." I paused, thinking. I could be correct. Then I remembered something. "What happened to Beck's brother, Calvin?"

"I don't know. China was dealing with him. Or maybe just making us think they were dealing with him. They could be the lead operator of the whole thing. You never know. Anyway, we think most of the people died in the explosion."

I attempted to ignore the last sentence of what John had said. I couldn't think about that. I had killed people. Even though it was to save our country, I still ended human life. I tried to change the subject, but it went right back to what we had just been talking about. "What have you been doing for the last month?" I asked. "What has my family been doing?"

"Let me make sure you remember this," John responded. "The outside world had no idea what was happening when the bomb was dropped on Beijing. They just thought it was an attack. But they're pretty scared of that thing. I don't think you realize how perfectly it worked. Not for them; for us. That weapon kind of scares me. You kind of scare me, no offense, if you can come up with that. You are a brilliant human, you know that, Alan."

I took a deep breath. I didn't know what emotion to feel. Pride? No. I created a *weapon*. Why should I be proud of that?

John spoke again. "Do you want to see a picture of what you . . . well . . . what you designed?"

"Yes."

John looked hesitantly at me then pulled out his phone. He used the voice assistant and said, "Bomb on Beijing." Instantly, thousands of photos popped up on the screen. I was almost blown away by what I saw in the first picture. The caption read, "Mysterious mega-weapon reigns terror on Beijing."

Above the caption was a picture of the destruction caused by my weapon. None of the buildings around it had been affected. But the one we intended to hit—the Chinese headquarters—was obliterated. Absolutely destroyed. There was a large crater in the ground where the foundation of the building should have been, and that was it. None of the building remained except for the bits of debris in the center of the crater.

"Where did the building go?" I asked John, astounded.

"No one knows. That's why it's so scary. All that was left was compressed debris in the crater. This photo was taken after most of it had been cleared away. Another thing that left the world questioning was the weight of the debris. It was for sure the compressed remains of the building. But it really scared China, even if they were aware of the Chinese quantum defense agency."

"Did this whole thing just amplify the cold war?" I asked John.

"Amplify it?" John laughed loudly. "It did about as opposite as you can get from amplification. It ended it."

"What?"

"As soon as the bomb hit, and China realized it wasn't just a regular bomb, they attempted to get any type of peace treaty they could."

"What do you mean?"

"The attack really freaked them out. They literally invited U.S. forces to come and occupy their nuclear-holding facilities."

"Really?"

"Yes."

"Did we do it?"

"Partly. We sent out some troops to monitor what was going on but didn't fully invade the country."

"That's good."

"Yeah. The two governments are still working out an official peace treaty, but I personally think it's going to be a while before anything is signed. The U.S. is in no hurry. No one knows what really happened other than the president, you, me, Boctrum, your brother, and your parents. We're the only ones who know it needs to happen fast. That is, if we don't include the USQDA or members of the Chinese—well, nevermind."

"What?"

"Nothing."

"What do you mean? The Chinese what?"

"The Chinese Agency."

"Why wouldn't they know what it really was? They were in constant contact with the USQDA."

"Not anymore."

"What do you mean?"

"They, uh, they—" He paused. "They died in the explosion. I didn't want to make you feel bad about that. You saved the entire world."

I nodded. "Thanks. I don't feel bad."

"Really?"

"Of course not." What I was really thinking was "of course so." I did feel bad. A little bit. No matter how much someone could tell me that I saved the world, I still killed people. And, being the person I was, that was wrong, no matter who it was.

"So," I continued, "What do we do next?"

"With Beck? Nothing. He's in prison, as are the rest of his people."

"There's nothing else we can do? There's got to be people on his side that were not at the USQDA when the fight went down. We need to find them."

"I think they are all gone. Either dead or in prison."

"What about Marisa? How long until the memory modification wears off?"

"I don't know. Her's was supposed to have worn off around the same time as mine. That must mean he was able to modify it a second time between the time you and Beck met and when I gave you the code. It's been around a little over a month, so it should be about worn off by now. Until then, she'll have little flashes where her brain has reverted some cells, but others are still modified. She will be all confused. Conflicting memories are not a fun thing to deal with. That's when you have about half of the story. Your brain thinks you are on both sides and it's really weird. Once the modification had completely worn off, she will know exactly why she's in prison, and she'll know when Beck actually performed the procedure that changed the memory. That's how it was for me at least."

"What do we do from there?" I responded. "The government doesn't know any of this, do they? They aren't going to just let her waltz right out of prison."

"I know. I've been thinking a lot about that. How are we going to get her out once she turns back into her regular self?"

I'd also been thinking a lot about it since I saw Marisa walk over to Beck's side. John had just asked how we would get Marisa out once she's back to her regular self. What if her regular wasn't a good regular? What if her regular was on Beck's side? What if that was John's too?

"You there?" John asked me. I was staring into the distance, submerged in my own thoughts.

"How do I trust you?" I asked John, after a moment. "I'm sorry I have to ask you that again, but how do I know you are really on my side?"

John took another deep breath. "Don't you think I would have killed you by now if I weren't on your side? You completely ruined all of Beck's plans and now he's in prison. Wouldn't you think, if I were on his side, I would want revenge?"

He made a good point. Maybe he was on my side. Why would he tell me everything he just told me if he wasn't? That wouldn't make sense. And, I mean, I had no reason to not trust him. He never did anything directly to hurt or stop me. Plus, he seemed like he was admitting everything. Anyway, what was there to lose by trusting him? Beck was in prison, which meant John couldn't do anything for him. I might as well trust him.

"Okay," I responded. "I trust you."

John smiled. "Thank you," he said. "I never thought I'd win your trust after telling you all that. You are the only one in the entire world who knows anything about memory modification."

"Does the world know I'm the designer of that weapon?"

He shook his head. "No. But the president said that if you come out of the coma, which you did, he'll want to have you and your family protected by the Secret Service. He also said that he doesn't want anyone to find out about who designed it because that would put you even more at risk. He's going to be really happy you've woken up."

"I hope so. How much longer does he have in office? You mentioned that there is a presidential election coming up really soon. How long?"

"Well, the election is in three days, but it won't be until the inauguration in January that the president-elect comes into office. I'm pretty sure our current president wants to get the treaty between us and China figured out before the end of his term, but I'm not sure if that's going to happen. Congress is still as slow as they've ever been."

I smiled. "That's a fact."

"I think that's all I needed to tell you. Want me to go get your family?"

"Sure." John stood up to walk out of the room and began to walk towards the door. Before he left, though, I needed to say one more thing to him. "Thanks so much. For everything."

He nodded sincerely as he stepped out of the room. I just needed to commit to memory everything he told me. I still couldn't be one hundred percent sure he was on my side and might need all of the information he just told me to help me decide later.

CHAPTER 29

A few seconds later, my family returned to the room with John. I was still amazed by what he had just told me that I did not hear my mother talking the first time.

"Alan," she began. "You with us?"

"Oh, yes," I responded, startled. I still couldn't believe everything John had just told me.

"So, what did you guys talk about?"

I looked at John and he spoke. "Just about work."

"Oh, I see."

I attempted to move the subject away from the USQDA. "When do I get to leave this hospital?" I asked everyone.

"They said you could leave today if you want," my mom replied. "I assume you want to?"

"Absolutely. Apparently, I've been stuck in here for a month. I've only been awake for a few minutes and I already want to leave."

Everyone around me chucked and I got out of bed. I looked at what I was wearing. It was a hospital gown, blue with pink flowers. "C'mon," I began. "That was the best they had?"

My brother smiled. "Obviously. The next best one had all different colors of flowers."

I smiled, then looked down at my gown. Then, to my great surprise, I realized something was terribly wrong with my right leg. I bent down to observe it more.

On my leg, there were remains of what looked to be third-degree burns.

How did it get there? Then it occurred to me. When I had been electrocuted once Beck had been defeated, that all occurred in my right leg. That must be what all that was from.

Also, mysteriously in the middle of the scars and broken skin, was a perfect circle, around one inch in diameter. There must have been some device that shocked me that was a perfect circle.

"It's not that bad," my brother assured me once he realized I knew what my injury looked like. "It makes you look tough with the scars."

"Thanks, man."

It did look like I had been through a lot, which probably was because I had.

"Let's get out of here," I said. "Do they have anything without flowers for me to wear?"

"No," my mom responded, "But we do." She handed me a stack of clothes that had been sitting beside my bed. "Come out when you've changed. We'll be waiting right outside the door."

I nodded and grabbed the clothes, throwing on the t-shirt and jeans, then laying the hospital gown on the bed. I stepped out of the room and we began going down the hallway. My parents stopped at one of the desks, and I assumed they were looking at the financial information. They told John, Dylan, and me to head out to the cars as they handed me the keys.

We headed out to the parking lot, looking for the cars. John had his own. We said goodbye and Dylan and I headed our separate ways. He assured me he would see me again soon.

"I haven't seen you in forever," Dylan said. "I guess I know why now. You were a little busy."

"True. I was just a bit busy."

We found the car and walked towards the doors. I opened mine, carefully avoiding the car parked next to us. I sat down in the seat and closed the door, looking around through the window to see what I had missed while

I was in the coma.

While looking, though, in the car next to us, I saw something that looked very familiar. There was a pair of men in black suits, looking at our car through their window. When I glanced in their direction, they immediately looked away.

My heart rate began to rise. Who were these men? Why were they looking at me? I'd seen enough suits to realize what this could mean.

Then, after looking away from me, they got out of the car. Instead of coming for our car, though, they were heading towards the hospital.

'My parents.' They must be after them. Why, though? All of the USQDA was supposed to be in prison.

"Dylan," I said.

"What?"

"Did you see those men?"

"Who?"

"They were in the car next to us. In all-black suits. They just got out of the car and they're heading towards the hospital. I think they're after Mom and Dad."

"What? Why?" He seemed very confused.

"I—I don't know. I've seen suits like that before. It never leads to good things."

"I don't think it's anything. What makes you think they have anything to do with us?"

He made a good point. "I don't know. I just—"

"You need to just calm down," he told me. "There's no problem here. I didn't even see anyone."

"I don't know. I just—I just." My breathing and heart rate had just increased by at least twofold.

"You're stressed by what has happened in the past. Everybody's gone now. People in suits have no relation to the USQDA anymore."

He was right. I just needed to calm myself. "Okay," I responded, trying to slow my breathing. "Mom and Dad should be back soon."

He nodded, and a couple of minutes later, they walked out of the front doors of the hospital. They walked towards our car, entered, and sat down. "Well," my mom said. "What should we do now? I think I promised something when Alan was awake." Dylan smiled.

"I think I know what you're talking about," he said.

"What?" I asked.

"We are going to go on a—" As she said this, my phone rang. I reached into my pocket to grab it.

"Sorry," I said. "It says 'unknown caller.'" I clicked to decline the call. "Keep going."

"Okay. We are going to go on a va—" My phone rang again.

"Goodness," I said, then clicked decline for the second time. "'Unknown caller' again. We are going to go on a vacation?" I asked excitedly.

"Yes! To—" My phone rang yet again.

"My gosh," I said. "It's still an 'unknown caller.' I'm just going to answer it. Give me a sec." I shot them a thumbs up and clicked accept.

"Mr. Barnes," said a familiar voice. "I've tried contacting you twice and you didn't answer." He paused, and I realized exactly who he was. He was the president of the United States of America.

"I'm sorry, sir. I didn't know this number." My family looked at me inquisitively.

"You didn't let me finish. I have tried contacting you twice and you didn't answer. But I am thrilled you did this time. I am so happy to hear you are awake. I called to thank you for your services to this country. I do not think you realize how much you did to help save us. By us, I mean the entire world. Thank you very much."

I didn't know how to answer this. "I appreciate your thanks," I began. "But it wasn't just me. It was—"

"Honesty is a man's greatest virtue." He paused. "I have also called for one more thing. I would like you to come to Washington tonight. We have some things to talk about."

"Sir, I would love to, but my family—"

"They may come as well. I will just need to have a meeting with you at some point during your time tonight."

"I—uh . . ."

"I will have a private jet waiting at the Philadelphia International Airport for you at three o'clock this afternoon. I insist on you coming."

"Thank you, sir. I'll think about it."

"If you decide you don't want to come, even though I insist on it, just call back on this number. I will be sending the flight information to your cell phone as soon as we hang up. Thank you again for your service." The president hung up the phone.

"You were talking about a vacation?" I asked everyone in the car after I had put away my phone. "Does Washington D.C. sound like a good idea?"

"What?" Dylan asked.

"The president wants to see me. He'll have a private jet here at three o'clock today. He's supposed to be sending me flight information right now." At that moment, a text came in from another unknown number containing the promised information. "There it is."

"Why does he need you?"

"I'm not sure. He needs to talk to me."

"Well, I'm sure we can find something to do in D.C.," my mom said.

"What time is it now?"

Dylan looked at his watch. "It's almost 1:30 in the afternoon."

"Then we need to get going," my dad said.

"Where's John going to go?" I asked.

"I think he mentioned that he was going to go back home," said Dylan. "He lives a little under two hours from here."

"If he lives so far away, why was he here?"

"The doctor had begun to see some signs of recovery and let us know. He decided to drive up here from his parents' house in Maryland. That's where he's been living since the battle."

"I see."

"Let's go," my father said, and we drove away.

Over the next hour and a half, we quickly drove home and packed suitcases. While we were there, I made sure to love on Bubbles. She had grown a lot since I had last seen her but was still the cutest dog I had ever seen. We hopped back into the car and headed to the airport. Once we were there, though, we ran into a problem.

"Where do we go?" I asked everyone.

As if the people outside of the car could hear our conversation, a couple of people in suits (which I forced myself to be calm about) approached our car and my mom rolled down her window. One began to speak.

"I am here on behalf of the president." He pulled something out of his back pocket and showed his badge. I confirmed to make sure it was legitimate. "I am in the Secret Service, and I am here to escort you to the private transport aircraft waiting for you here. If you would please come with me, that would be greatly appreciated."

We all nodded and exited the vehicle, taking our luggage with us.

"Please follow me," he said, and the two of them began leading us through the airport to the newly added private airline area. Philadelphia had recently had an excess of private activity, so the airport decided to make a private sector of the airport.

Once we were there, we headed to one of the gates and immediately walked through the door onto the bridge. I had never been to this part of the airport, but it was very fast. Before we knew it, we were sitting on the plane and ready to take off.

As a surprise when we had boarded the plane, though, we found someone familiar sitting in one of the seats in the very back of the plane.

"John?" I asked him.

"Hey Alan!" he responded. "They told me you would be soon."

"Why are you here?"

"Why are *you* here?"

"I don't know," I replied. "The president called and said he needed me. I'm not sure why."

"That's what he said to me as well. I'm not sure why we need to go there."

"Me either." I looked at my watch. "It's 2:57. I should probably get seated before the plane lifts off."

"Yeah. Good idea."

My family and I made our way towards the chairs near John, stowed our bags in the overhead compartments, and sat down. As soon as we were buckled in, one of the Secret Service members who had escorted us here told his radio that we were ready to go.

The plane took off, and during the hour-long flight, John and my family talked. It was just like old times, before we knew the true intentions of the USQDA. And I was still talking to my parents.

Finally, after the short flight, we touched down at the D.C. airport. We all exited the plane, and the two Secret Service agents offered to help us with our bags. They did and we walked out of the plane to the car parked a short distance away. It was crazy to be able to instantly get into a car right after landing in a plane. I guess this was what it was like all the time if you had a private jet.

One of the Secret Service agents walked to the driver's side and the other entered on the passenger side. They instructed us to get into the backseat, adding that we would be heading to the White House so John and I could have a meeting with the president.

After a short drive of around fifteen minutes, we looked out of the window and saw the White House. I had forgotten what it looked like, as it had been years since we visited D.C. I thought it was really neat to be able to see the capital of the United States.

The car drove through the open gates and onto the White House grounds. When we were told to get out, we were met by a group of more Secret Service agents who would take us inside.

We followed them and they took us through the metal detectors. I took my phone out of my pocket and set it on the x-ray tray.

After making it past security (and Dylan's glasses setting off the alarm), we were finally into the main part of the White House. It was such a neat experience to know who had been here and what had happened there over the last hundreds of years.

We began walking towards the West Wing, following the Secret Service agent at a brisk pace. As we were heading into the wing that held the Oval Office, I assumed I would be visiting the president right now.

I seemed to be correct. We continued to walk in the direction of the president's office, drawing many eyes from nearby workers. Coming into the West Wing did not happen very often, especially when being led by Secret Service agents.

Finally, we approached the door of the world-renowned office. We could hear the president talking inside on the phone. One of the Secret Service agents slowly opened the door, as to not disturb him, and gestured to show that we were waiting to talk to him.

"I'm sorry," we heard him say, "But I am going to need to call you back." He paused. "It is not your business why. Now, I will call you back in about an hour. Thank you." We heard him hang up the phone.

The Secret Service agent looked at us and told us to wait while he went in to see if the president was ready. He returned momentarily, telling John and me to enter. My family was not allowed to come with me.

"Mr. Ross," the president began. "Mr. Barnes. Please take a seat." His face looked like it had rapidly aged compared to the last time I had seen him. He also had deep bags under his eyes. Nevertheless, he still seemed energized to have us here. He gestured to the chairs awaiting us. "You are probably wondering why I have called you here."

"Yes, sir," John said.

"I guessed you would quickly figure out it involves the USQDA and Alan's awakening. When I got the call, I was very delighted. No offense, but I wasn't sure you would make it out of there. I am absolutely thrilled that we still have a brilliant mind like yours in the world."

"Thank you," I responded.

He nodded. "Now, to let us get to the reason I brought you two here. As you know, the United States is now being questioned by many people about the weapon we created and used on the Chinese quantum agency. I believe John has already filled you in about how the whole situation has created mass fear, as well as anger, around the world. I believe that the reason China reacted the way they did is that they do not want a larger version of that weapon used on their country. They knew what it did to the one building. I do not think they can imagine what would happen if we could use it on the entire city of Beijing. It's a similar situation to the end of World War II. When Japan surrendered due to the two nuclear bombs, which were a new type of weapon at the time like the quantum bomb, I do not doubt they were terrified that we would drop another on Tokyo. China is fearful we will drop a bomb on Beijing with the Quavert, also known as 'The Plane They Couldn't Catch.'

"The end of my second term is looming nearer, meaning we need to take action before the president-elect comes into office. I would like to have a new Quantum Defense Agency developed by the end of my time in office."

John and I looked at each other. "Really?" I asked. After everything that had happened, he wanted to create another agency? Why?

"Yes. We need to be able to defend ourselves against any incoming threats. Now that your work is in the world, Alan, it is vitally important that we are *ahead* of the rest of the world. As you were the designer, you should be ahead of everyone else anyway."

"So, what are you asking us to do?" I asked.

"If I am going to create a new agency, I'm going to need some new people. Who else better could I recruit than someone who designed the first used quantum weapon and worked for an undercover agency called the *United States Quantum Defense Agency*? Then, as my other first employee, I would have someone who also worked for the USQDA and was held captive by its old boss because of his extensive knowledge. I mean, who could be better qualified for the job?"

"I—uh . . ." I began.

"I don't know," John began. "I'm not sure if we're the right people for this. Just look at what happened last time we tried to create an agency. It—"

"It won't turn out the same way," the president interrupted. "There's no possible way I could make such a mistake again."

"You won't be the one making the mistake," I said. "It will be your successor who does so."

He looked sternly at me. "I recognize your concern. You did just recover from a coma because of the entire operation. I understand if you would like to leave this behind you." He sighed. "Enough with that. You can think about it. There is still something else I would like to award you."

"Award us?"

"Yes. You put your lives on the line for our country. There isn't much more you can do to assist our great nation. In appreciation of your services, I would like to award you the Department of the Army Distinguished Civilian Service Award in gratitude for your acts. Under normal circumstances, we would have a ceremony for you. As we cannot expose your identity, you must receive this in private." He pulled out two plaques, as well as two medals from inside his desk, nodding to show us to hold our heads out for him.

"Alan Barnes," he said. "Your brilliance has stopped the decimation of the United States of America and prevented the corruption of our country from the inside out. I thank you." He placed the medal on my neck, shook my hand, and turned to John. "Now, Mr. John Ross. You communicated the information necessary to allow Mr. Barnes to do what he did. You were also taken hostage under Timothy Beck. I thank you." He shook John's hand and put the medal on his neck. "I have a few more things for you." He picked up the plaques off of the desk and handed them to us. "I would like you to turn over the plaque and read the attached paper."

I did as he said and pulled off the paper. I began to read.

THE WHITE HOUSE

WASHINGTON

Mr. Alan Barnes:

I am deeply honored to present this award to you. Your services to this country have benefited the entire world. I sincerely thank you. I am apologetic that we are unable to honor you furthermore for your acts of courage and bravery. As compensation for this and your services to the United States, I have granted you a lifetime monthly pension of $5,000.00.

'Five-thousand dollars per month?' He couldn't be serious. I couldn't imagine all I could do with this money. It could support me for the rest of my life

and I would never have to work again if I didn't want to. I continued reading, astounded by what had been contained by the previous part of the letter.

Along with this monthly allowance, I have recently passed an act increasing military funding. This funding, if applicable, will not be going to the Army, Air Force, Space Force, Marine Corps, Navy, or Coast Guard. Instead, it will benefit the United States Quantum Research Agency. The value of this act is 1.3 billion dollars. Thirty percent of this will benefit the USQRA. That is 390 million dollars. This is an official government grant for the initial funding of this agency.

I realize the United States Quantum Defense Agency has had an enormous impact on your life and your family. I would completely understand if you decided to reject this job offer, although I would highly recommend that you take this. I am officially offering you the position as a co-director with Mr. John Ross. In the event that you are to accept, more information will come then. I need your help. Your nation needs your help. I do not think you realize the dire situation the United States is in. We must have some type of defense against this new and emerging threat. Other countries are forming their agencies. We must be ahead of them all. I feel that, with you, we can succeed in this goal. Without you, I feel as though we would put the entire world at risk.

Still, I realize you may want to move past this and continue with your life. You may want to continue your education and find a job within the private sector. You will still receive your monthly pension, as you rejecting this offer would not take away from the past deeds you have performed for this country.

As a final thought, I would like to add that we will be renaming the new agency from the United States Quantum Defense Agency to the United States Quantum Research Agency. The reason for this is simple. We will be transferring our focus from defense to research. The research can be put to use if needed, but I would like for us to research more than to attack. The United States has never been known for attempting to take the rule of other countries. We have been known for assistance and peacekeeping. I would like to keep it this way.

In conclusion, I greatly thank you for your services. I also would like you to consider my offer for you to work for the United States Quantum Research Agency. Thank you very much for everything you have done, and I look forward to what comes to us in the future.

With deep respect,

The President of the United States of America

The president had signed his name below the document. After I had finished, I set the paper down on the table and looked to John, who had finished slightly before me and was staring at me. The president broke the silence.

"I take it that you have finished reading the letter. I hope you realize that the United States is—I hate to use this word to describe our country—desperate. We need a way to defend ourselves against the emerging threats of the world. In no way, Mr. Barnes or Mr. Ross, do I regret your actions. You saved the lives of billions of people. Nevertheless, these actions have brought new troubles in the place of the old ones. I want to make it clear that these issues will be addressed and taken care of. So, I am formally offering this job to both of you: The Director of the United States Quantum Research Agency. As this would be a promotion from your previous position, you will see that reflected in your pay. You will also receive the initial grant of 390 million dollars. This will encompass the building of the new headquarters, equipment, finding employees, and anything else that has to do with the new agency. But, I need to know now. This is a very pressing issue and the position needs to be filled. I understand if you would like to put this behind you and move on with your life. In that case, we will still be finding staff for the new agency."

John and I again looked at each other, all of the information buzzing through our heads. If the president really was going to start this new research agency, no matter who was on the staff, John and I would definitely be the best options. We had the most experience with this type of agency.

Also, he had said there would be a raise in pay and an enormous government grant to start this agency over. With 390 million dollars, we could make a lot happen.

Then my final thought made it obvious what my choice should be. 'What did I have to lose?' I mean, my family already knew about the agency, so no conflict would arise there. If I didn't join the agency, I would constantly be wondering what was happening behind the scenes. Plus, if I were to leave, I wouldn't have a job. I mean, I now had plenty of incoming money as a result of the Department of the Army Distinguished Civilian Service Award, but still . . .

Then, it occurred to me. The president had mentioned and offered multiple times that I could leave this in my past and move on with my life. Could that mean really leave it in the past? So much that I wouldn't remember what had happened in the last month before my coma? Or more?

If the USQDA had the power to erase and modify memories, couldn't he just do that for me and make me forget everything that had happened? Could I live without knowing about the secrets of the United States and the world?

The answer was yes and no. Yes, I could live without knowing. But was it even a life worth living? I had the opportunity to hang onto this priceless knowledge for the rest of my life. I could know what nearly no one else in the world knows. And I would be able to do what nearly the rest of the world couldn't do.

The answer was simple, yet incredibly complex, but John looked like he was thinking the exact same thing.

Simultaneously, as though we had communicated it before, we looked intently at the president's waiting eyes and spoke.

"Yes."

CHAPTER 30

"Wonderful," the president responded. "Construction of the United States Quantum Research Agency will begin immediately." He paused, pleased with us and himself. "I appreciate this more than either of you will ever know. I would like for you to enjoy the rest of the day. Do not think about this for at least today and go enjoy yourself." He stood up, headed to the door, and opened it for us, shaking our hands on our way out. "Wait. You should take off your medal and plaque for now. Your privacy is now a top priority." He walked back to his desk, pulling out a very high quality felt box, and handed it to us to put our medal in. "Thank you," he said. "If you have anything you need to talk to me about, anything at all, just call."

We nodded and walked through the door. Once it shut behind us, I saw the astounded looks on my family's face. They had seen the things I was carrying out with me.

"What is that?" my father asked.

"The president just awarded us the Distinguished Civilian Service Award."

"Congratulations," he said. "That is a huge honor." The rest of my family told me congratulations as well.

"Thank you."

We followed a Secret Service member out of the West Wing and towards the main entrance. Before we stepped out, the Secret Service agent shook John's hand, followed by mine.

"So," my mom began. "What do we do next?"

"Let's do something fun," my dad responded. "What are you guys thinking?"

"There are so many things to do in D.C." I thought about it. "We could go to the Smithsonian." I looked at John and he nodded his head in approval.

"That sounds great," Dylan said, and we began walking in its direction. We soon remembered that we did not have a car, though. We didn't have a hotel either. Nevertheless, we ignored this and kept walking, as the Smithsonian was only a half mile away. We would need to do something about it, though.

I pulled out my phone, went to the recent calls, and clicked "unknown caller."

"Hello, Alan," the man on the other end said. "What do you need?"

"Hello, Mr. President. I was wondering if there was any way we could get a car and a hotel." Midway through the phone call, I realized how immature the reason for the call was. I immediately attempted to correct it. "Sorry, sir. I shouldn't waste your time like this."

I was about to hang up when he responded. "No, absolutely not! You have the right to waste my time for the rest of my life. I will get you a car and a hotel. Just give me a few minutes and I'll send you the information."

"Thank you so much," I said, and hung up.

My dad spoke. "I'm going to hope you didn't just call the president to get a hotel and car for us."

"He's sending the information now." He smirked, shaking his head, and looked away.

***

The rest of the day was very enjoyable. We had a wonderful time at the Smithsonian. I forgot how much I loved being with my family. Going away to college at the age of sixteen had not been easy, much less typical.

This entire experience with the USQDA and Beck really brought me closer to my parents. Before all of this had happened, I wasn't as close to them, but this had brought us together.

Still, there was so much to do. Building the USQRA would not be easy, especially with John and me as the directors. In addition to building the new research agency, the world was undeniably in a state of questioning. No one knew what that weapon was—much less its full potential—but it wouldn't be long until they did.

Once everyone figured out what it was, there would be a new wave of questioning, involving accusations and most likely searching for the designer. That would put me in high amounts of risk at all times, although I wasn't sure how word could get out that I was the designer behind the destruction.

Then, another issue would be the new president. Our current leader was reaching the end of his time in office. All of these tensions would be passed to the new president, and he wouldn't know what entirely to do. For John and me, there would be a lot of explaining to do to him if our current president didn't do it for us. The entire transfer would be very rough.

Nevertheless, the world was now safe from Timothy Beck. He was imprisoned. He was gone. He was gone out of our lives forever.

Or was he?

Although he was in prison, he knew exactly what had happened. He knew I was the designer and destroyer of his master plan to destroy the United States. How could we really be safe until he didn't know any of these things?

The death penalty was absolutely fitting for the crimes he had committed. But what had he actually done to make him deserve that? He never committed murder. He attempted murder but never actually committed it. That was the thing that put you on death row. You had to end the life of another. And was it really my choice to make?

Legally, he wouldn't be put to death. In prison, he was just as dangerous because of his extensive knowledge. If only there was a way to remove this knowledge . . .

Then it came to me. Beck had helped develop the Quantum-Brain Interaction Unit. What if there was a way that we could use the memory deletion against him? We could remove his memories so he no longer had a recollection of the event.

That would work. It was, obviously, a less severe punishment than death row, but it would work. It would do the same job. Theoretically, it was still removing the dangerous Timothy Beck from the world.

I needed to tell someone about this. And who better to tell than the president?

I pulled out my phone again and found the unknown caller. I clicked it. He answered. "Did your car and hotel not go through? The car should be there any minute now," he said.

"No, no. That wasn't the reason for calling. And yes, they are about to pick us up."

He sounded slightly confused on the other end. "Okay . . . why were you calling then?"

"I think I've got an idea." From there, I told him how I didn't feel Beck was safe until his knowledge was truly gone.

He thought about it. "That could work." He paused. "So, essentially, you are proposing we make him forget all of the things he has done and seen?"

"Yes, sir."

He took a deep breath. "I think that is something that needs to be done. Let me see what I can do." He hung up.

"What was that?" my mom asked.

"Oh, nothing," I responded. She looked at me with skepticism, but decided to not question me anymore.

We continued on with our day, having a nice and relaxing time at the museum. Unfortunately, the question of what to do with Beck was still nagging at my brain. I didn't know what needed to happen.

Finally, after the long but enjoyable day, we got into the waiting car, which took us to the hotel. We were exiting the car when my phone rang, reading the same unknown caller ID as I had seen earlier today. I clicked accept. It was the president.

"Hello, Mr. Barnes. We have decided to use your idea. Timothy Beck will indeed have his memory cleared from the past five years. Marisa Palmer will not be a part of this." He paused. "I wanted to let you know this so, if you would prefer to, you could come. If you wanted to, I will be able to admit you and Mr. Ross to assist in the memory deletion."

Why did he need me? Couldn't they do it by themselves? And what was going on with Marisa? I decided to put that last part out of my mind. "Why do you need me?" I asked.

"It is your equipment now. You are the new director of the USQRA. I would also like to make it clear that if you would not like to see Beck, you don't have to." He paused again. "We will be doing this as soon as possible. It will happen tomorrow at the latest. If you would like to come, I can get you there. I will be leaving early tomorrow morning, so you may fly along with me."

I thought about it. Did I really want to be there? I wanted to, but I didn't at the same time. I was here with my family, and we were all together. Did I really want to ruin that by leaving? Leaving to go where?

"Where are we going?"

"We are going to the old USQDA on the Air Force base in Nevada."

I thought about it some more. I would be going back there. Did I really want to do that? Then again, would I regret my decision to stay here? What did I have to lose?

"I'll go."

"All right, then. I will be in front of your hotel at six o'clock tomorrow morning. I should have you back before one o'clock tomorrow afternoon. I will see you tomorrow."

Again, I would have to tell my parents that I would have to leave. There was no way around it, though.

"Mom," I began. "I am going to have to leave tomorrow morning for just a few hours. I should be back by one o'clock in the afternoon." She looked at me sadly.

"What do you have to do?"

"Well, the president wants me to go with him to Nevada. He's going to pick me up at six o'clock tomorrow morning. He's going to fly me there and bring me back by around one o'clock."

She thought about it. "That's fine. If you need to do that, then go ahead. There'll still be plenty of time in the afternoon to do whatever we want."

"Thank you."

Once we were in the hotel room, I took a long shower, put on some pajamas, and hopped into bed for the night. After all that had happened, including being asleep for a month, I was still tired. I instantly fell asleep, but not before setting my alarm.

Much too soon, it rang and I hopped out of the bed, still tired, but rejuvenated. I quietly got dressed, attempting to not wake up the others any more than I already had, but my mom knocked on my door after I had finished changing. I opened it.

"I thought I'd wake up to see you off," she said, yawing. "Are you about ready?"

"Yes," I said, grabbing my phone and putting it in my pocket.

"Good. I'll see you later today." We hugged, and I walked out of the room toward the lobby. Like he had said, the president was waiting in front of the building.

As I approached the Presidential Limousine, one of the Secret Service agents got out and opened the door for me. I thanked him and hopped into the vehicle.

"Good morning," the president said. "How did you sleep?"

"Good," I responded. "Thank you so much for getting the hotel for my family."

"It's the least I could do." He nodded. "We should be to Nevada pretty soon. Your friend Mr. Ross has chosen to not accompany us today."

I wondered why he hadn't wanted to come. I guess for the same reasons I would have stayed behind.

It took around three hours until we reached the USQDA. We had gotten to ride on Air Force One. It was one of the most marvelous things I had ever seen. Every vehicle that the president got to ride on was amazing.

By now, we were able to see the USQDA—or what was left of it. The entire base still looked like a war zone. Luckily, the weapons and people had been removed, but the rest remained as I had expected it had been when the battle was over.

It was terrifying, yet oddly comforting, to be back here. So much had happened on these premises, but it was all over now.

Still, though, it made me shiver to look down at what had changed the world. Over the last few months, I had transformed from a naive prodigy to having the weight of the world on my shoulders. I discovered that my country I once trusted with my life wasn't really as it seemed. The world I never thought twice about was against me.

The killer mass weapons, the instantaneous, overwhelming knowledge and power, the fact that I no longer had the views of a sixteen-year-old . . . it was all so much. And now, more than ever, I could create the opportunity to reconnect with my family, take a nice time off, and feel what it was like to be a normal teenager—the normal teenager that I had never been. I could put all this behind me and move forward.

But I couldn't. That was the simple truth. This would always be in my past. I had to learn how to live with it. And now with all of the responsibility I held, I could—I would have to—make the best of it.

These were the simple truths. They were something so simple yet so complex. Like everything else in my life.

EPILOGUE

As we felt Air Force One land on the runway, a new wave of energy rushed over me. It was different from just flying over it. I was back. I was back in the place where so much had happened. I took a deep breath and followed the president and his Secret Service members down the stairs to the ground.

Once we were on the ground, we immediately began walking towards the USQDA building. While on our way, all I could remember was the night Marisa and I had snuck around out here in order to get Beck's keys.

We kept walking and, eventually, reached the building with access to the USQDA. One of the Secret Service agents opened the door for us and we all walked in. We then found the Special Operations door and entered.

I walked the route I had walked so many times before. We approached the elevators. The president took out an ID badge from his pocket and scanned it for entry. It dinged open and we all walked in. It was very odd to have the only noise in the entire place be the ding of an elevator.

We all took the silent ride into the earth. Finally, we reached the USQDA and the doors opened. Like a flood, the memories came rushing in. After all this time, I wouldn't have ever believed that I would be back here.

I took a deep breath and focused. We all stepped out of the elevator, revealing a dark and deserted main floor. There were a couple of emergency lights with power, but that was it. They all led in one direction—one that I had never been before.

Now that I thought about it, I had never been in the Quantum-Brain Interaction Unit. I never was able to see what was in there. I followed the group in that direction. I began to hear small noises that sounded like shuffling around and it wasn't us who were making them. It must be the people who had brought Beck here.

We opened the door that said QBIU to reveal a short hallway with six doors, three on either side. We knocked on the nearest door, noticing the light was on inside and the door was cracked open.

We heard some footsteps inside and a man with a lab coat pulled open the door.

"Greetings, Mr. President," he said.

"Hello. How is it going?"

"We are almost there. In around three minutes, we should be ready to go." The president nodded and gestured for everyone else to go in, but he held me back with his arm.

"Go ahead," he said to his other companions. "I want to talk to Alan for a second." They all nodded and shut the door behind them when they had filed into the room

"Alan," he said. "I wanted to just tell you, if you feel like you don't want to or should not go in, you can stand out here. I realize so much has happened here at the USQDA and you may not want to see this."

I thought about it. I had already come this far, so I might as well go in. "I'm fine. Thank you, though." He nodded slowly and pushed the door open so we could walk in.

When I did this, I realized I should have evaluated my options better. Sitting in the chair in the room, tied down and handcuffed, was Timothy Beck. He looked as disheveled as ever and was wearing his orange prison uniform. When I entered, his neutral expression turned into a sly grin. "So . . ." he began. "I see you have come to witness my downfall. You know, I was doing something great. Something only a hero could do." I ignored him and reminded myself he was insane. He continued. "But instead, you decided to come and get in my way." He took a deep breath, and the president interrupted him.

"That's enough," he said.

"But I am just—"

"I said that's enough," the president said more forcefully.

"Sir," the man in the lab coat said to the president. "It's ready."

"Then let's get on with it." For the first time, I noticed there were two other people with lab coats in the room. There happened to also be a handful of guards. Also, for the first time, I thought I saw something in Beck's eyes. That cool, collected, sly look was gone for an instant, replaced by what almost seemed like anger, but then his cold stare returned almost instantly.

The main doctor in a lab coat grabbed something off of the table behind him. It looked like a helmet and had many multicolored wires attached to it. He set it on Beck's head, then turned around to his computer.

But I had just remembered something. That helmet. The exact same one that was placed on Beck's head right now was the same one that had gone on my head while we were rescuing my parents. It was also the same helmet that went on Marisa's head and the FBI members at the time of the rescue.

Could that mean . . .

If that helmet was what altered memories, what did that mean for us when it had come down on our heads?

As though she could hear my thoughts from wherever she was, I felt a vibration on my phone which was in my pocket. I took it out and looked at the number. It was random. But I decided to answer it anyway. And the person on the other end made me just about pass out from shock.

"Alan," Marisa said. "We need to talk."

ACKNOWLEDGMENTS

My inspiration to author a book came to me in the midst of COVID-19. Before I started, I had no idea I would enjoy creative writing this much. I took pleasure in writing about something I was passionate about. For me, this was science-fiction.

The genre of my book is technically sci-fi, but it leans more towards the science side rather than the fiction side. Many times, this is categorized as hard sci-fi, a type of science-fiction that encompasses real ideas and logic that could actually work. My current goal in life is to go to school to study Aerospace Engineering or Robotics Engineering and eventually work for NASA.

Of course, there are so many people who have supported me and my book. Without them, I would not be where I am today.

To my mom, Jennifer. You are the greatest mother anyone could ask for, and I am so very blessed to have you in my life. You are one of the most inspirational people in my life and always encourage me to do my best.

To my dad, David. Without you, my motivational levels about anything and everything I do would be lowered. You push me to always strive to do my best, and you are the greatest dad I could ask for.

To my sister, Clara. You will always be my lifelong, greatest friend and we will always be there for each other. You will go so far in life, and I love you so much.

To my grandparents, Nana, Lito, Grandma, and Papaw. You are also some of the most major components to my success and have been here every step of the way with me.

To my 7th Grade teacher, Mrs. Hill. You have taught me so much more than the subject of English and supported me before I ever began writing my book. Thank you so much.

To Ross, you helped me not only strengthen my Christian spiritual life but also supported me in so many other ways. Thank you.

To City Limits Publishing, thank you for your commitment to my book. Thank you for giving this 14-year-old a chance.

And finally, to all of my friends, who have stood by me through my life. There are so many of you and I appreciate you more than you will ever know.

Thank you so much for your dedication to me and my life, and celebrating all of my accomplishments with me. I can't thank you enough.

ABOUT THE AUTHOR

Abram Smith, a 14-year-old student from Owasso, Oklahoma, is the author of the novel, The Quantum State. Inspired by the COVID-19 pandemic, writing became his newfound retreat. In his free time, he plays classical violin, golf, and enjoys writing.

MORE FROM CITY LIMITS PUBLISHING

Mary Claire has always hidden. During the week, she feels like every other child—but on Fridays, she slowly becomes invisible. Hiding is how she remains safe.

At ten-years-old, Mary Claire begs God to take her father away, but someone else has plans for him.

Years later, Claire Stanton struggles with the secrets of her past. After her daughter becomes sullen and angry, she fears history may be repeating itself, and she takes matters into her own hands, vowing to make the abuser pay.

Life is complicated. Secrets are destructive. But the truth is explosive.

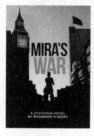

The EU is dead. The UK is gone. London's political climate is one of fear, death, and distrust. Into this comes Mira, a young punk with nothing left to lose. An ensemble cast of intertwining plotlines collide when Mira must choose to save herself - or an innocent boy.

Agritania was a small kingdom of mostly farmers and merchants but, as the Lord Chancellor Fengold knew, was sitting on vast deposits of silver and gold. But the king was a fool and wouldn't allow Fengold to develop these resources even though the wealth could be used to improve the lives of all the citizens... but especially Fengold himself. When the new prince is christened, Fengold enters into a conspiracy with a counselor from Ferristein to ambush and assassinate the royal family so he can become king and begin mining the silver and gold. It takes seven years, but the opportunity finally arrives and when the royal family was about to enjoy a picnic, they were attacked. As the attack began, the king told Prince Stephen to run into the woods and not to stop or look back. While he was running, he suddenly came to a cliff and fell. At the bottom of the cliff, an old man named Barnabas picked up the injured prince and carried him off to his cottage in a hidden valley. Fengold sent soldiers to look for them but he never found them. Over the years, others began living in the valley until they became a village of outcasts and outlaws. Becky Dixon's parents were getting divorced and they were moving to her mother's parent's ranch. But, once they arrive, she found it wasn't so bad. Especially since her best friend Emily Washburn was going to spend a month with them. The two girls were exploring the ranch when they found a cave and decided to investigate. While they were crawling through a narrow passage the floor gave out and they tumbled into another world. They soon find themselves in the middle of a desperate war to restore Prince Stephen to his throne. Do they succeed? Do they all survive? And if they do, do the girls ever get home?

Everyone knows vampires aren't real, and the vampires need it to stay that way. Adrian has managed their Human Resources department for over a century, keeping their true activities hidden from human eyes.

Journalist Clare can barely contain her eye roll when asked to do an article on the Heliophiles. It's indulgent to play to the delusions of people who change their lifestyle based on a belief in vampires.

But when Clare's work is flagged by the vampire organization, she has to depend on the rules in The Survivor's Handbook to stay alive. And Adrian is hunting for her.

CPSIA information can be obtained
at www.ICGtesting.com
Printed in the USA
LVHW030720140721
692648LV00006B/867